OVER THE KNEE

'Do you want a smacked bottom, my girl?' he asked, again in a much louder voice than necessary.

Mortified, I pleaded with my eyes. Now even more people were staring. Behind me the French boy sniggered and I heard him translating what Peter had said for his girlfriend. My face burnt so hot it was painful.

'Well?'

'No,' I whispered, cringing.

'No *what*?'

'No, sir.'

'Well, I'm not so sure. I think a smacked bottom is just what you need.' He took me by the hand and led me forcefully to the nearest bench. Still holding my hand, he sat down in front of a giant advertisement for the Royal Ballet.

'Right, young lady,' he said sternly, enunciating the words with crisp and awful precision. 'Over my knee.'

My legs threatened to buckle and I stared at him in abject horror. He couldn't mean it. He couldn't be serious. Not here. Surely he wouldn't . . .

Other titles available in the Nexus Enthusiast series:

LEG LOVER
DERRIÈRE
BUSTY
UNDER MY MASTER'S WINGS
THE SECRET SELF

OVER THE KNEE

Fiona Locke

The LAST
WORD *in*
FETISH

enthusiast

This book is a work of fiction.
In real life, make sure you practise safe, sane and consensual sex.

First published in 2006 by
Nexus Enthusiast
Nexus
Thames Wharf Studios
Rainville Rd
London W6 9HA

www.nexus-books.co.uk

Typeset by TW Typesetting, Plymouth, Devon
Printed and bound by Clays Ltd, St Ives PLC

ISBN 0 352 34079 7
ISBN 978 0 352 34079 5

For the Professor

My homework, sir.

Prologue

Standing in the corner, I place my trembling hands on top of my head. The movement causes the punishment gown to lift and the flaps fall to either side, revealing the pale tender cheeks of my bottom. The air is cool against the unprotected skin, heightening the feeling of exposure. I lace my fingers tightly together to still the tremors. Behind me, on the edge of the school desk where I have placed it, the birch rod waits. I feel its presence like a ghostly chill in the room.

Soon I will hear the slow purposeful tread on the stairs. It might be five minutes or fifteen. But I must be in position when he comes to punish me. In the corner, he wants me to reflect on what I have done. Or rather, not done.

Downstairs in the entrance hall, the grandfather clock ticks away the seconds. I try to count them, to mark the passing time. But it's impossible to concentrate on anything but my impending punishment. The burning stripes he will paint across my bottom.

I had to make my own rod. It's part of the punishment. It's a short walk out to the small stand of trees in the woods behind the house, but the reason for my visit makes it seem much longer. I know what he expects and I dare not return with switches that are too flimsy. I've learnt that lesson.

I cut thirteen slender sappy switches, the straightest I could find. I took them back to the house and bound them into a bundle. I'm always afraid of meeting someone on the way back, but so far I've been lucky. I don't know what I'd say.

I presented the rod to him for inspection and he nodded his approval and told me quietly to change and wait for him in the schoolroom. I took the rod back upstairs, staring at it with frightened eyes, knowing that in a short time it would be in pieces on the floor while I cried and atoned for my misdeeds.

Finally, I hear his footsteps. The agony of waiting is almost over. The floorboards creak as he enters the room and stands behind me. The flaps of my gown sway slightly at the displacement of air, tickling my thighs. I can feel his eyes on me and I try hard not to fidget.

'Angie,' he says softly. 'Come here.'

He doesn't raise his voice. Authority never shouts.

I creep from the corner and stand before him, ashamed and apprehensive. My unfocused gaze rests on the oak floorboards, chilly beneath my bare feet. But he waits until I raise my eyes to his face.

'Fetch the rod.'

My fingers feel glued together, but I pry them apart. My arms ache from the position they've been in. How long has it been? I cannot tell.

I pick up the rod. Individually, each switch is almost weightless, but bound together they are capable of astonishing pain. It's like a hybrid of cane and whip and I fear it above all other implements. My respect for it borders on awe. With shaking hands and downcast eyes, I present it to him.

He swishes it through the air and I flinch. With the rod he indicates the birching block against the wall. I implore him with my eyes, knowing it will do no good. He waits. The silence is intolerable. I fetch the block and place it in the centre of the room. Then, reluctantly, I kneel on the lower step. Bending right forward over the upper step, I place both hands flat on the floor. The position raises my bottom high in the air, with my head much lower. The gown parts even further and my sense of exposure is complete. A deep flush spreads over my body and I close my eyes in dread.

He lays the birch against the vulnerable flesh of my bottom, tapping it lightly to measure the first stroke. 'Two dozen,' he says. 'Count them.'

One

Spanking (noun)
A traditional form of punishment in which a series of slaps or smacks are delivered to the buttocks, usually with the open hand.

Even the definition was enough to make me squirm. I couldn't pick up a dictionary without looking it up. And all the attendant words: whip, thrash, flog, paddle, strap, cane, punish, discipline. For as long as I could remember they had held a special power for me.

I'd never been spanked in my life, so I had no idea where my strange fantasies came from. My parents were permissive and inattentive. And while corporal punishment technically still existed at my school, I didn't know anyone who had actually received it. The cane was little more than an urban legend. Instead, my teachers assigned detention and made us write lines. I hated both. And yet the very concept of punishment and someone authorised to administer it tickled something deep inside.

I often wondered if I'd have felt the same if the cane had been a real threat. And if I'd been bad enough to earn it, would the cane have reformed me? Or would it only have left me wanting more?

Mr Ellis, the history master, was fond of reminiscing about 'the good old days', when teachers used the cane and slipper. 'Pupils knew the meaning of discipline back then, by God,' he would rant. But he was a blustering ex-army power tripper. A bully with no true authority. No one took him seriously.

The headmaster, Mr Chancellor, was another matter. Soft-spoken and eloquent, his old-world features and public-school education seemed out of place at Ravenscroft School. I hung on his every word in assembly, lost in the sound of his voice, no matter how dull the subject. I never confided my schoolgirl crush to anyone; my friends would only have teased me.

Only the headmaster had authority to cane. And while I'd never heard of Mr Chancellor caning anyone in my time, he must have done it in the past. I couldn't stop thinking about it. It led me into fantasies. Internal re-enactments of scenes I'd read in vintage school stories and Victorian novels.

Before long, the images began to preoccupy me. They became intrusive, dominating my thoughts. I couldn't rid myself of the confusing feelings they evoked. If I saw a picture of an actor or a musician I liked, I would picture myself being spanked by him.

Then, one day in assembly, Mr Chancellor brought the flat of his hand down sharply on the lectern to emphasise a point. My pulse quickened as I imagined his hand coming down like that on my bare bottom. The image consumed me with shame and embarrassment. But for the first time I understood the source of my confusion. I glanced furtively at my classmates, certain that they could see the disgusting thoughts in my mind, certain that the word 'pervert' was emblazoned on my forehead.

That one moment marked a definite sexual awakening for me. A revelation. I suddenly understood exactly what I was into. No wonder candlelit romance stories left me cold. I didn't want to be a pampered princess. I wanted to be dominated. I wanted a man who would punish me.

And right then I wanted Mr Chancellor to punish me.

There was only one problem: I was a good girl. Despite my parents' disinterest, I went to my lessons and did my homework diligently. My record and my character were unblemished. So my decision to play truant one day was a hard one to make. But I had no choice. It was a serious offence – one that would warrant a visit to the headmaster.

Most girls would have enjoyed their day off, but I spent mine in guilty paranoia. Several times I regretted my decision and was on the verge of going back to school, concocting whatever flimsy excuse I could to explain my tardiness. Tardiness was nowhere near as serious as truancy. But I managed to screw up my courage and stay away. I had to do this.

The next morning my hands shook so much I could barely knot my tie. And I felt faint when the English master read the note he'd been given and announced brusquely, 'Angela Harker, you're to report to the headmaster's office immediately.'

A collective gasp reinforced my sense of having crossed the line. My fellow pupils were aghast. Swotty had been summoned to the headmaster! What could I possibly have done? Their expressions of stunned disbelief stayed with me all the way down the long corridor.

Smartly turned out in my crisp white shirt and striped tie, I pictured myself submitting to physical chastisement. Would Mr Chancellor order me to lift my dutifully ironed skirt? Or would he do it himself?

My stomach churned with anxiety. I was a bold but reckless explorer taking my first steps in an unknown hostile land. Armed with an all-consuming desire to confront my obsession, I knew the experience would change me forever.

After an eternity, I reached my destination. The headmaster's secretary, Mrs Willis, eyed me with cold disdain and waved me towards the row of hard plastic chairs outside Mr Chancellor's office. On the wall opposite a bland monochrome clock loudly counted the seconds as its bent second hand lurched from one number to the next.

I sat down, imagining myself as the last girl in a long queue of miscreants sent here to be dealt with. I fancied I could even hear the terrifying swish of the cane from within. The headmaster didn't enjoy it, of course. He was just doing his duty. His motivation was purely disciplinary.

And that was the element that obsessed me the most. I didn't want it for sexual reasons; it had to be punishment. The fact that I did really want it was my little secret.

My train of thought was making me feel dizzy and overheated. My lungs felt too weak to expand fully. And the interminable ticking was beginning to wear on my already ragged nerves. I shook my head to banish the images, afraid he would sense the true motive behind my misdeed. My shoes scuffed back and forth on the floor as I swung my legs nervously.

Mrs Willis raised her head and glowered at me, completely unsympathetic to the fear anyone would feel in my position.

Another agonising minute crawled by and then, at last, Mrs Willis told me I could go in.

I raised my clammy fist to the door and knocked timidly.

'Come in.'

I took a deep breath, held it in for three seconds and let it out slowly. Showtime. I entered and stood before his desk like a criminal in the dock. He studied me, his fingers steepled beneath his chin.

'What were you thinking, Harker?' he asked gently. 'That you wouldn't be missed?'

'No, sir, I just . . .' It was hard for me to lie, but I forced the words out hastily. I'd rehearsed them the day before, saying them over and over to the mirror in as flippant a tone as I could manage. 'I just couldn't be bothered.'

He frowned and sat back a little in his chair. 'I beg your pardon?'

With an audible swallow, I pressed on. 'I didn't feel like coming to school yesterday. I had better things to do.' He raised his eyebrows expectantly and I added, 'Sir.'

'I see.' He stood up and walked round to the front of the desk.

I began to tremble, already regretting my foolish endeavour. I was terrified, yet dying of curiosity at the same time. Even so, I remembered that no one – not even Dale Grisham, who'd thrown stones at the school windows and broken one – had ever been caned. I wasn't a known offender, a troublemaker who was always being sent to the headmaster. This was my first offence, after all. My first *ever*. There was no real chance that he would cane me. But perhaps he would at least threaten . . .

Mr Chancellor crossed his arms and leant back against the edge of his desk. 'I'm surprised at you, Harker. This isn't like you.'

I was surprised he knew what I was like at all. Good girls never got noticed. They blended into the scenery while the bad girls took centre stage and got all the attention.

His expression softened. 'Now, I know you're a good student and I can only hope this is an isolated incident. But I want you to know that I'm very disappointed in you. I rely on girls like you to set an example for the other pupils.'

It was the killer. My eyes filled with tears and I looked forlornly at my shoes. This wasn't the way it was supposed to go. He wasn't supposed to be *nice* to me!

'I'm sorry, sir,' I heard myself say.

The rest of the interview was a disaster and I was thoroughly ashamed of myself by the time he handed me a tissue and told me I could go. Detention. No caning.

Disgusted with myself, I resolved to repeat my adventure. And this time I would be merciless. I wouldn't break down and I wouldn't apologise. I would give him a reason to raise his voice, to reprimand me severely, to tell me what I really deserved – and, with any luck, administer it.

Cruising the high street in my uniform, I boldly met the eyes of nosy passers-by who knew I was playing truant. Being bad was exciting. It was liberating. I could definitely get used to this. The disapproving looks gave me a cheap thrill, but no one said anything to me.

I loosened my top button and pulled my tie askew. I untucked my shirt. But I kept my blazer on so everyone could see the badge and know which school I was profaning. Representing the school so disgracefully was a grave offence as well. Someone was certain to report me. The pinch-faced old lady with the yappy Yorkshire terriers, perhaps. She glared at me, the delinquent schoolgirl. I offered her a sneer in return, silently daring her to ask me why I wasn't at school. I would catch it the next day. Oh, yes.

Sure enough, Mr Chancellor didn't coddle me this time.

'Would you care to explain yourself, Harker?' he asked severely.

'Not really.'

'Sir,' he prompted.

I rolled my eyes. '*Sir.*'

He was unfazed. 'I was told about your little display in town yesterday. And I'm shocked at your behaviour.'

He wasn't even bothering with the guilt trip this time. He was really affronted.

'I had trusted that you wouldn't abuse my lenience, girl. But, as you clearly didn't learn your lesson last time, you leave me little choice. I'm forced to adopt sterner measures.'

Here it was! A hot flush covered my face and throat. I raised my eyebrows, mimicking the look he had given me last time. 'Oh yeah?'

'Yes, Harker. You would normally be given a third chance, but your flagrant insolence leaves me no choice.'

I heard the last two words as a portentous echo. *No choice*. Was I mad? The cane would hurt. Terribly. It was meant to. But there was no way out now. Backing out was not an option. I held my breath as I waited for him to pass sentence.

'I'm suspending you for a week.'

I froze. 'What?'

Mr Chancellor looked slightly bemused. 'What did you expect to happen, girl? Anyone would think you were deliberately provoking me. Were you trying to get expelled?'

I gaped at him. 'No, sir, not that, I just . . .'

'Yes?'

Flustered, I shook my head. 'Nothing. I'm . . . not myself. Sir.'

'I can see that. So I suggest you make good use of your time away. Reflect on your actions and their consequences and see if you can get back in my good books when you return.'

I was shell-shocked. I didn't know what to say. Not only had I failed to elicit the desired result; I'd earned a black mark on my record. And my parents would hear all about it. Not the imagined caning, six strokes of agony and no one the wiser.

'You're dismissed, Harker.'

'Yes, sir.'

Disaster. Absolute bloody catastrophe. No survivors.

I winced at the memory. No, that hadn't been my finest hour. I still thought about Mr Chancellor from time to time, wondering if he was still at Ravenscroft. I'd been tempted many times to go back and see him, to confess the real reason for my failed offensive. There would be no question of ethics or professional misconduct; we were no longer teacher and pupil. This time he could cane me without fear of the consequences. Or would he see it as a vulgar seduction attempt?

I was confident enough about my looks. I had a willowy frame with long athletic legs and small breasts. I had wide brown eyes and soft full lips. These feminine features were offset by the short pageboy cut of my gingery brown hair.

I knew how to dress to flatter my grown-up charms, but I had a penchant for girlish tartan skirts. An independent uniform fetish, I suspect. I rarely wore anything else. When people asked, I simply shrugged and confided that it made me feel more studious. They laughed it off as a charming eccentricity. They had no idea.

But, though I fantasised about it often, I never got up the courage to go back to Ravenscroft. And as the years passed, the preoccupation lost its urgency. University kept me busy and before I knew it I was buried in my thesis: 'The Victorian Chat Room: Covert Sadomasochism in Nineteenth-Century Family Magazines'.

Victorian England was alive with deviant undertones. The sexual repression coupled with the harsh discipline of the period created an ideal environment for fetishes to flourish. There was a wealth of flagellant literature and I was certain that if I had lived then I'd have been writing my own as well. But the obsession with corporal punishment went beyond overt pornography. The 'English vice', it was called.

A group of enthusiasts infiltrated mainstream periodicals like *The Family Herald* and *The Englishwoman's Domestic Magazine*, publishing spurious accounts of spanking and birching, rendered in obsessive fetishistic detail. There were accounts of the birching of young ladies by schoolmistresses. Floggings in monasteries and nunneries. Whippings administered by strict governesses. Discussions of whether it was decent for gentlemen to whip girls, ladies to whip boys. The disciplinary merits of such chastisement. And on and on.

But the most enticing aspect was the fact that these detailed letters were to be found sprinkled amongst the commonplace crises of etiquette. The moral implications of kissing before marriage. How to break off a tender acquaintanceship. Where one may purchase birch rods for the chastisement of unruly daughters.

Ah, the glorious hypocrisy of Victorian sexuality. The lengths to which they went to repress their urges. They staunchly refused to acknowledge that there was anything inherently erotic underlying their obsession with corporal punishment. Heavens, no – that would be perverse!

Many of the letters were obvious hoaxes, pornography masquerading as morality. Some of them purported to condemn the practice of corporal punishment. The moral outrage only lent further credence to the discourse, however.

> A HATER OF THE SYSTEM (our old friend) writes to inform us that even she does not disapprove of flogging, but only indecent flogging; and she says that in the most aristocratic schools flogging is of daily occurrence. She describes the system pursued in one near Edinburgh, where the terms are 120 guineas per annum. 'A book of offences is kept by one of the young ladies,

in which every fault is regularly entered. There is a graduated scale of punishments, the highest of which is corporal. When an offence of sufficient magnitude takes place, the culprit enters it in the book herself, and carries the report to the lady superintendent, who writes under it the amount of punishment. For the first offence, the delinquent is prepared for punishment, but generally pardoned. For the second, she is whipped privately. For all subsequent delinquencies the punishment takes place in the schoolroom, on 'the horse'; and, in addition to the pain it inflicts, it costs in money about 1s., paid in fees. The system is as follows: 1st. She proceeds to the housekeeper, to procure the rod, a leathern thong. She pays 2d. for the use of it. 2nd. She has then to be partly undressed by the maid, and this costs 2d. 3rd. The culprit has then to walk barefooted to another part of the house, to be robed for punishment, a peculiar dress being used, to add to the disgrace. It is a long linen blouse, short cotton socks, and list slippers, all of which each offender has to provide for herself. The young lady, thus costumed, now proceeds to the drawing-room, to be exhibited to the lady superintendent. Having been approved, she is then conducted to the schoolroom, when she has to pay 6d. to the governess, who inflicts the amount of punishment awarded. A wooden horse, covered with soft leather, is the medium of castigation. The delinquent subsequently thanks the governess! kisses the rod!! then thanks the superintendent, and retires to her own room, to appear no more until prayer-time the next morning.' Our correspondent says the ceremony has more effect than the punishment. The young ladies are in other respects tenderly dealt with. Even the horse has a soft cushion.

The letter had the same effect on me as on my predecessors. The extravagant ritual was a form of protracted foreplay and the detached mannerly voice only heightened its eroticism. It was all perfectly proper and above board. And all in the name of old-fashioned English discipline.

My supervisor hadn't batted an eye when I'd proposed my thesis title. Dr Morrison was a humourless, asexual pedagogue who was oblivious to my personal interest in the subject. The irony was delicious; the vanilla readers of *The Family Herald* didn't realise they were watching fetishists at play either.

My academic life was steeped in erotica, but my reality remained steadfastly bland and boring. At twenty-four, I was getting desperate for sympathetic company. I'd had boyfriends, of course. But none of the guys I went out with could measure up to my fantasy of Mr Chancellor. They completely missed the hints I dropped. But I couldn't spell it out for them. They had to be the ones to initiate it.

I had no trouble attracting vanilla boys; the trick was finding the kinky ones. There was the Net, of course. But I was wary of visiting dubious sites from the university library's computers. There were strict regulations about that. If I were caught, the humiliation would be too much to handle. Then again, perhaps it would be worth it.

There was a wealth of material about the spanking fetish – so much that I could never hope to read it all. But I tried. Naturally, the Victorian offerings were my favourites. I was fascinated by the harsh class division and the wicked things the upper classes could do to the lower. Power was hot, but power *abused* . . . well, that was something very special indeed.

One of my fondest fantasies cast me as a maid for a prurient gentleman who punished me when I didn't perform my duties as he expected. I had no option but to submit to his touch as well as his correction. It was that or be cast out on to the streets. No choice. No responsibility. No guilt.

My favourite book was the Victorian classic *Frank & I*, the story of a girl who disguises herself as a boy and lives with a strict guardian. When the guardian orders 'Frank' to take down his trousers for a birching, he discovers her secret, but keeps it to himself. Frank must continue being a boy, unaware that her guardian knows full well she is a girl. And her guardian, a self-proclaimed 'lover of the rod', delights in finding fault with his young charge and administering sound punishments for every offence.

Of course, there is nothing more traditional, more quintessentially English, than the cane. A short sharp shock. Skirt up, knickers down. Six of the best in the headmaster's study. But, even more than the implement, it was the ritual that obsessed me. There were prescribed conventions that I saw played out compulsively in both my fantasies and the stories I read. The English had made an art of discipline.

But all things considered, I couldn't imagine anything more intimate and humbling than an old-fashioned bare-bottom, over-the-knee spanking. The exquisite embarrassment of being treated like a child, my clothing adjusted just enough to expose my bottom for smacking. My ears would burn as my disciplinarian scolded me, telling me what a naughty girl I'd been and how I deserved punishment. He would bring his palm down on my pale cheeks, turning them pink and red while I kicked and squirmed over his lap. Perhaps then he would move on to the hairbrush, the most domestic implement of all. The polished ebony would elicit cries of pain and promises of better behaviour from me.

I sighed and flipped through my notebook. It hadn't been a productive morning. I'd spent most of it lost in daydreams. The possibility that there could be someone out there who wanted to spank me as much as I wanted to be spanked was driving me to distraction.

Perhaps I could justify visiting spanking websites and chat rooms as part of my research. After all, I couldn't very well compare Victorian magazines with modern chat rooms if I didn't visit some of them myself. But I'd have to fill in a special application form for that and I wasn't sure if I was ready to out myself to the librarian just yet.

Frustrated and torn, I returned to the comfort of the dictionary. I could always rely on its clinical descriptions for a little fix. This time I looked up 'birch'. I pictured the embarrassment and dread of having to cut switches and bind them together to make my own birch rod. Presenting it to my disciplinarian and asking to be punished.

Sometimes I liked to fantasise about being a boy. Or just a modern-day 'Frank' disguised as one. I wondered how I would look in short trousers and a schoolboy cap. Or an Eton suit. There was no shortage of corporal punishment accounts about the elite public school. I'd gone to the Eton museum once to see the famous birching block. Imagining myself as a boy during Dr Keate's reign of terror, trembling before the rod, stretching myself across the block . . .

'Hey, Angie.'

I gasped and slammed the dictionary shut, startling several students near by. They raised their heads and looked at me reproachfully before returning to their studies.

'Sorry, didn't mean to scare you.' It was Karen, the librarian's assistant.

I blushed as though I'd been caught with a pornographic book instead of the *OED*.

'Thought you'd like to know that this is back in,' she said, handing me *A History of the Rod*. Again.

It was a curious little book, written in the late 1800s by the Reverend William M. Cooper, BA. Subtitled *Flagellation and the Flagellants*, the cover displayed an embossed gold-leaf etching of the Eton birching block, complete with birch rod. The spine bore etchings of other instruments of correction. Not a masterpiece of subtlety, but a potent wellspring for those in the know.

'Thanks,' I said. 'I just needed to check some references in this chapter.'

I tried to act nonchalant, but I could see her puzzled expression. She'd probably flipped through it and seen the delights on offer. She must have wondered what all the fuss was about – why two people were fighting over it, recalling it back and forth.

She raised her eyebrows, as though waiting for me to let her in on the joke. 'I expect it will be recalled again next week?'

'I expect so.' I refused to elaborate.

Shaking her head, she left.

It was an odd but alluring little game of cat and mouse. I didn't actually need the book at all. I'd already read it. But I did want to know who else was borrowing it. He – and I was convinced it was a man – had to be a kindred spirit.

He wasn't quite what I'd had in mind.

Two

'Lift your skirt.'

I heard the direction clearly, but my response came unbidden. 'What?'

'You heard me. Lift. Your. Skirt.'

My skin felt chilled as my tremulous fingers crept down to the hem of my kilt. I hesitated, glancing up at him with pleading eyes.

'Would you like me to do it for you?' he asked, squarely in control.

'No!' Slowly, I dragged the fabric up until he could see my knickers.

'Very good. Now turn around.'

Closing my eyes, I obeyed.

I was the one who had started this. I was the one who kept recalling *A History of the Rod* so that he had to do the same. It was like a possessive game between children. 'Mine.' 'Mine!' 'No, *mine*!'

So, when he recalled the book again, as I knew he would, I returned it. Then I staked out the circulation desk, waiting for him to come in and reclaim it. I wondered who he could be. Did I know him? If not, would I recognise him as a fellow pervert? Would it be obvious? All my life I had felt like the last of my kind. I assumed they had all died out after the golden age of Victorian prudery. I was not going to miss the chance to meet another like me.

The sturdy little volume sat in a stack on the desk with a slip of paper inserted halfway into it. I knew it must have his name on it and it was all I could do to resist darting behind the counter and snatching it.

I stationed myself where I could see everyone who approached the desk. I could hardly concentrate on my work. I was delighted by a *Family Herald* letter from a lady who disapproved of the word 'flog' when referring to the chastisement of young ladies. She offered instead 'the elegant and soft English expression, "chasten"', administered – of course – with all due affection and gentleness. But even this titillating bit of trivia couldn't distract me from my quarry. I skulked about all day, waiting.

At last, I saw the librarian take the book from the stack. At the desk was a young guy, clearly a student. He was tall, with longish dark hair and a goatee. Strong arms and muscular legs. I didn't much like the Bohemian scruffiness, but he would clean up nicely. The baggy trousers would have to go.

He was at the desk for a long time, talking to the librarian. She nodded in my direction and he turned, following her gaze. I ducked my head, pretending to be engrossed in my writing. I casually put my head in my hand and watched out of the corner of my eye. He was coming towards me.

'Excuse me,' said a slightly terse voice.

I looked up. 'Hmm?'

He gave me a tight little smile. 'Pardon my asking, but are you the person who keeps recalling the Cooper book?' He had a strong northern accent, but it lent him a certain boyish charm. He was a long way from home.

'Yes,' I said, refusing to elaborate.

He stared at me for a few seconds and his eyes flicked down to my tartan skirt. He clearly liked what he saw and it must have confirmed my own fascination. 'Well,' he said at last. 'We – ah – seem to have some shared interests.'

'Oh?' I tried to play it cool, but inside I was ecstatic. No, there were no obvious signs that he was kinky. I never would have picked him out of a lineup. But the fact that he had come to *me* was exciting.

He slid into the chair next to me, a grin spreading over his face. The discovery must have been as exhilarating for him as it was for me. My stomach fluttered and I coyly shifted my papers to hide what I was working on. He set the book down on the table between us, like a challenge to a dual.

I looked at it, then back up at him.

'You need it for research?' he asked.

'Research,' I confirmed.

He nodded knowingly, still grinning. 'Perhaps you'd like to compare notes.'

I pretended to consider. 'That might be . . . instructive.'

'Well, my flatmates are going to a concert tonight,' he said slowly. 'So if you'd like to stop by . . .'

The offer was irresistible and it was all I could do to restrain my glee. 'Sure,' I said. 'I'd love to. Just give me your address.'

He took the pen from my hand and wrote the address on the page I'd been working on. He also wrote his name: Paul Milburn.

I smiled. 'Angie Harker.'

'A pleasure. I'll see you around eight, then.'

Not eight sharp, just 'around eight'. He was no authority figure, but he was kinky. That was the important thing. He got up, leaving the book on the table.

'Bring the book,' he said.

I changed in and out of several outfits over the course of an hour. My bed was a giant discard pile. At last I settled on a short black and green tartan skirt with a white blouse and matching crossover tie, white knee socks and low-heeled black shoes. It wasn't exactly a school uniform, but it had the look. Finding the right pair of knickers took me almost as long. In the end I decided I couldn't afford to be subtle. If he got that far I didn't want any mistake. I wore the white boyshorts with 'naughty' scrawled across the bottom in girlish purple letters.

I arrived at the dreary little house at ten past eight. I wanted him to have an easy excuse. My knickers were already embarrassingly wet.

When he answered the door he looked slightly anxious. I guessed that he'd been watching the clock for the past half-hour, wondering if I was really coming.

'Sorry I'm late,' I said.

Paul closed the door and looked me up and down admiringly. 'That's all right.'

He was probably grateful I hadn't been more punctual. The flat was much tidier than I had been expecting and I was touched that he would go to the trouble. It was unlikely he'd been cracking the whip over his flatmates to get them to help. He looked a lot neater as well. He was wearing smart black trousers and a dark-blue collared shirt.

He gestured for me to walk ahead of him – either politeness or so that he could get a look at my bottom. I obliged him and found myself in a cramped but cosy living room. A well-worn sofa stood against one wall, but I was too keyed up to sit. I produced the book and gave it to him.

'Here it is,' I said. 'Which bits do you like best?'

'I'm not sure yet,' he said, flipping through it. 'I've only just started it.'

'You've recalled it three times!'

'And so have you,' he said carefully, his eyes glinting. 'But we both know this isn't really about the book, don't we?'

I blushed and looked down, listening to the soft slicing noise as he turned the pages.

'But, since you asked, I rather like the chapter, "On the Whipping of Young Ladies".'

The title alone made me blush.

'What about you?' he asked pointedly.

The question didn't come out of the blue, but it still put me on the spot. 'Well . . .'

All at once I felt nervous and unsure of myself. I'd played teasing games with a complete stranger simply because he'd checked out a book on corporal punishment. I'd gone to his house dressed like a tart. Up to now nothing had been decided. But, once I'd told him what I liked, I'd be committed. It wasn't that I didn't want it. But the recklessness of it struck me. His flatmates were away. No one knew where I was.

I swallowed.

My sudden unease seemed to give Paul even more self-assurance. Like a dangerous animal sensing fear. 'Well?' he prompted.

Blushing deeply, I tried to regain some pluck. 'Isn't it obvious?'

He looked at me hungrily. 'Yes, I suppose it is.'

The tables had turned dramatically. There was no trace of reticence now. I hadn't realised just how devilish the goatee made him look. Standing a little straighter, a little taller, he stepped back for a better view of the girl who had delivered herself to him.

'Lift it higher,' he said. 'Let me see. I can't quite make out what that says.'

My eyes flew open. I'd forgotten all about the knickers. The obvious amusement in his voice made me feel even more exposed as I complied.

'Well, well.' He chuckled. 'Hardly regulation issue, are they?'

I smoothed the skirt back down, squeezing my legs together.

Behind me I heard a schussing noise and I glanced over my shoulder to see him pulling the coffee table aside, away from the sofa. He sat down.

My stomach was tying itself in knots.

'Come here,' he said, his voice barely a whisper.

My feet felt rooted to the floor and it was several seconds before I was able to summon the willpower to move. For one panicky moment I thought of calling it off. But calling *what* off? Nothing had been explicitly discussed or agreed. It was all insinuation. And yet unequivocal messages had been exchanged.

I stood in front of him, unable to meet his eyes.

Paul took me by the hand and guided me to his right side. Then, without a word, he patted his knee.

My face burning, I hesitated. The moment had arrived. I couldn't move. But he was in control now and my hesitation only gave him courage. He waited. When I couldn't bear the standoff any longer, I stretched myself across his lap. I rested my arms on the sofa and buried my face in my hands. The position wasn't exactly comfortable, but it wasn't uncomfortable either. His muscular thighs felt strong and solid beneath my hips.

When he lifted my skirt it was with excruciating deliberation, as though he was unveiling a work of art. He traced the outline of the word on my backside with his finger, spelling it out. 'Yes, "naughty" is exactly the word I would use.'

Involuntarily I clenched my buttocks, stimulated by his touch. I held my breath as he rested his hand on my right cheek. He was going to spank me. I'd known since he spoke to me in the library that he would, but still the imminence of it was overwhelming. All my life I had fantasised about it, imagined what it would be like and how it would feel. Now I was about to find out, and the reality of it seemed more unreal than any of my fantasies.

I felt his hand lift away from my cheek and hover in the air, like a bird of prey about to dive. He brought it down sharply across the fullest part of my bottom and I made a tiny sound, muffled by my hands. *My first ever smack*. He did it again and my cheeks clenched as his palm made contact. He was barely hitting me and yet the position was so belittling that I imagined it stung intolerably.

I cried out at the next smack and continued to whimper as he increased the tempo of the spanking. His hand rained brisk little slaps on my bottom and I drummed my feet on the floor in petulant protest.

I heard him laugh and he began to smack me a little harder. It still wasn't painful, but it did make me writhe over his lap.

After a few more smacks he stopped. His finger explored the outline of my knickers again and then he said, 'We'll have these down now.'

I moaned as he peeled them over my cheeks. He slid them all the way down to my ankles. They offered precious little cover anyway, but now I was in danger of kicking them right off if I moved too much. And the only way I could keep them around my ankles was to spread my legs. That was too much exposure.

Paul spanked me again, harder now. And when he stopped he caressed my pinkened cheeks. I sighed and relaxed at the gentle treatment as his fingers trailed over the inner curves, teasing me. At last the wandering hand slipped along the cleft of my bottom and in between my legs. He drew his fingers along the slick folds of my sex and I felt even more exposed by the treacherous wetness there.

Then his hand returned to my bottom, delivering another volley of smart slaps. These were much harder and I couldn't help kicking my feet. I felt my knickers slip off my right ankle, but I couldn't do anything about it. Besides, resisting was part of the appeal. Silently I urged him to do it harder, but he was being very cautious. He stopped again and resumed his exploration of my sex, probing the wetness. When he dipped his finger inside me I gasped, then lowered my head back to the sofa. I parted my legs, inviting him further. He obliged, swirling his finger deep inside, making me clutch at the cushions.

Then his hand was back on my bottom, smacking me sharply. I struggled feebly and twisted on his lap, hungry for release. But I couldn't think how to get my own hand underneath to assist.

The spanking stopped and the touching began again. I was less concerned about the noise now and I panted and gasped loudly as the stimulation made me quiver. He teased me with his right hand while his left found the buttons of my blouse and began to unfasten them. I lifted myself up enough to give him access and he undid two of them, before slipping his hand inside to cup my breasts. My nipples stiffened in response to the attention and he pinched them through the fabric of my bra.

I was hyper-stimulated from the spanking, on the point of overload. He slid his fingers up and down the groove of my sex, finally pinching the hard little nub at the top. That was all it took. With a wild cry I surrendered to the barrage of pulsing, undulating waves, clinging to the sofa as though I would float away without an anchor.

As the tremors began to die away I became aware for the first time of the hard uncomfortable bulge of his erection and I reached underneath myself to touch it, squeeze it. He drew in a ragged breath as I did and he froze until I released him.

My limbs still unsteady, I clambered off his lap and dropped to my knees, eager to reward him. I unzipped him and freed his cock, then caressed it and kneaded it in my hands. I ran my tongue along the underside and it twitched and stiffened in response.

Wrapping my fingers around the base of the shaft, I exerted a little more pressure, encircling his balls and pulling the flesh taut. He gave a sharp intake of breath and I watched as a glistening pearl of moisture appeared at the tip. The salty drop was gone with a flick of my tongue and he murmured something incomprehensible. Lapping at the little fold just underneath the head I heard him groan and I took him in my mouth.

He clutched my head in his hands, pushing me up and down along his length. It wouldn't take him long. I let him guide my rhythm and within seconds I felt the shudders of his climax and he emptied himself into my mouth.

I swallowed every drop and then raised my head. Paul's face was flushed and it took him several moments to catch his breath. He tousled my hair affectionately as I smiled up at him. I rubbed my bottom, wishing now that it had been harder. The sensation was fading already.

'That was nice,' I said at last, not knowing what else to say.

'You weren't bad either,' he joked, still breathless. 'In fact, I think you've earned the book. Just be sure to return it on time or you'll be in trouble.'

I smiled and curled up on the sofa next to him. 'Promise?'

'Promise.' He pulled me on to his lap and I affected an exaggerated hiss of pain. His hands cradled my bottom, squeezing gently. 'Mmmm, you're still very warm. Positively radiant.'

'You have no idea how long I've wanted to feel like this,' I told him.

'You have no idea how long I've been wanting to do that,' he countered. 'I remember drawing handprints on girls' bottoms in magazines when I was a little boy.'

I giggled, charmed by the image. 'Well, I used to lie across the lap of my giant teddy bear and pretend he was . . . well, you know.'

Paul laughed. 'That's dead clever,' he said, giving my bottom an affectionate squeeze. 'If a bit deviant.'

'I was a strange little girl.'

Suddenly, Paul stiffened.

'What is it?'

'Shh!' He cocked his head, listening intently. Then he sprang to his feet, doing up his jeans in a panic. 'Oh, bollocks!'

'What?' I demanded, getting frightened.

'She's home!'

It took me a few seconds to process the situation, but it suddenly came clear. The spotless flat. His initial nervousness. Flatmates indeed.

I scrambled up off the sofa as he shoved the coffee table back into its place. He grabbed the book and thrust it at me, nearly making me drop it. He waved his hands wildly at me in a shooing-away gesture. I shook my head in bewilderment. Where the hell was I supposed to go?

'Hi, sweetie!' came a cheery female voice from the front door.

'Hi!' Paul called back. 'Be right there!'

'That's OK, I'm gonna have a bath. I'm knackered.'

There was the sound of footsteps clumping up the stairs and Paul waited until he heard the bathroom door shut before dragging me by the arm to the front door.

The panic was contagious and the outrage didn't hit me until I was past the threshold. I crossed my arms over my chest and shook my head at Paul in scathing disapproval.

He offered me a pathetic shrug and glanced back behind him miserably. 'She doesn't know,' he whispered, a look of desperate pleading in his eyes.

'I gathered that much,' I said with a frosty smile. 'Thanks anyway.'

And I turned on my heel and marched away. It was only when I got to the top of the street that I realised I'd left my knickers behind. But somehow the idea of Paul's girlfriend finding them seemed only fair.

Three

'What that girl wants is a damned good thrashing.'

I would never forget hearing my father say those words. Not about me. No, never about me. It was a little girl around my age, throwing a screaming tantrum in Marks and Spencer having been refused sweets.

Like a tableau vivant, the scene was frozen in my memory. I could recall every detail. The shrill little harpy stamping her pink ballerina shoes on the lino floor. Her ineffectual mother looking around her in embarrassed desperation, as though hoping a passing stranger would offer assistance. The disgusted expressions on the elderly couple as they shuffled past.

The inauthentic howls of misery became more and more outrageous each time the little girl shaped her quivering lips around the word 'chocolate'. My parents, at first startled, quickly lost patience. And then there was my father's comment, which he intended to be overheard.

It would never have occurred to me to act like that and I was frightened on a deep level by the extremity of the girl's behaviour. That my father could say she deserved a thrashing for it only magnified that it was quite beyond the pale. I watched, transfixed, to see if the thrashing would happen. In the end, the harried mother gave in to the child's demands and there were audible mutters of disapproval from the elderly couple. I was both thrilled and conflicted by my father's remark. Curious yet repelled. What was a thrashing like? Some dark confused part of me desperately wanted to know. But I would never be able to bring myself to act like a two-year-old brat to earn a spanking. Even as a child, I had my dignity.

I'd never seen a proper over-the-knee spanking. The ones in cartoons didn't count. Those old classics from the 1940s and 50s always seemed to have some character being pulled over someone's knee and smacked. I was drawn to those particular scenes, with no idea why they fascinated me.

Then there was Bad Hospital – a peculiar game I used to play with my cousin Gina when we were little. There wasn't really a story. We were just two girls trapped in a giant hospital and the object of the game was to avoid the wicked doctors with their evil needles. (We had a paralysing fear of needles.) The game involved crawling under beds and behind sofas, screaming whenever we encountered our imaginary pursuers. Then we would run frantically to find another hiding place. In my mind, there were other things these unseen evil doctors would do to us if they caught us, but Gina remained fixated on needles and wouldn't follow my hints of other torments.

One day Gina's brother Davy asked if he could play too. At first Gina said no, but I was quite keen, especially when he said he wanted to be one of the doctors. He was only a few years older than us, but he was almost a teenager, so he seemed worldly and wise to me. He was my first crush. And when he found me hiding behind the long velvet curtains in the sitting room I shrieked and ran from him, but not fast enough. He pounced on me and sat on my back, pinning me to the carpet. Then he whacked my bottom, exclaiming triumphantly that he'd just given me a shot that would knock me out so I couldn't escape. It was only a little smack, but it had resounded through my entire body like an electric shock.

I was giddy with strange excitement and I feigned succumbing to the knockout drug. I watched as Davy raced after his squealing sister and overcame her as well. We lay grinning at each other across the room while our conqueror stood, hands on hips like a superhero, nodding proudly at having vanquished us. And all I could think of was escaping so I could be captured and smacked again. And again. And again.

My feelings were a maelstrom of heady ambivalence. And they only intensified as I grew up. I couldn't articulate it. There was something unfathomably appealing about an unruly girl being hauled across a strong man's knee and spanked, yet I had no wish to be beaten or abused. I didn't really know where the line was. Sometimes it frightened me and I wished I could be rid of the bizarre fascination. I tried to think of other, so-called *normal* things. But it was no use; images imposed themselves on me unbidden. Whatever this affliction was, it was wired into me.

In primary school, Juliet Fairfax told me how she used to get her brother into trouble just to see him spanked. Naturally, he did the same to her. This thrilled me and I played at her house often, mainly in the hope of seeing it happen. I longed for a brother or sister of my own. Someone to get *me* into trouble.

Once Miss Baker smacked Sara Robinson for drawing something 'vulgar' I never got to see. The teacher hauled Sara up out of her desk and gave her two brisk swats on the rear. That was all. But Sara's eyes went wide with astonishment and then they filled with tears. It couldn't possibly have hurt, but she wailed as though she'd lost a limb.

My heart hammered in my chest and I replayed the event obsessively in my mind. I embellished it, making Miss Baker pull Sara over her knee and bare her bottom for a long hard spanking. Just like in the cartoons and movies that made me feel so funny. What would the teacher's pale hand feel like against my own bottom? What was it like to be bent over someone's knee?

Some part of me knew enough to feel ashamed and that only confused me more. Worse, I was certain that everyone knew what I was thinking, that my mind was somehow broadcasting the images for all to see. Miss Baker would think I really *wanted* to be spanked. But then, didn't I? When the other little girls played school, I always secretly hoped there would be a spanking. None of them ever mentioned it, though, and I was left feeling alienated. Isolated. Dying both of curiosity and the fear that it would be satisfied. But in spite of (or perhaps because of) my fixation, I was well behaved in school.

The only time I did misbehave in Miss Baker's class, I was doodling instead of paying attention to the lesson. She called my name and told me to stand up. Instantly I feared the worst. My skin turned to ice as I clambered out of my seat, my legs weak and uncertain. But she didn't spank me; she put me in the corner instead. I couldn't reconcile my simultaneous feelings of relief and disappointment. Humiliated, I cried softly as the lesson continued behind me while I stood with my nose pressed into the angle of the walls, excluded. It was a feeling I would come to know well – the loneliness of the one who knows she is 'different'.

As a teenager I kept a secret video library of all the movie and TV spankings I could find. In the films made before political correctness, there were plenty. *Kiss Me Kate* and *McClintock* were two of the best. Naturally, BBC drama was a fertile source, replete with Dickensian floggings and canings. I hooked up two VCRs and copied scenes from TV movies and rented videos. I was devastated when I finally wore out my grainy pirated VHS cassettes, victims of too much obsessive rewinding and pausing.

I pretended to share my father's fascination with the days of fighting sail. But what really hooked me was the severe discipline of the Royal Navy in its glory days. Rum, sodomy and the lash. Common sailors were flogged, and midshipmen were bent over a cannon and caned across the seat of their tight white breeches. *Damn the Defiant* had a tantalising subplot with a sadistic first lieutenant and a hapless midshipman who found himself kissing the gunner's daughter at every opportunity.

One of my dad's books gave me fantasy fodder for weeks. It was about 'female tars' – women who went to sea disguised as men and boys. A sailor's wife could expect a miserable existence on shore. The sea offered freedom, adventure and the chance to earn her own money. There was so much scope for fantasy there. The captain might agree to keep her secret and make her his personal cabin boy, subject to his discipline, naturally. Or perhaps the ship would be captured by pirates and the 'boy' taken prisoner. There was no shortage of punishment scenes in the books and movies set in that era.

My mum liked Elvis, so I bought her *Blue Hawaii* for Christmas one year. I'd heard there was a spanking scene in it. I was unprepared for the suggestion that we all watch it as a family. I had counted on being able to see it on my own sometime later. So I watched it with my parents, burning with embarrassment at what I knew was coming. I was sure they would know why I had chosen that particular movie. And when Elvis dragged the bratty girl over his knee for a few well-deserved smacks, I slid down into the cushions of the sofa, turning away so they couldn't see my scarlet face.

But Hollywood spankings were, by and large, unfulfilling. What really pushed my buttons were the longer and more elaborate scenes in novels. Even ones that the author cruelly skimmed over gave me a place to start. My imagination could supply the rest.

To this day I can't be sure if my memory of a certain TV adaptation of *Tom Sawyer* was real or not. Mark Twain only hints at the scene in the book. But I can remember every detail with vivid clarity. The angry schoolmaster demanding to know who was responsible for the prank. Lovely red-headed Becky Thatcher quaking in terror. Tom leaping valiantly from his desk – 'I done it!' – and taking Becky's whipping in her place. I even remember him having to select the switch from the rack on the wall.

But on the whole books were better. Classic school stories naturally yielded the richest harvest and historical fiction was consistently reliable as well. I couldn't bring myself to read romance novels, but skimming one once rewarded me with a scene where a dashing highwayman kidnapped and spanked the haughty lady he accosted on the road.

There was even a horror author who could always be depended on to include a spanking or a caning in nearly every book. In one he described a movie called *The Battle of the Villa Fiorita* and I promptly went out and got it. The father–daughter spanking in it struck the right chord, but the scene was nowhere near as enticing as the psychically altered version watched by the character in his novel. It was a talent I fantasised about cultivating.

I had to know what a real spanking felt like, but there was no one who could help me. Not that I could have asked anyway. So, one day when my parents left me alone in the house, the inevitable happened. I stood in front of the mirror, pulled down my pants and, feeling like a right fool, I spanked myself.

It was just a few tentative little slaps at first. It felt strange. Slightly stingy, but not unpleasant. However, I couldn't tune out the ridiculousness of what I was doing. It was all I could do to keep from laughing. I tried to pretend that someone else was spanking me. But it wasn't just pain I was after; I needed to feel punished. It had to be harder. It had to hurt.

Emboldened, I drew my arm back a little farther and brought the flat of my hand down harder on my right cheek. It stung a bit more, but it was impossible to hit myself hard enough to feel like a proper spanking.

Looking around the room I spied an electrical cord. I doubled it over and swung it round to hit my bottom. I didn't measure it out, though, and the cord wrapped all the way around my hips, landing across my abdomen. I cursed and rubbed the angry red welt.

I wasn't about to try that again, so I grabbed a book instead. *David Copperfield*, as it happened – a hefty hardback. I barely felt it.

Frustrated, I went to the kitchen, where I dug through the cupboards and drawers. I came across a wooden spoon and I returned to the mirror. I drew it back and landed a good sharp swat right in the centre of my right cheek. That did it. With a yelp of surprise and pain I dropped the spoon and clutched my cheek, massaging away the sting. I retrieved the spoon and smacked the other cheek even harder. Then I watched, mesmerised, as two bright-red ovals with white centres deepened against my pale skin.

I smacked each cheek several more times, wincing and hissing at the pain. I didn't like the actual sensation when the spoon landed, but I enjoyed the warm tingling as the sharpness began to fade. And I loved the marks that decorated my bottom. I imagined that having someone else doing the smacking would make all the difference.

I set myself a number: twenty. I would give each cheek ten hard whacks, not letting up when it hurt and not cutting it short. I owed it to myself not to wimp out. And I didn't. There were several rings of tender bruises when I was done and I hoped none of the other girls would see when I changed for gym. Though there was a perverse appeal in the idea that they might think I got spanked at home. They might share their own stories with me then.

It was soon after that that Mr Chancellor began to invade my fantasies.

Four

I trembled as I knelt in the confessional, intimidated by the shadowy silhouette of the priest on the other side of the grille. I had no idea what to say. Was I supposed to speak first? Was he?

The sound of his voice made me jump. He offered some sort of blessing, but all I heard was a low murmur.

I felt like a bad undercover spy. I didn't know the proper response. Now that I was here, what was I supposed to do? My mind was spinning. Finally, I took a deep breath and plunged ahead with the one bit I knew.

'Bless me, Father, for I have sinned.'

I tried not to think about my adventure with Paul, but I kept circling back to it. It had been fun, but the untimely interruption of Paul's girlfriend had rather spoilt it. I did feel sorry for him, though, and I was in no position to claim the moral high ground. If I had been faced with a similar opportunity and a vanilla partner conveniently out of the way for the evening . . .

Still, there was something left wanting in the scene. It was too loving and gentle. Too sensual. Too *nice*. In my fantasies the focus was on discipline, not sexual pleasure. I wouldn't deny that punishment turned me on, but somehow it was the very non-sexual nature of it that was so hot. Just like the Victorian letters. The game was pretending it was one thing while knowing that underneath it was something else entirely.

I didn't regret the sexual play. But, in retrospect, I wished it had happened independently of the spanking. Especially if I could have pretended it was against my will. It made me feel guilty, but there was a strong non-consensual component to my kink. Spanking was a vehicle for intimacy, yes, but it still had to be punishment. Otherwise I retained some control. And much of the appeal lay in being *out* of control.

The Royal Oak was crowded, but not overly noisy. I settled in with some notes and picked at my food while I studied them. I needed to put Paul out of my mind so I could concentrate on my thesis.

'And then he . . .' The voice came from my left.

'What? Tell me!'

The girl lowered her voice. 'He spanked me.'

The word got my attention instantly and I nearly choked on the leathery haddock I'd been trying to force down. No, that couldn't be what she had said. Surely not.

I shifted in my seat to get a sidelong look at the two girls at the table next to me. They were on the other side of an oak pillar and they probably thought they had privacy.

The one who had said the magic word was a young blonde, probably no more than eighteen. Busty and wearing too much makeup. Her friend was a mousy redhead with glasses. I inched closer to the beam so I could hear the details.

'Oh my God, you are *so* not serious!'

'No, I swear it. He told me to see him in his office after confession and he'd – well, he'd give me a different kind of penance.'

My heart was in my throat as I listened.

The friend seemed just as hungry for details. 'So how did it happen?'

'Well . . .' Now the girl seemed embarrassed. 'I told him what happened at the hen party with Jose and Maurice.'

'You told him about that?' The redhead sounded incredulous. 'No way! Even the part about Sarah's mum?'

I stifled a laugh. It must have been one hell of a hen night.

'Of course. You, like, have to confess everything or you can't be absolved,' the blonde explained impatiently.

'Well?'

She had clearly been bursting to share the details and the words came in a rush. 'Well, he's, like, really strict. So when I told him what I did he goes, "You're acting like a spoilt teenager, Gemma. You've always been wilful and deep down you only want attention." Then he's like: "What you need is a good spanking."'

The redhead gasped.

'Yeah, I know! I couldn't believe it. I mean, he's, like, been a friend of the family for years, so he's known me since I was a little girl. He knows what a brat I was. So I'm like: "Well, go on, then!" You know, never thinking he's gonna really *do* it!'

'And he actually did it? He spanked you? Promise you're not taking the piss?'

Shut up, I thought. *Let her tell the bloody story*!

Gemma took a big gulp of her pint. 'Uh-huh. He said, if I'm gonna act like a child, I'll be treated like one and have my bottom smacked. Then he, you know, pulled me over his lap and spanked me.'

'What, over your clothes?'

'Yes. Well, over my knickers.'

Disappointed, I readjusted the image in my mind. I'd been imagining a bare-bottom spanking. But still the picture made my pulse race.

'Wow! Did it hurt?'

Gemma laughed. 'Absolutely! But here's the weird bit: there was something sort of comforting about it too. I mean, I really did feel guilty about what happened at the party. I guess that's why I went to confession in the first place. But, omigod, I hope Brandon never finds out. He'd go totally mental. But I did feel, you know, absolved. I can't really describe it. It was so much more intense than just saying a few Hail Marys. You know?'

'I can imagine.'

I could as well. My face felt warm and flushed and I stared at my plate, suddenly no longer hungry. My mind was racing. How many Catholic churches were there in the area? I was desperate to know which church, which priest.

The girls were silent for nearly a minute. At last the redhead spoke. 'So how were things left?'

The blonde sighed. 'I told Father Michael I was truly contrite. And I promised never to do it again'

'Just like that? Did he say he'd spank you again if you did?'

'I didn't ask.'

It was maddening! How could the girl be so blasé about it? She didn't even sound embarrassed. I would have been mortified in the same position.

'Will you ever go back?'

'Of course,' the blonde said, sounding shocked. 'Why ever not? I've always gone to St James's.'

I made a mental note of the names. St James's church. Father Michael. I wasn't Catholic, but it was time to go to confession.

'Bless me, Father, for I have sinned.' It was like speaking a foreign language. The cloying silence made the confessional seem even smaller as I waited for him to respond.

'How long has it been since your last confession?'

I had expected him to call me 'my child'. But I'd probably just seen too many movies. There was a hint of impatience in his voice and I decided there was no way I could pull off the charade. I was only here for one reason anyway.

'Um . . . well, never.'

There was silence from the other side.

'I should probably tell you I'm not a Catholic.'

More silence. Was he making the sign of the cross at me? Could he see into my sinful little mind?

'Is that OK?'

'I'm not sure why you're here, then,' he said. His voice was low and sombre. 'I can't offer you absolution if you're not a Catholic.'

'Oh, I know,' I said. 'But I had to tell someone. And they say confession is good for the soul. Even for heathens.' I gave a nervous little laugh.

The priest didn't reciprocate. He didn't seem like a man who laughed easily. But he said, 'Go on.'

The blonde in the pub had clearly got up to something wildly sexual with two men at a hen party. Perhaps they were male strippers. It followed that Father Michael took a dim view of such promiscuity. I closed my eyes and plunged ahead.

'I cheated on my husband,' I said. The word was alien to me and I instantly felt guilty about the lie, certain he could see through it.

The priest prompted me with his silence.

'More than once. I just couldn't help myself. There are things he won't do for me, you know?' I resisted the urge to take it further. It had to be believable. Otherwise he was likely to think I was just using him to enact some perverse fantasy – baiting a man of the cloth. Besides, while I wasn't religious, the idea of lying to a priest felt like tempting fate.

He didn't say anything.

'Father?'

'Yes.'

'I need help. I just have so many dirty thoughts. I can't control them.' That certainly *was* the truth.

'Do you try?'

'Well, yes. I mean – I try to, but the fantasies just take over. They consume me and it's all I can think about.'

There was a long pause. I was beginning to feel claustrophobic in the dark box. My knees were stiff from kneeling and the collected scent of incense and candles made me feel slightly drunk. I wasn't really lying now. My fantasies certainly did consume me. And the confession was having the opposite effect. In theory it was supposed to unburden me, but it was only making my body respond in what this stern priest would call sinful ways.

At last he spoke. 'If you have no desire to stop, there is little anyone can do to help you.'

Floundering, I said, 'I just need a way to cope with the guilt. Some sort of forgiveness. Or catharsis. I don't want to be bad.'

I waited for him to take the hint. As the silence deepened I began to lose faith. Mr Chancellor hadn't taken my hints back at school. There was no guarantee this priest would either. And there was always the possibility that I was in the wrong church, that this was the wrong priest. Worst of all – what if the blonde had been making it all up?

'How old are you, my child?'

There. He'd said it that time. 'Twenty-four, Father.'

A moment's silence. Then he said, 'Perhaps there is a way . . .'

I couldn't breathe. The moment was so fragile. Any sound or movement from me could shatter it.

'It's a little unorthodox. But, if you truly wish to purge your sins, I could counsel you privately, in my office.'

It was all I could do to keep my voice calm and steady as I said, 'Yes. Thank you.'

'Very well, then. Come back in an hour. I'll be waiting.'

My fate was sealed. It was one of the longest hours of my life.

As I knocked on the priest's door I thought of my failed attempts with Mr Chancellor. Just seeing Father Michael's name on the door gave me a jolt of adrenaline. It wasn't the wrong priest or the wrong church. It was going to happen.

His office was strikingly different from my headmaster's. Gloomy and dark, with dusty teetering stacks of books on every surface. Light struggled in through the window blinds to lie on the floor like distorted ribbons. Father Michael sat behind a huge oak desk and he looked up as I entered.

'Close the door,' he said. He had the authoritative voice of a general. Deep and booming in the cramped little cell.

I pushed the door shut and stood in front of him, clasping my hands behind me. I wore a short red tartan kilt with black over-the-knee socks. A generous expanse of thigh showed between the hem of the skirt and the tops of my socks. He was bound to disapprove.

'So, my child, you have sinned and you came to me for forgiveness. Is that right?'

'Yes.'
'But forgiveness requires penance, does it not?'
'Yes.'
'Have you ever been punished?' he asked.
'Punished?'
'Spanked.'
The simple sound of the word sent shivers through me. I had been waiting for this for so long. A week ago I could have answered him honestly. But then, that hadn't been a punishment. 'No,' I whispered, adding 'sir' out of habit.
'I'm not a schoolmaster,' he said tersely. 'You may address me as "Father".'
'Yes, Father,' I corrected, already beginning to squirm.
He sat studying me for several intolerable seconds before standing up. The ancient chair shrieked in protest. As he moved closer I fought the urge to take a step back. He was tall and imposing. The immaculate white dog collar stood out in stark contrast to the austere black cassock, enhancing the formality of the situation. Father Michael's face bore the deep lines of one who has spent a lifetime in grim contemplation. Mr Chancellor had been hard enough to cheek; there was no way I could be anything but respectful with Father Michael.
'What is your name?'
I stammered it out. 'Angie.'
His eyes glinted, though not with humour. 'Are you nervous, Angela?'
I winced at the use of my full name. 'Yes, sir – Father. I am.'
'Good. Punishment *should* be feared, if it is to act as a deterrent.'
I looked down at the floor, chewing my lip.
'Do you accept my punishment?'
'Yes, Father.' My words were barely audible.
'Then ask me for it.'
I flushed so deeply my ears burnt. It was more than I was prepared for. I opened my mouth, but couldn't form the words. At last I choked out what I thought he wanted to hear.

'Please punish me, Father.'

'How?' he persisted sternly.

I lowered my head even further. I had never actually said the word aloud to anyone. 'Spank me.'

'And why do you need to be spanked?'

'Because I'm a dirty little girl.' Saying the words to a priest made my legs weak and I longed for a chair to sink into. Now that I'd asked for it I was having second thoughts. I was in over my head. This wouldn't be a gentle, erotic scene like I'd had with Paul. Father Michael was going to spank me hard and it was going to hurt. The old maxim about being careful what you wished for was about to be demonstrated. But it was too late to chicken out now.

Father Michael watched the play of emotions on my face with satisfaction. Then he moved away. He took a straight-backed chair from the wall near the tiny window and placed it in the centre of the room. He sat down with the air of one accustomed to ceremony and ritual in all things.

'Very well, Angela,' he said, as though pronouncing sentence. 'Come here.' He indicated the spot to his right, exactly where Paul had made me stand.

I forced my feet to comply, painfully aware of the tremor in my gait, as though I'd just run a marathon.

'Your profligate behaviour is disgusting,' he said with vehemence. 'And it must stop. It shows a childish lack of regard for consequences and will only lead you to damnation. You must learn to resist the temptations of the flesh.'

With that he pulled me down across his lap.

I uttered a little squeak of surprise and embarrassment, but didn't fight him. I rested my hands on the carpet and straightened my legs behind me so that only my toes were touching the floor. The position made me feel intensely vulnerable and childlike.

Father Michael placed his left hand in the small of my back and without another word he brought his right hand down on my skirt with a muffled thump. It didn't hurt at all. He smacked me several more times, but the woolly tartan offered too much protection.

He stopped.

'For this to have any effect,' he began slowly. 'You need to have less protection.'

I made a mournful protesting sound, but I didn't resist as his fingers dragged the tartan kilt up over my bottom. He exposed the frilly French knickers that barely covered my cheeks, revealing more than they concealed. I trembled in the silence. I knew how alluring my bottom must look, with the lower half of it on display and his distaste was unmistakable.

'Even for confession,' he said. 'You wear the garments of a whore.'

Quietly thanking God I hadn't worn a thong, I took hold of the chair leg as I felt his hand rise again.

He brought it down hard, with a resounding smack. I yelped. But before I could process the sensation he smacked me on the other cheek. Again and again his hand connected with the smooth skin of my bottom, the smacks ringing out in the dim poky office.

I struggled and writhed over his lap, crying out at the stinging pain. I arched my back, but he pushed me down firmly and carried on. This was not play. It hurt much more than I had thought it would. Father Michael laid on with a will, alternating from cheek to cheek, peppering the whole of my bottom with brisk smacks. As the knickers left my lower cheeks uncovered he aimed most of the blows on the bare flesh. And he didn't neglect the tender crease where my thighs joined my bottom.

I twisted from side to side, but there was no escape. A stack of leaflets lay on the floor in front of me and I tried to focus on them to distract myself from the pain. But the spanking was too intense. In desperation I flung my right arm behind me, but he simply clamped my wrist against my lower back, smacking me even harder.

It was exactly what I had always wanted. And now all I wanted was for it to stop. It was too much. There was nothing enjoyable or pleasurable about it at all. It was intensely painful. But I was helpless to escape it. I heard myself yelping and begging him to stop, but he had no pity for me.

'No, young lady,' he said over the unrelenting cadence. 'I will not stop. You agreed to this. It's intended to hurt because it's intended to teach you a lesson. One you won't forget.'

'But I've learnt it!' I cried. 'I'm sorry!'

'You're sorry it hurts,' he corrected me. 'But you're not contrite. I have no intention of stopping until you feel genuinely remorseful.'

The words filled me with horror. Remorse for what? A fabricated affair? I kicked wildly, howling with pain. I could almost see my bottom turning from pink to red to purple as his hand rained merciless blows on it. There was no escape.

I heard myself pleading, promising, cajoling. Anything to make it stop. Tears pricked my eyes and, just when I thought I couldn't possibly take any more, a strange thing happened. I flashed back to an incident from my first year at university. A time when I had felt overwhelming guilt and no one to confess it to.

I'd been out clubbing with my best friend Diane and her new boyfriend, Nikolai. He was from Moscow and spoke almost no English. But there was a forthright intensity about him that fascinated me. I listened, transfixed, to his rich lyrical language as he talked to Diane in Russian and she translated for me. I couldn't help seeing him through the obsessive veil of my fetish, which cast him as a KGB officer and had him inflict creative tortures on me. His large hands were *made* for smacking a girl's bottom. I couldn't keep my eyes off him. And, as the evening wore on, it became clear that he felt much the same about me. And Diane – sweet, naive, trusting Diane – was oblivious to the sparks.

As the night wore on and we got drunker and drunker, my resolve weakened unforgivably and I fell into bed with him that same night – while poor Diane was asleep in the next room. He murmured incomprehensible Russian to me while I drowned in wicked fantasies that would probably have horrified him. He was a rough selfish lover and he left me feeling cheap and dirty as he slipped away, back to bed with my friend. Unsatisfied, I had no choice but to get myself off. The shame only enhanced my climax.

Diane never accused me outright, but I could tell by her eyes that she knew what we'd done. We drifted apart not long after that and I never saw her or Nikolai again.

I had forgotten all about the incident. I'd felt terrible at the time, but I'd moved on. Now it was all I could think of as I gasped out apology after apology. I'd found a hidden pocket of guilt, a dirty little secret that needed purging. The tears began to spill down my cheeks and I surrendered to the release. I deserved this.

I was unaware when the spanking finally stopped.

I lay over Father Michael's knees, sobbing convulsively. Gradually I became aware of his hand on my back, stroking me gently. Comforting me. The unexpected tenderness released another flood of emotion and he gathered me on to his lap, letting me soak his cassock with my tears.

When I was finally able to calm myself, I looked at him in bewilderment, sniffling like a little girl. His expression had softened and his eyes crinkled in a slight smile.

He offered me a handkerchief and I took it gratefully, wiping my eyes and blowing my nose loudly.

'Do you feel better?' he asked.

Disoriented, I nodded. 'Uh-huh.'

I felt as though I had dived off a cliff and abandoned myself to the reality of death only to discover that I could fly. My body felt lighter and the pain in my bottom had shaded into a tingling pleasant warmth.

I left the church in a daze, marvelling at the experience and the intensity of my response. The spanking was nothing like I'd expected. I had genuinely hated every minute of it, but now that it was over it was all I could think about. My backside was still smarting, a constant reminder. Confused thoughts and emotions whirled round in my mind, dancing just beyond the reach of reason.

I knew instinctively that if he hadn't held me while I wept it would have been traumatic for me. It had signalled an end to the punishment and reassured me that I was forgiven. I had let down my walls and let him inside my head. I had been completely vulnerable and exposed and he had not abused my trust.

No other form of punishment could ever reach me as deeply as the spanking had. Tedious impositions and detentions had never touched the emotional core. There was no surrender there, no submission to caring authority. And, most of all, no intimacy. That was the key.

The sexual escapade with Paul hadn't had the depth of what I'd just shared with Father Michael. And yet there had been nothing sexual about this spanking at all. It was pure punishment. Why, then, was I so aroused now that it was over?

As soon as I got home I yanked up my skirt to see my bottom in the mirror. It was glowing red and sore to the touch, speckled with tiny purplish bruises from particularly hard smacks. His fingertips. Eager to experience the sensation fully, I sat on a hard wooden chair, wincing at the sting. It hurt to sit. Overcome with the joy of my discovery, I felt my eyes begin to water again. I had entered a strange and wonderful place and there was no going back.

The euphoric awareness was like an alternate reality. I felt lighter, as though I could fly. I could only compare it to descriptions I'd read about spiritual epiphanies. My insides burnt with a strange new fire and I wanted to share my discovery with the world. But there was no one I could tell, no one who would understand.

Suddenly my racy thesis seemed colourless and uninspired. Perhaps I could ask Dr Morrison about incorporating an experiential element. Field research. He would probably just nod distractedly, as if I'd suggested using Century Schoolbook instead of Times New Roman.

Still high on endorphins, I climbed into bed. I closed my eyes and replayed the afternoon as my fingers crept inside my pyjamas. Now that I'd been punished, I could allow myself some pleasure. It only took a few skilful swirls of my finger to bring me to a shattering climax.

The crash came the next morning and tore the bottom out of my heart.

Five

My sleep was disordered and fitful. When I woke, the pillow was soaked with tears. I'd been crying in my sleep and waking hadn't made it stop. Even the lullaby of the shipping forecast, usually so soothing and reassuring, had lost its power to comfort me. My head felt heavy and there was a rolling, queasy feeling when I tried to move.

I couldn't get out of bed. I didn't want to. I didn't want to do anything. The high was gone and in its place was an oppressive leaden weight. I had felt complete. Connected at last in a real way to the elusive conflicted part of me. Now there was only a cold aching void.

All I could think about was Father Michael. I heard his voice in my head and felt his hand on my bottom. Cold rain streamed over the windowpanes like a mockery of my tears.

I moped around, in mourning for the profound intimacy I'd experienced. It wasn't sexual; it was something I couldn't define. But the ephemeral bond had taken me to a fantastic height and then forsaken me at its apex. It was all downhill from there.

The marks lasted a week. I examined them every day, replaying the confession and penance again and again in my mind, yearning for more. Gradually, they began to fade and with them went my inconsolable mood. It had happened once; it could happen again. I wondered how long I should wait before going back to St James's. How soon would be too soon? I didn't want to put him wise to my game, but I needed what he could give me the way a junkie needs a pusher.

Desperation finally gave me the motivation I needed. But not to see the priest. I understood now that this wasn't just a frivolous quirk; it was something I couldn't live without. And I couldn't possibly be the only one who felt this way.

As soon as I could, I filled in the university forms to get access to the online spanking community. I claimed it was necessary for my research. But my thesis was the last thing on my mind. I had to find my kink's companion.

It was surprisingly difficult to type the word into the search engine. *Spanking*. It looked so plain, so matter-of-fact. But it was a potent word; it had the power to weaken me and make me writhe with dread and delight. The cursor blinked unhurriedly while my finger hovered over the ENTER key. I was on the threshold of a discovery, one I knew would change my life forever. I made myself savour the moment, drawing out the suspense until the word began to lose its meaning.

At last I pressed the key. Immediately a list of URLs appeared. Millions of hits. More than I could ever hope to investigate. There were websites filled with stories, photos, fantasies, drawings, discussions and personal ads. Newsgroups, forums, messenger services and chat rooms. Of course, there were countless porn sites as well, but the sites for true spanking enthusiasts weren't hard to spot. The discovery brought back some of the euphoria I'd felt after the catharsis in the priest's dusty office.

Gateways demanded to know if I was old enough to enter and I felt like a knight on a quest. I clicked my way in, delighted and amazed. I'd found them at last: others of my kind.

Within the spanking world I was intrigued to discover two distinct camps. There was an erotic contingent for whom sex and spanking were inextricably linked. The one had to lead to the other. Spanking was a sexual act, intended to arouse and designed for mutual pleasure. Though I'd enjoyed playing with Paul, I still couldn't quite get my head round the idea of a mutually pleasurable spanking.

I'd heard someone say once that whatever you thought about while you masturbated to orgasm was what you were into. Well, the only thing I ever thought about was being spanked. Sex could be enjoyable, but it just couldn't compete with a well-smacked bottom.

The other camp was where I belonged. They were into punishment. Pure and simple. And punishment wasn't meant to be enjoyed; it was meant to hurt. To teach a lesson. To correct and reform. The enjoyment came afterwards – in the warm glow of sore cheeks and the sense of relinquished control.

One of the most fascinating websites was a vast archive of factual documents and personal accounts of corporal punishment around the world. At first sight it looked like a purely objective resource, but it had all the hallmarks of a fetishistic mind behind it. Likewise, the overinterested Wikipedia article on spanking had clearly been written by people who shared my predilection. I was overjoyed. Here were my Victorian flagellants, strutting their stuff in the guise of detached reportage.

I didn't waste any time; I registered with a site for personals and posted an ad of my own.

> DEAR SIR,
>
> I'm waiting nervously in a queue outside your study, listening to the awful SWOOSH-THWACK! from within. All too soon the wait is over and a tearful girl rushes out. Now it's my turn. I'll fidget while you scold me, flexing the cane in your hands. When you order me to bend over I'll be shaking so much it will be impossible to keep my legs straight. But you're accustomed to girls being frightened. You'll instruct me to raise my skirt and tuck it well up over my back. Then you'll hook your fingers in the waistband of my white cotton knickers and pull them down to my knees. I'll shudder as you lay the cane against my bottom. 'Count them, girl,' you'll say sternly. Then the cane will draw back and land sharply,

painfully. 'One, sir. Two, sir.' All the way up to six. Twelve if I've been especially naughty. How long will you make me wait, sir?

Yours respectfully,
Angie

I got more responses than I could have wished for. And there were some frighteningly clueless ones. Guys who had obviously read too much of John Norman's Gor series and taken every word literally. 'True masters' who didn't seem to understand that I wasn't into whips and chains. I couldn't possibly have been clearer about what I wanted. I didn't have anything against D/s or BDSM in general; they just weren't my kink. And if these guys were truly into it themselves, they ought to have known that.

Some of the emails I got were as much an assault on the English language as on me. I deleted them. The grammar and spelling were so appalling I marvelled that the writers were able to operate a computer at all. I knew I was being a snob but, if these men couldn't be bothered to proofread three lines of text, why should I bother to read it? The stern headmaster of my fantasies would never write, 'wow u sound hot, send me a pic of ur ass and im me for cyber!!!'

I likewise deleted anything with the phrase 'On your knees, bitch'. There were dismayingly many of those. But I wasn't alone there either: the forums were filled with rants about swaggering, posturing wannabe doms. 'Lord' this and 'Sir' that. Social invalids who wouldn't know what to do with a vanilla girl, let alone one with my needs and desires. It wasn't the titles that bothered me; it was the profusion of blustering men who mistook domineering for dominance.

Even the sincerely kinky ones could be frustrating. No sooner would I enter a chat room than an instant message would pop up with some crude Gorean sex command or graphic description of how I would serve them. The presumption of not capitalising my name and expecting me to call them 'Master' on the basis of their self-proclaimed dominance really rankled.

'Oh, but spanking is just part of S&M,' one man insisted.

I pictured a naked slave girl kneeling at the feet of a headmaster brandishing a plastic Ann Summers whip. 'Sorry,' I replied, trying hard to be polite. 'The physical act may well be, but the ethos is completely different.'

He changed tack, assuring me that slaves got punished too, that it wasn't all about pleasure.

'I'm not a slave,' I bristled. 'Nor do I want to be.'

But he wouldn't give up. He was the leather equivalent of a Jehovah's Witness, determined to convert me from schoolgirl to submissive. I finally had to slam the cyber door in his face.

Most surprising of all was the number of people who were seriously conflicted by their feelings. In my naivety I had assumed that anyone 'out' enough to admit being into spanking was as unapologetic about it as I was. But for some the fetish was a sickness, a morbid fixation, a kind of self-inflicted torture. Compelled to find ways of justifying their offbeat sexuality, they agonised over the guilt they experienced for not being normal. I'd had my moments of doubt too, but that was ancient history now. The kink was too large a part of me to try to quash it. It defined me.

Day after day I haunted the chat rooms and forums, gushing about how wonderful it was to find a community of fellow enthusiasts – people I could share my fetish with. It was like being in love for the first time.

The librarian commented that she'd never seen me so engrossed in my work. I was at the library every day when it opened and had to be chucked out when it closed. Thinking quickly, I explained that I had just come up with a new angle for my thesis and was very excited about what my research was uncovering.

If she doubted my story she didn't let on, but I considered it a warning nonetheless. I tried to be good and focus on my naughty Victorians, but the lure of real spanking chat was always there and impossible to resist. I slipped into an unproductive cycle: I'd write a few words, decide I needed to look something up, surf the kinky sites, glance back at my thesis, declare myself uninspired, indulge myself with some spanking chat for 'inspiration', look again at my thesis, respond to email . . .

And so on. My thesis languished.

'And how many words have you written today, young lady?'

The instant message gave me a jolt. I cast a surreptitious glance around the library. When it was available I always used the computer at the far right end of the long table. I could angle the screen away from the one beside it and have relative privacy. No one could see what I was doing. I had mentioned in chat that I was working on a thesis, though I hadn't shared any details about the topic.

'Who wants to know?' I wrote back, trying to convey a challenging tone.

A few seconds later he replied. 'Someone who takes an interest in the education of young ladies.'

I blushed. I didn't know what to say to that. Luckily I didn't have to respond.

'Is your research proving fruitful, Angie?'

I wasn't surprised he knew my name; I'd used it in my personal ad. Rash, perhaps, but it was hardly an unusual name. 'So far,' I replied. 'But you have me at a disadvantage.'

'I'm Peter,' he said, adding a smiley. 'I was about to write you an email, but then I saw you were online.'

'Yes, I'm supposed to be working, but I'm a little blocked.'

'I don't let *my* students get away with that excuse.'

My fingers hesitated above the keyboard as a little flicker of warmth went through me. But before I could formulate a reply he wrote again.

'Would you like to chat?'

Would I ever.

Peter was in his early forties. He was a history professor and self-admitted pedant, both of which appealed to the intellectual snob in me. He wasn't into erotic spankings; like me, he favoured discipline and punishment.

'I'm not interested in the slutty schoolgirl look,' he wrote. 'I believe in proper school uniform.'

'What about underneath?' I asked.

'Regulation school knickers, of course. Anything else would be inauthentic.'

Oh yes, we would get on well.

Peter had been in the scene for many years. He'd been in spanking relationships and had friends who shared the fetish. He told me he was a keen roleplayer, which was something I'd never considered. I had my fantasies, but in fantasy you were already whoever or whatever you wanted. You weren't playing a role. I had never imagined acting out my fantasies. But Peter piqued my curiosity.

He was away on business, but would be back in London in a week. We agreed to meet for dinner on the Friday. Over the next few days, when he could escape from work, we exchanged email and played in the chat room.

I was amazed that simple chat could push my buttons so easily. And Peter could talk the talk. I constantly found myself looking up from the screen, blushing and shifty eyed, paranoid that someone was reading over my shoulder. I worried that Paul might turn up to try to entice me back for more consensual spanking play. But I knew who I was now.

In one email Peter asked for my measurements. I sent them, nervously wondering what use he would make of them. I was a kid counting the days, the minutes, the seconds until Christmas.

I gave him my mobile number, hoping he'd oblige me with the spanko equivalent of phone sex. But instead he sent me an email telling me to be careful.

'You must be more cautious, young lady,' he scolded me. I could just see him wagging his finger at me. 'I know it's thrilling to find where you belong, but you need to be careful about sharing sensitive information with people you haven't met. I could be Jack the Ripper for all you know.'

'He's probably not much of a threat any more,' I wrote back cheekily. 'What's the big deal? I'll be meeting you in a week anyway.'

'And if I had bad intentions it would be too late then.'

'Yeah, but maybe it will have been worth it!'

'Young lady, do I need to set you an essay on internet safety? You'll find it difficult to concentrate on writing it with a sore bottom.'

I writhed in my seat, my cheeks burning. I lived for his words and I printed out every squirmy email. They were my bedtime reading.

When he asked me if I'd ever been spanked, I told him about my recent experiences. He especially enjoyed the story about Father Michael. 'I have a friend who will want to go to confession when she hears about that,' he wrote.

I also told him about the terrible emotional crash I'd suffered afterwards.

Peter diagnosed it instantly. 'Sub-drop,' he said. 'It happens to lots of people. You'd just been through an extremely intense emotional experience. The elation can't last forever and, when the endorphin high wears off, it triggers a sort of grief. It's like a holiday you never wanted to end. Suddenly it's over and it's back to reality again. You're not equipped to cope with the mundane after that.'

That made perfect sense to me. And just knowing I wasn't alone in it was a comfort. I wondered if I would suffer it again after meeting Peter.

He directed me to several websites I hadn't yet found and my education progressed. I was amused to discover that America in the 1950s had its own equivalent of the Victorian correspondence column. *Your Romance*, a magazine for teenage girls, boasted its famous 'Pats and Peeves' column. Nearly all the letters were about spanking. Husbands who took their wives in hand and over the knee. Boyfriends who'd caught their girlfriends flirting with other guys and were keen to teach them a lesson. Bosses who knew how to deal with their secretaries' misdemeanours. All in the innocent chirpy voice characteristic of the period. All this could go into my thesis and I was relieved to have justified my quest.

He also sent me pictures and stories he'd scanned from old issues of *Blushes*. The magazine depicted another world – one where lecherous old goats were free to indulge their penchant for punishment with shop girls and nieces and maids. In the *Blushes* world, the girls expected no less and submitted, embarrassed but compliant, to whatever humiliating chastisement was inflicted on them. It was everything a modern, sexually liberated woman should scorn and despise. I loved it.

There was one thing I was dying to ask, but I wasn't sure how to bring it up. At his age, he must have some interesting school stories to tell. He'd mentioned boarding school but, when I asked him where he'd gone, he was coy.

'Oh, a place in Shropshire,' he responded glibly. 'You'd like the town, though. A maze of small streets filled with half-timbered houses.'

I was pretty sure I knew where he meant.

[illegible]

[illegible] away, the [illegible]

[illegible] minute I [illegible]

[illegible]

I wander[illegible] the rest of the [illegible] park [illegible]

[illegible] of the [illegible]

[illegible]

Six

I looked at the clock and sighed. I'd been chatting with Peter for nearly two hours. Reality was calling. My mum's birthday was approaching and I hadn't got a present yet. She had very upmarket tastes and I'd forgotten her completely the year before. This year I knew I had to make amends and the simple high-street shops just wouldn't cut it. Reluctantly, I explained the situation to Peter and said I had to go. I wanted to get to Selfridges before it closed. He wished me luck and I set off for Oxford Street.

I meandered around the immense store, unable to focus on the task at hand. I'd been unable to focus on much of anything since getting online and connecting with kindred spirits. I couldn't resist a stroll through the lingerie department, where I managed to talk myself out of a criminally expensive pair of designer silk pyjamas. But then my eye fell on a display of frilly panties and before I knew it I was digging for my credit card. As if I really needed another pair of French knickers. But these were blue. I didn't have any in blue. I was good at rationalising: I wanted to be wearing something new when I met Peter. That was only one day away. The red ones tempted me as well, but at the last minute I found the willpower to put them back.

I wandered around the rest of the departments for nearly an hour, feeling intimidated by the price of most of the merchandise. But at last I found a pashmina that wouldn't plunge me into too much debt. It was the usual fall-back gift, like ties and socks for my dad, but it was something she could show off to her class-conscious friends.

It was dark outside by the time I was finished. A tall redheaded woman almost knocked me down as I left the store, shoving between me and the door frame. Her attention was riveted on her mobile phone and she seemed totally oblivious to me. Appalled at her rudeness, I stood staring after her for several seconds before shaking my head in disgust. Then I continued on my way, heading for the Tube station at Bond Street.

Just as I rounded the corner a man stepped out in front of me, startling me. I gasped, almost dropping my bag.

'Excuse me, miss,' he said. 'But I'm afraid you'll have to come with me.' He wore a dark-blue uniform with a peaked cap. There was a slight London twang in his voice, but he had the authoritative bearing of one who was accustomed to being obeyed.

I blinked in confusion. 'What?'

'Store security.'

I just gaped at him.

'I'm sure you know what this is about,' he said with cool confidence.

Utterly baffled, I shook my head. 'I have no idea.'

But the guard wasn't having it. He took me firmly by the arm and guided me back in the direction of Selfridges. 'Then we'll have to discuss it with the manager.'

In shock, I allowed myself to be led a few steps before digging my heels in. 'Look, I really think you ought to tell me what this is about.'

'Very well,' he said. He had a nice face with finely carved features. Bright hazel eyes. He was probably a handsome man when he relaxed his fascist demeanour. 'Would you mind telling me what you bought in the store, Miss . . .?'

'Harker,' I said, a hint of indignation creeping into my tone. I wasn't going to be intimidated. 'If you must know, I bought a pashmina and some underwear.'

'What kind of underwear?'

Now he was trying to embarrass me. Well, it wouldn't

work. 'Sexy little things,' I said brazenly. 'French knickers, if you must know.'

'What colour?'

God, he was unflappable. 'Blue.'

'Not red?'

The question took me aback and I shook my head slowly.

'Would you mind showing me?'

I hesitated, then reached into the bag and took out the knickers I had bought. I waved them in front of him like a flag and several passers-by paused to watch the display. 'See? Blue. Like I said. Would you like to touch them?'

'That won't be necessary, Miss Harker,' he said, completely unruffled. 'Would you mind showing me what you have in your coat pockets?'

My eyes flashed. 'Oh, now this is going too far.'

'If you have nothing to hide . . .' he began reasonably.

He had accosted me on the street, where people were watching and making the obvious assumptions. It was humiliating. Galling. Fuelled by the fury of the wrongly accused, I snapped, 'Right. You want to see?' I plunged my hands into both pockets, intending to find my Underground pass and nothing else. But, to my surprise, my left hand met something soft and lacy. Slowly, I drew out an incriminating scrap of scarlet material.

The guard raised his eyebrows at me.

I could scarcely get the words out. 'Those – those aren't mine,' I protested feebly. 'I mean, I looked at them. I considered getting them – *buying* them – but I didn't!'

He nodded grimly. 'Yes, I can see you didn't buy them.'

'No, you don't understand!' Desperately, I cast back in my mind. Was it possible I could have been so absent-minded? That I had just shoved them into my pocket instead of putting them back? No. It *wasn't* possible; in fact, it was inconceivable.

But, all the while, the security guard was watching me impassively, his face betraying nothing, not even triumphant glee over this turn of events.

A nervous laugh escaped. 'Look,' I said. 'This is clearly a misunderstanding. I'm sure the girl at the lingerie counter will remember me. I'm happy to pay for these, but you have to understand I didn't steal them.'

'Do you know how many times I hear shoplifters say that?' the guard asked wearily.

'But I'm not a shoplifter!'

'No, I'm sure you're not,' he said with patient condescension, as though I'd claimed to be Joan of Arc and was now insisting I wasn't mad.

Several people had stopped to watch our little drama. I wanted to scream at them that I hadn't done it.

The guard took my arm again. 'You can explain it all to the manager. Now, come along.'

Dread began to gnaw in my stomach like a hungry rat. My eyes burnt with tears of shame and my legs felt too weak to carry me. A sour-faced woman with two little kids stood watching me with righteous gratification as I passed them in disgrace, the contraband knickers dangling from my hand. For a crazy instant I pictured myself collapsing on the street. I'd wake up in hospital to find the whole mess sorted. A simple misunderstanding and good-natured apologies all round. No hard feelings.

Suddenly, I remembered. 'Wait! That woman at the front door . . .'

'Come along, Miss Harker,' he repeated, this time more firmly. 'Fifteen years ago I might have dealt with this on my own, but nowadays I'm afraid that's beyond my authority. So it's a matter for the police.'

I knew full well what would happen if the police got involved. There was no way they'd believe such a ludicrous story. A strange woman came from outside the store and shoved something into my coat pocket as I left? Why? It had happened so fast I doubted if I could even identify her.

But what had the guard said? If he had the authority? The police hadn't been called. The manager didn't even know yet. 'What do you mean?' I asked cautiously. 'Deal with it on your own?'

The guard stopped. We had almost reached the front of the store. He gave me a long considering look. 'I suppose it depends,' he said.

'On what?'

'On how sorry you are.'

'But I didn't –'

He held up his hand, silencing me. 'I might be persuaded to let the matter drop if I felt you'd been sufficiently punished for it.'

He'd looked me straight in the eye as he said it. There was no mistaking his words or his intent. My face and ears burnt so intensely I felt feverish.

'Well?'

'What – what do you mean?'

His hand dropped to his belt buckle. 'I think you know what I mean. This. Across your bottom.'

This couldn't be happening. I hesitated and, when he made as if to drag me into the store, I capitulated. 'All right, all right.'

The guard nodded curtly and led me back the way we'd come, back down the street. I could hardly believe this was happening. It didn't seem real. But there was no other way. I had no idea where he was taking me, but as long as it was away from Selfridges I would go without complaint.

He led me down a private street, a narrow alley somewhere beyond the Tube station. I supposed I should be relieved he wasn't going to do it in the middle of Hyde Park. I stood trembling beside a scattering of rubbish, waiting for him to make the first move.

The guard held out his hand and I realised I was still holding the red knickers. I'd forgotten all about them. The two of us must have been quite a picture as we strolled by. I surrendered them to him, along with the bag of things I'd legitimately paid for.

'Your coat as well.'

I hesitated, but when he sighed and made as if to take my arm again I hurriedly slipped it off and passed it to him. He set the shopping bag down on the ground and folded my coat, before tucking it carefully into the bag. Then he tore the price tag from the knickers.

Holding them back out to me, he said, 'Put them on.'

I took them and lifted one leg to step into them, but he stopped me.

'No. Take off the ones you're wearing first.'

There was nothing lecherous in his tone. He wasn't here for cheap thrills. In a way, that would have been easier. If he had demanded sexual favours in exchange for his silence I'd have felt empowered. I could have insisted on seeing the manager then, to report his indecency. Perhaps my outrage would get me off the hook. But he wasn't interested in a blow job or a quick shag in a stairwell.

Miserably, I reached under my skirt and slipped down the white panties I was wearing, blushing deeply at the damp patch in the gusset. I wadded them into a ball so he wouldn't notice and relinquished them to his outstretched hand. To my horror, he unfolded them and inspected them closely. I hurriedly stepped into the red lace knickers and yanked them up, then smoothed my skirt down over my bottom. Then I stared at the ground, waiting.

He returned to the Selfridges bag and dropped my panties inside. 'Right,' he said.

I clutched my hands behind my back.

Without another word he began unbuckling his belt. It was a wide fearsome leather strap. He pulled it briskly through the loops and it made a sharp flapping noise that set my nerves on edge. He doubled the belt and pulled the ends taut, snapping it. I jumped.

He indicated a spot on the wall to my right. 'Hands up there, girl,' he said gruffly. 'Hands and feet apart.'

Shaking, I turned and pressed my hands against the cold clammy bricks.

He lightly kicked my feet apart until my legs were spread to his satisfaction. Then he lifted my skirt. He took his time tucking it up into the waistband to hold it out of the way.

'Bottom out.'

I squeezed my eyes shut, but I did as I was told. I expected him to take my knickers down, but he didn't. Not that they would afford me any protection.

'How much did the knickers cost?' he asked.

Too much, I thought ruefully. 'Fourteen pounds.'

'Hmm. Fourteen strokes, then, I think.'

I swallowed hard.

He laid the leather belt across my bottom. It was warm from his body heat and I tensed in anticipation.

'No screaming, now.'

The belt whipped into me with terrible force, its resounding slap echoing in the closeness of the alley. I gritted my teeth against the slashing pain, just managing to keep quiet. The pain dwindled until the punished skin was a wide throbbing welt. I shuddered to think of thirteen more like that.

Another stroke and I gasped, pushing hard against the wall to keep from flying up and grabbing my bottom. The flesh must have been as red as the knickers.

Another. I threw my head back with a groan, gritting my teeth and digging my nails into the wall as he lashed me again.

The next stroke followed so soon after the previous one that I cried out, writhing and dancing in place.

'Not a sound,' he instructed softly, aiming the strap again.

Biting my lip, I nodded frantically, urging him to get it over with.

As the belt painted scorching stripes across my cheeks I did my best to take them without making too much noise. I couldn't help gasping and hissing through my teeth. And I couldn't suppress the occasional yelp, especially when the strap licked round into the crease, just catching my sex. Tears sprang to my eyes and I pressed the back of my hand against my mouth so I wouldn't cry out.

I lost track somewhere around number eight and had to trust that he was keeping count. It was so much more painful than the spanking from Father Michael and I knew I would be marked from it. And yet the sensation was exhilarating. The sheer terror I had felt over the prospect of being arrested for shoplifting was a rush unlike anything I'd ever experienced. And the pain of the whipping that was saving me from that awful possibility, however terrible to endure, was welcome.

I bent my knees at the impact of each stroke, my fingernails clawing at the wall. But each time I gathered myself and straightened my legs again, arching my back and presenting my bottom for the strap.

'Last one,' he said.

I held my breath as the leather slashed into me and this time I didn't even try to restrain my howl of agony. I sank to a crouch on the cobblestones, clutching my sore bottom. Intense throbbing heat emanated from my rear. I felt like I'd sat on a stove.

At the same time, my body was trying to process the bewildering fusion of pain and arousal. I was flying again. Inexplicable guilt and shame washed over me and I resisted the tide of emotion that threatened to reduce me to a sobbing girlish wreck.

The guard calmly slid his belt back through the loops of his trousers and buckled it. 'Very well, Miss Harker,' he said, still adhering to formality. 'We will consider the matter settled.'

'Thank you,' I said, choking back my tears and lowering my head in genuine gratitude. I didn't blame him or resent what had happened. While he couldn't claim he'd just been doing his duty, I couldn't argue that he'd dealt with the situation in a firm but fair manner. My inner turmoil was nothing to do with him.

Like a gentleman he helped me into my coat, only making the moment seem more unreal. He held the Selfridges bag out to me and I took it with shaky hands. Dazed, I glanced around at my surroundings.

'I can escort you back to Bond Street if you like,' he said. 'That's where you were heading, wasn't it?'

I nodded meekly, reduced to a submissive little girl in need of guidance. 'Yes. Thank you. I don't know where I am.'

He offered me the barest hint of a smile. 'No, I don't expect you do.'

I stood for most of the Tube ride. And I was right about the marks. I had several wide red welts to show for the evening's adventure. The individual stripes were about two inches wide, overlapping in a curious fan shape. Pink in the centre and a colour approaching burgundy along the edges. They shaded towards purple where the doubled end of the belt had struck my right cheek. An impressive display.

There was no way they'd be gone by the time I met Peter. How was I ever going to tell him about this?

Seven

'I'm meeting someone here,' I told the maître d'. 'Peter Markworthy.'

After a deprecatory glance at my legs, he consulted the list before him. 'Ah. Yes. This way, please.' He gestured for me to follow him and I had to scurry to keep up as he led me through the restaurant.

I was ten minutes late and I was worried Peter would think it was deliberate. But it had nothing to do with fashion. I was fretting about the marks and agonising over which knickers to wear right until the last minute. I'd bought the blue ones for him, but I'd paid such a steep price for the red ones it seemed a shame not to wear them. In the end I decided on the red and I had just shut the door behind me when I changed my mind again and had to go back and change.

The maître d' took me all the way to the back of the room, to a small table for two. A man with close-cropped dark hair and glasses sat with his back to me. The maître d' pulled my chair out across from him.

'I'm sorry I'm late,' I said. And as I turned to face Peter my breath caught in my throat. It was the security guard.

I stood gawping at him until the maître d' gave a little cough behind me. I sat hurriedly, wincing at the discomfort in my bottom. Peter smiled.

The maître d' stood to the side of the table. 'Something to drink?' he asked.

Peter ignored him and reached for my hand. 'Angie,' he said. 'You look lovely.'

Still dazed, I gave him my hand and he squeezed my fingers affectionately.

'Which knickers did you wear – the red or the blue?'

I coloured deeply and glanced at the maître d', who seemed completely unfazed by the exchange. He was clearly not going to leave until we ordered something.

Peter raised his eyebrows to prompt me.

'Blue,' I said softly, casting my eyes down at the table.

He smiled and released my hand. Then he turned to the maître d' and ordered a bottle of wine. Something with an eight-syllable German name that he pronounced flawlessly. At last we were alone.

'It's interesting,' he said. 'You were so bold the other night. And now you're blushing like a schoolgirl.' He'd spoken with a bit of a London twang then, but there was no trace of it now. His accent was pure RP.

Still reeling from the initial shock, I forced myself to look him in the eye. 'I can't believe it. How did you . . .?' I shook my head, not knowing where to start.

'My dear girl,' he said, laughing. 'Didn't I warn you about sharing too much information? You weren't very difficult to track down.'

'But you said you were out of town. On business.'

He shook his head slowly, amused by my naivety.

I blushed again. 'Oh,' I said. I replayed the events at Selfridges in my mind, marvelling at the planning that must have gone into it. 'So how did you plant the red ones on me? It was that woman at the front door, wasn't it? But how did you know it was me?' I felt like a child demanding to know the secret behind the magician's trick.

'Well, you still have no way of knowing I'm not a serial killer, but that doesn't invalidate the safety lesson.' He sat back in his chair. 'You gave me your first name, of course. And your university-based email address makes no secret of your surname. A bit of searching turned up a school photo of you on the website of a former Ravenscroft pupil. Your hair was longer then, but of course you'd told me in chat that you had short hair now. Remember?'

I nodded, biting my lip. I hadn't told him the name of the school, but I must have unwittingly said something that confirmed it. He had probably led me into all sorts of unintentional disclosures.

'My friend and I followed you to Selfridges. And when I saw you change your mind about the red knickers and put them back I told her to buy them and wait outside until you left the store. Then I simply trailed you and waited. I phoned her as you were buying the scarf and went out ahead of you. Then my friend slipped the knickers into your pocket when she pushed past you in the doorway.'

He was like Sherlock Holmes or Lord Peter Wimsey coolly laying out the facts of a case – the sequence of criminal steps.

'You'd be an easy mark for a pickpocket,' he concluded. 'You never felt a thing.'

I was impressed. 'What are you, a detective? A secret agent?'

Peter beamed proudly. 'No, but I'll take that as a compliment. Ah, here's our wine.'

Peter tasted the wine and approved it while I considered his words, absorbed in retracing the steps.

When the waiter had left Peter raised his glass. 'To head games,' he said.

I clinked my glass against his. 'To recklessness,' I countered.

He inclined his head and we both drank.

'Tell me,' he said, looking serious again. 'How did you know I was a Selfridges security guard?'

'But – you're not. Are you? What do you mean?'

'When I told you I was store security, what proof did you have?'

I saw where he was going and I looked down at the menu, caught again.

'Exactly,' he said. 'Are you normally that imprudent?'

'But you knew about the red knickers,' I offered lamely, knowing it was no defence.

His indulgent smile confirmed that it was pathetic. 'Someone needs to teach you a firm lesson about not trusting strangers.'

'Well, why on earth would anyone wear a security guard's uniform and lie about working for Selfridges?'

He gave me a stern look.

I shifted uncomfortably in my seat.

'Angie,' he said, his voice low and serious. 'If I'd suggested you meet me at my house instead of a restaurant, would you have done it?'

I was a hitchhiker being warned about the dangers of hitchhiking by the driver who'd picked me up. 'Yes,' I admitted. I'd done exactly that with Paul. He'd been harmless, of course, but one could argue that I'd been extremely lucky.

'Yes what?'

Such a simple question, yet loaded with so much authority. I squirmed as I said, 'Yes, sir.'

'Then we'll discuss this again after dinner. At my house.'

I squeezed my legs together, lost in the delicious mixture of fear and elation.

He was silent for a few moments. Then his expression softened into a friendly smile and he opened his menu. I followed suit and, by the time we ordered, the conversation had drifted away from my impending doom.

'I always thought I was a freak,' I said, still reeling over the simple joy of being able to talk to someone about it.

'I think most of us felt that way at first. Just imagine how much harder it was in the days before the Net.'

'You should see my thesis.' I giggled, draining my glass.

Peter refilled it. 'Oh?'

I grinned slyly. 'What? You mean you haven't already hacked into my supervisor's computer and read it?'

Peter laughed. 'Sorry to disappoint you. Some things are beyond my humble abilities.'

I found myself regaining my enthusiasm for it as I told him the title. And I was stunned and delighted that he not only knew about the flagellant correspondence column; he had actual issues of *The Family Herald*!

'It's mentioned in Cooper's book,' he explained as though it was common knowledge. 'I had to see it for myself. I've quite a collection.'

'I wonder if you have my favourite?' I mused aloud.

He raised his eyebrows at me and I described the letter from A Hater of the System. His arch smile told me he did.

It was an embarrassment of riches. 'I feel like I've entered some kind of parallel universe. It's like every crazy thought and fantasy I've ever had exists in this other world as a reality.'

'Yes, it's a bit like a secret society,' he said. 'We all had the same strange feelings from certain movies and books when we were kids. We know what it's like to worry that we're sick or perverted. We've all been rejected or denounced by vanilla partners who just didn't understand. And we've done a lot of self-analysis. Read everything we could get our hands on, as though it were some disease we were trying to find the cure for.'

I nodded eagerly throughout his description. 'Yeah. But now that I know there are others just as sick as I am, I don't want to be cured.'

'Nor should you. There's nothing unhealthy about it. It takes a lot of strength, trust and courage to submit. It sounds elitist, I know, but I think you reach a higher level of intimacy through this kind of power exchange than you ever can through ordinary sex.'

I knew exactly what he meant, though I'd never have been able to put it into words so easily. It was a truth I'd always known.

'But it's not just about sex,' I said. 'And, really, the scenes that turn me on the most are the *least* sexual ones. Does that make sense?'

'Absolutely. I don't want to spank a girl who *enjoys* it. You're not meant to enjoy being punished.'

'Oh, I know! It's the ultimate paradox. Someone who finds the idea of spanking so arousing, yet only if it's in the guise of non-sexual discipline.'

'For your own good,' he added, grinning.

I thought of the way he had tricked me into the alley. Lured me with the threat of arrest and the alternative of punishment. In retrospect it had been incredibly risky. As he said, he could have been Jack the Ripper. But he wasn't.

I knew I would pay the price for my foolhardiness later. And I would hate every minute of it. But I would love hating it. I was already savouring the dread, the way I loved the roller coaster's slow climb to that first big plunge. But afterwards I would relish the marks and replay it in my mind for days.

'You know what the real irony is?' he asked. 'The fact that you have to rely on mainstream fiction for the kinds of scenes that we find the hottest. Almost every publisher's guidelines say that erotica has to be consensual. But you can get away with anything in mainstream.'

I shook my head in wonderment. These weren't things I had shared in chat or email, but they were my thoughts exactly. 'School stories,' I supplied. 'All those school punishments where no one is aroused by what's happening. Dickens knew how to push my buttons, though I'm sure he intended those scenes to have the opposite effect.'

Peter laughed. 'Yes, as did your Father Michael.'

'And a certain security guard.'

'Well, I can't claim his motives were entirely disciplinary.'

'But I didn't know that. And that was all that mattered at the time.'

'It's a funny idea, isn't it?' he mused. 'That vanilla discipline can be more exciting than overtly kinky discipline.'

'But it makes sense. Mr Chancellor is the perfect example of that.'

'Ah, yes,' Peter said. 'Your uninitiated headmaster.'

Finally spying an opening, I took it. 'Was yours as uninitiated?'

He steepled his fingers and looked at me, a gleam in his eyes. 'Oh, no,' he said. 'No, mine was rather more of a disciplinarian than your Mr Chancellor.'

I waited for him to continue.

He smiled. 'Very well,' he said, as though indulging a child with a bedtime story. 'At my school we had both boarders and dayboys. I was a boarder and dayboys were at the bottom of the food chain. The way we saw it, they had it easy. They went home every night to their families and proper meals and their own comfortable beds. I'm sure it's the same in every school. It wasn't their fault, of course, but there's a *Lord of the Flies* mentality in every closed society, especially those dominated by teenage boys.'

'Believe me, girls are just as bad,' I said, remembering the cliques and popularity contests of my own adolescence.

'I expect that's true,' he said, refilling our wineglasses. 'Anyway, the dayboys were the perfect victims for bullying. Especially the younger ones who were still wet behind the ears and eager to be accepted. They got coerced into doing all sorts of things whether they wanted to or not. And, quite often, they got caught. But it wasn't done to sneak. No matter how unfair, you took your stripes and you didn't complain. And you certainly didn't blub.'

I knew about this schoolboy code from the countless stories I'd devoured. I had always admired it. There was something very special about the boys' school dynamic that was completely missing from the girls' one.

'Dr Litchfield, the headmaster, was a product of his time. A Wykehamist and a strict no-nonsense disciplinarian. It's difficult to explain, but we feared him, respected him and liked him all at the same time.'

I understood perfectly. I felt exactly the same about Mr Chancellor.

'There was one dayboy – Fletcher, I think his name was – who had bragged about nicking sherry from his father's liquor cabinet. Said he did it all the time. So a group of lads in my dormitory insisted he bring them a bottle. He tried to get out of it, but they were very persuasive. In the end they sent him to Coventry until he agreed to it.'

'Coventry?'

'Made him invisible,' he explained. 'It was the worst thing you could do to a boy. Everyone pointedly ignoring you, pretending you don't exist. For days. Weeks. It may not sound much, but it gets to you.'

My eyes widened in horror.

He lifted his shoulders in a guilty little shrug. 'Fletcher was the one who boasted about his exploits. If he was making it up to impress us, he should have known we wouldn't be satisfied with mere talk. In the end he did what we wanted. He nicked a bottle of sherry and brought it to school. And of course he got caught. He could hardly plead innocence; the Latin master caught him sneaking it in. We all knew what he was in for, but none of us felt very sympathetic. He should have been more careful.'

'They' had suddenly changed to 'we'. 'So you were involved in it?'

Peter looked down at his plate and sighed. 'Yes,' he said at last. 'I'm not proud of it now, but back then I wasn't about to stick my neck out for a dayboy, especially a little showoff like Fletcher.' He spread his hands. 'It doesn't excuse anything, but it's just . . .'

'The law of the jungle,' I supplied.

He nodded his head with a wry smile. 'Well, either Fletcher broke down and told Litchfield who was behind it or one of our lot confessed. We never found out. But Litchfield was furious. He hadn't exactly punished an innocent boy, but I've no doubt Fletcher made it seem that way. Litchfield wanted to make an example of us. He knew everyone in the dorm must have known about it and even the ones who weren't directly responsible he considered guilty by association. No matter how bloodless, it was still bullying. We were all in for a damned good thrashing.'

I was short of breath and I tried to act nonchalant as I drank my wine, barely tasting it. I squeezed my legs together, feeling guilty for my response, but still dying to hear the denouement.

'That night Mr Carew, the housemaster, had us stand at the foot of our beds and wait for the headmaster. Fourteen boys, standing in our bare feet, shivering in our thin cotton pyjamas. It was deathly quiet. No one said a word.

'Finally, Litchfield arrived. I remember how the silence grew even more ponderous at the sight of the cane. I'd never been caned before, but I'd seen what it could do. Boys showed off their marks, you see. And just a month earlier my two best mates, Caithness and Mercer, had shown me theirs. Each of them had two vivid red raised weals.

'The headmaster held the cane behind his back as he stalked up and down the room, between the lines of anxious boys, as if we were soldiers on parade and he was the general about to have us shot. Mr Carew was standing by the door, watching coldly. Our actions had reflected just as badly on him as on us; our reign of terror had occurred right under his nose. No doubt he was there to prevent us from bolting.

'The headmaster pursed his lips and said nothing for a long time. When he finally spoke, it was just one word. "Four." I had been expecting six, but four was no relief. The fixed number suddenly made it more real. As though up to that point it had all been just a bad dream and we could still wake up.

'We all knew it would hurt. Some of us even knew we deserved it. He had pronounced sentence and now he would carry it out.

'With one last sweeping glare up and down the lines he chose his starting place. Dering, a boy in my row, two beds down from me on the right. He was cox of the First Eight and something of a natural leader.'

Peter paused to take a sip of wine and I realised I had been holding my breath. I could actually feel the crackling tension in the air, hear the soft rasp of frightened shifting feet on the cold floorboards.

'Dering stood to attention as the headmaster stopped in front of him. "Turn around, boy," he said. "Feet apart. Elbows on the bed." Dering glanced fearfully down the row at us and got into position, bending across the iron-framed bed. I couldn't tear my eyes away. The position pulled his pyjama bottoms tight across his seat. Litchfield stood almost directly to Dering's left side and measured the cane out across his bottom. Then he drew his arm back and raised it high in the air. It seemed to hang there forever before he finally brought it down like a sabre. It carved the air and there was an almighty whack as it met Dering's backside. I think we all flinched as one, but Dering made some kind of horrible yelping cry. An animal in pain. He sank halfway to the floor, reaching around with his right hand to clutch his cheeks. Litchfield didn't say anything. He just waited. And Dering pulled himself together and got back in position. The cane went up again and Dering handled that stroke with a little more dignity. The last two were real stingers and I could tell the headmaster was laying it on as hard as he could. I shuddered. It was almost my turn.

'When he finished with Dering he moved to the next boy, Underhill. Dering got up stiffly and stood in front of his bed. I stared intently at his face. He did his best to disguise the pitiful sniffle, but his eyes were streaming with tears. He was a pretty tough customer, normally, and that scared me more than anything. Suddenly my flimsy pyjamas felt like a winter coat, glued to my skin with icy sweat. Dering slipped his hands behind him and gingerly touched his bottom, baring his teeth with a soft hiss.

'Underhill was stoic and I was immensely grateful for that. If he'd howled and wriggled I think I'd have been even more terrified. But he'd been caned before and knew what to expect. His legs vibrated madly with the effort of staying in position while the cane slashed into his bottom four times. Only the last one dragged a noise from him, a sort of half-yelp, half-grunt that he couldn't quite suppress. He looked pale, but there were no tears in his eyes as he stood up. Then Litchfield stopped in front of me.

'I assumed the same position I'd seen the first two adopt, my face burning as I awaited my fate. There was a reeling, light-headed sensation, as though I were slightly drunk. And I remember being thankful for my position in the queue. I really felt for the ones at the end, having to watch all of us get it first. The waiting must have been torture.

'I heard the swish and crack and then my backside came alive with pain. I made some strangled gasping noise like Dering had and bent my knees. The headmaster waited for me to get back in position before continuing. I decided it was better not to delay it. I locked my legs in place and gutted it out, anticipating the pain, taking it and letting it course through me like an electric shock. A detached part of me was watching with morbid fascination, analysing. This was a proving ground. For each of us and our masters. None of us could argue that it wasn't fair. It was richly deserved.

'I stared at the bedclothes, in a kind of trance, as the cane rose and fell. And a strange sort of exhilaration came over me as I imagined having that kind of power over someone else. Having someone offer their bottom up to me like that, wanting to make me proud by taking it. I was removed from the pain by my thoughts, as though I'd made a great discovery. And, just like that, it was over. My bottom throbbed with a pulsing fire, until I seemed to feel every line separately. But I had survived. Litchfield moved on to the next boy and then the next. Right the way round the room until we'd all been dealt with.'

I was right back there with Peter, watching the mass execution, feeling their strokes and feeding on their pain like a vampire.

'There was one boy who'd worn underpants beneath his pyjama trousers. That just wasn't done. It was stupid too. Litchfield saw it as soon as he bent over and he got an extra stroke for it. Two of the boys broke down in tears before the end, but that didn't make Litchfield go any easier on them. After all, it was considered to be character building.' He thought about it and added with a touch of irony, 'It certainly helped build mine.'

I laughed, shaking my head at the story. 'Amazing,' was all I could say.

'That's what I thought at the time. And, of course, once Carew had left, we inspected one another's marks. They were good ones, too. Red tramlines and blue bruises. Flawlessly aimed and well laid on. You had to admire it. Litchfield was a bloody good swisher and we held him in even higher regard after that. I was never closer to any group of boys at any time in my life. We'd been through something intense together. I guess that's what they call male bonding.'

I felt a little stab of envy. 'Did you leave the dayboys alone after that?'

He nodded solemnly. 'Oh yes. We all learnt our lesson. They weren't any higher in the hierarchy, but they didn't get bullied any more.'

I sighed. 'I wish I'd had that sort of experience. I wonder how it would have changed me. I was a good girl at least, though. Mr Chancellor should have known how hard it was for me to break the rules just to be sent to his office.'

'True. But what if it had been effective? Curbed your behaviour and cured you of the kink?'

'It certainly didn't cure you!'

'No, but who's to say it hasn't cured others?'

'Well, it would be a tragedy,' I admitted. 'Though it would have saved a lot of frustration in later years. God knows what I'd be doing my thesis on in that case.'

Our waiter appeared to clear away our empty plates and asked if we wanted to see the dessert menu. I looked pleadingly at Peter until he relented. We shared a decadent slice of raspberry cheesecake, Peter feeding me like a cherished pet.

The unspoken threat of what awaited me at his house hung in the air like fog. I couldn't see anything else for it.

Peter asked for the bill and my heart began to flutter. I had reached the front of the queue for the roller coaster and was about to climb aboard. All I could think of was Peter's description of the dormitory caning.

He gave his credit card to the waiter and looked at me. His whole demeanour had changed. 'Are you nervous?'

'Yes.'

He nodded once, no trace of a smile. 'So you should be.'

I picked up my wineglass, disappointed to find it empty. So I plucked distractedly at crumbs on the table, my chin in my hand.

'Angie,' he said in a low tone. 'Stop sulking. Sit up straight.'

I obeyed instantly, lowering my head as the waiter returned with the credit card receipt.

'You'll have plenty to sulk about when I'm finished with you,' he continued, well aware that we weren't alone. 'Just wait till I get you home, young lady.'

The waiter stopped short, blinking in surprise at Peter. I chewed my lip, wishing I were invisible. The waiter cleared his throat awkwardly and fumbled with the receipt as he set it on the table, darting a surreptitious glance at me. 'Have a good night,' he said, before hurrying away.

[illegible] aside [illegible] the [illegible]

[illegible] dragging [illegible]

[illegible]

[illegible] [illegible] [illegible]

up and [illegible]

[illegible] the medical [illegible]

[illegible]

[illegible] the [illegible]

[illegible] standing [illegible]

[illegible] thank [illegible]

[illegible] Perhaps [illegible]

[illegible] closed [illegible]

[illegible] in [illegible]

the [illegible] stood [illegible]

[illegible] parts of [illegible]

[illegible] Rather [illegible]

Eight

I moaned softly and clenched my cheeks in dread. Goose-flesh stood out on my arms and legs and I repressed a shiver as I watched his hand close around the cane, lifting it up and out of my line of sight.

'The Old Vicarage' said the placard on the stone wall. Set well back from the road into the village, the double-pile house stood at the end of a short winding drive, nestled among the trees. Chimney stacks rose from the side walls of each of the four gables. The keystone above the panelled front door gave the date: 1726.

I had never been intimidated by a house before. But the simple elegance of the Georgian façade seemed to enhance the formality of what was about to happen to me. Its symmetrical proportions promised order and stability. Uncompromising tradition.

I lingered on the drive, gazing up at the house. The dark brickwork glistened from the recent rain. Elaborate stucco architraves surrounded the five bays of sash windows.

'It's beautiful,' I said, sincere but also playing for time.

'Thank you.'

With a knowing look, Peter took me by the hand to lead me inside. As the door closed behind us, I had the sense that I was stepping back in time. I couldn't help but admire the period details. We stood in a wide panelled entrance hall flanked by two pairs of doors. Regency chairs sat between each pair and a faded Oriental rug ran the length of the hallway. The farther door on the right led to the kitchen, but the other three doors were closed. At the rear of the hallway stood a painted pine staircase with slender turned balusters, three to a tread. The handrail swept down over the newels, ending in a spiral flourish over the bottom tread. A stately grandfather clock stood facing us beneath the landing, ticking loudly.

I'd grown up in a rather plain Victorian terraced house in Camden Town and had only ever gazed covetously at the exteriors of the fancier Georgian elevations. And this was a simple vicar's house.

'You didn't tell me you worked for English Heritage,' I said casually, trying to restrain my awe.

He acknowledged my compliment with a modest smile.

'You'll have to give me the grand tour,' I continued, in no hurry to be beaten.

'Afterwards,' he said, brushing aside my clumsy attempt at distraction. 'Right now you're to go upstairs. Second door on the right. Everything you need is in the wardrobe. Report to my study in fifteen minutes.' He indicated the closed door to the left of the staircase.

I glanced up at the clock to note the time. 'OK,' I croaked, my throat suddenly parched.

He raised his eyebrows and I corrected myself quickly. 'Yes, sir.'

I took a moment to stroke the gracefully curved hand-rail before heading upstairs to the room he'd directed me to. I supposed it was a guest bedroom, as it didn't look lived in. A mahogany armoire stood against one ochre wall. Inside it hung a crisp white shirt, a navy-blue pleated skirt and a matching school blazer. On the floor of the wardrobe was a paper shopping bag with my surname written on it in neat black marker. Inside I found a pair of white knee socks, white cotton knickers and a blue and grey striped tie. I knew everything would fit perfectly. The precision and planning both fascinated and frightened me.

Inside the bag was an envelope labelled 'Angie'. With shaking fingers I fumbled it open.

'You've been warned before about safety,' it read. 'And you've always seemed to feel that rules are there for others and not for you. Last night, your housemaster, Mr Taylor, caught you sneaking back into your dormitory in the small hours, having slipped out to meet a boy. The next morning you are summoned to see the headmaster, Mr Markworthy.'

I bit my lip as I read. True, it was just a roleplay, but the offence was real and serious. A genuine safety issue. Authenticity would demand an equally serious punishment.

I'd felt I was stepping back in time when I crossed the threshold of his period house, and putting on the school uniform regressed me in age. Suddenly I was that shy desperate sixteen-year-old again, preparing to meet her fate. This time, though, the headmaster was a disciplinarian. It wouldn't just be a simple telling off and a hand cramped from writing lines. If Peter wielded the cane as heavily as he had his belt, I would have a very sore bottom indeed. I thought about the story he'd told me at dinner and how the cane had reduced boys to tears. What would it do to me? My heart fluttered against my ribs like a bird desperate to escape its cage.

I glanced anxiously at my watch every few seconds. The Ravenscroft uniform had been bottle-green, so navy must be his personal preference. The blazer badge bore the name 'Westfield'. I tried to imagine Peter going into a school outfitter's and picking out the uniform. He'd probably told the clerks he was buying it for his daughter. The image made my knees weak.

I didn't dare present myself as anything but impeccably dressed. I fastened my top button and knotted my tie dutifully – actions that were still second nature to me. Then I lifted my skirt and pulled down my knickers, bending over to see my bottom in the mirror. The marks from his belt were still vivid, but I didn't think that would earn me any leniency. I suddenly regretted having shared so many details about my punishment fantasies with him. I'd invited him right inside my head and he knew exactly what pushed my buttons. He had to know I'd be disappointed with anything less than the real thing. He had set the bar the other night in the alley near Bond Street. This would be even more intense.

I hesitated so long that I suddenly realised twenty minutes had passed. Tardiness was not likely to make him sympathetic. With no more time to stall I made my descent. My shoes clattered noisily on the wooden treads, making me wince with each step. I stopped outside the study door, struck by the sense of déjà vu. My unsteady fist knocked softly on the wood.

'Enter.'

I took a deep breath and opened the door. The room was darkly panelled and imposing. Bookshelves lined the wall to my left and egg-and-dart plaster mouldings encircled the ceiling. Peter – Mr Markworthy – sat at a large oak desk with an envelope before him. He was wearing a formal schoolmaster's gown. Behind him was a small fireplace with a lavish surround decorated with scrolls. I gaped at my surroundings like a museum visitor.

'Ah, Harker,' he said. 'Close the door.'

I turned the knob and pushed the door soundlessly into its frame, before turning to stand in front of his desk.

Mr Markworthy stared at me for several seconds, his eyes travelling up and down, scrutinising my uniform. It was a long uncomfortable silence and I shifted my weight nervously, twisting my fingers behind my back.

'Hands at your sides,' he told me sharply. 'And stand up straight.'

I obeyed. At least he could find no fault with my uniform.

He picked up the envelope and I saw that it had already been opened. He slipped the letter out and unfolded it. I watched as his eyes scanned it and then flicked back to me.

The cruel suspense made me tremble and I looked down at the floor.

When he spoke there was a hard edge to his voice. 'I expect you know what Mr Taylor's letter says, girl.'

I pictured the scenario. A schoolgirl – me – slipping her bonds to meet a lad from the neighbouring boys' school.

After some adolescent fumbling in the dark woods between the schools, one or the other would decide that they should be getting back to their respective dormitories. But sneaking back in would prove even harder than sneaking out.

'Yes, sir,' I said.

I could actually feel the rising panic of being caught. Tiptoeing down the hallway, my shoes in my hand to muffle my passage. The sudden male voice curtly telling me to turn around. I could see myself facing the housemaster, frightened, ashamed, apprehensive. Being given the dread command to report to the headmaster in the morning. I wouldn't have slept the rest of the night.

Mr Markworthy adjusted his glasses and cleared his throat. 'Tonight I caught Angela Harker trying to return secretly to school after lights out. When confronted, she was insolent and disrespectful. I believe this incident requires stricter measures than I am authorised to administer. Harker shows a persistent disregard for school rules and contempt for authority. This is not the first time that she has broken bounds at night to meet a boy, and she has repeatedly shown poor judgement in matters of personal safety. She seems to feel that danger threatens others, not her.'

He set the letter aside and looked at me gravely. 'Well, young lady? Do you have anything to say for yourself?'

I gulped. I couldn't very well criticise Mr Taylor for his opinion or call him a liar. But, as the roleplay had one foot in reality, I had to defend myself. 'I wasn't really in any danger, sir. It was perfectly safe.'

'Perfectly safe,' he repeated. 'In the woods, with a boy, after dark, out of bounds. Is that right?'

It sounded positively criminal coming from him. 'Well, yes, sir,' I had to admit.

'Are you aware that there was a murder committed in those woods a few years ago?'

'Erm, no, sir.'

He shook his head disapprovingly. 'That only emphasises your temerity, Harker. You took no steps to find out how dangerous it actually was. But let us come back to the letter. I want to hear your explanation for last night.'

'I just . . . I mean, I was only . . .' I didn't know what to say. His natural authority had transformed me into a naughty teenager, reduced to stammering lame excuses. He was completely different from the security guard who'd strapped me in an alley two days before. In my head he was really my headmaster.

'Come on, girl,' he said testily. 'Explain yourself.'

'It was stupid, sir,' I confessed. 'And reckless.'

His eyebrows rose nearly to his hairline and he looked down at the letter again, clearly appalled that I hadn't said what he wanted to hear. 'Is that all, Harker?'

I fidgeted, plucking at the hem of my pleated skirt. 'Sir, I –'

'Hands at your sides, girl!'

I snapped them back to my sides. 'I'm sorry for sneaking out, sir,' I said. Then I added pathetically, 'I won't do it again.'

'No, you most certainly won't,' he said severely. 'I intend to make sure of that.'

He stood up, pushing back his chair. He came round the front of the desk to stand in front of me. The black gown framed him like an executioner's robe. I instantly felt smaller.

'There are three issues here,' he began. 'The first and most serious is your recklessness. You're a clever girl, Harker, so it's not stupidity or naivety. So it must be negligence. You know you ought to take precautions, but you just can't be bothered, is that it?'

'No, sir,' I mumbled, lowering my head.

'Then what is it? Look at me, girl.'

Meeting his eyes was hard, but I forced myself to do it. I floundered for an explanation, but nothing would come. 'I don't know, sir. I guess I just assume I'll be all right.'

'You find the idea of a little peril exciting, do you? Romantic? Is that it?'

It was. Damn, he was good. I mumbled a sheepish 'Yes, sir.'

Mr Markworthy eyed me for several uncomfortable seconds. 'Do you know what hubris is, Harker?'

I turned scarlet and looked at the floor again. 'Yes, sir.'

He sighed and shook his head, returning to the desk. I thought he was going to sit down again and for a moment I felt relieved. But he stopped at the stand by the fireplace. A selection of crook-handled rattan canes stood there, a silent threat.

'Now we come to the second issue,' he said.

I chewed my lip as he withdrew one of the thinner canes. He considered it for a moment and then put it back.

'Flouting school rules,' he continued.

He chose a thicker cane and pulled it out. He flexed it in his hands and I was instantly reminded of an old Hulton Archive photo of a woman in a lab coat testing school canes at a factory. She was bending a cane into a dramatic arch in the foreground while in the background her colleague was surrounded by bundles of canes finished and ready for use on the backsides of errant pupils. I shuddered. The moment was approaching.

Mr Markworthy returned to the centre of the room to stand before me again. My legs began to tremble and I felt my breathing grow shallow at the nearness of the cane.

'I'm sorry, sir,' I said, knowing it was no defence.

'Yes, you will be, girl,' he said seriously. 'Very sorry indeed. This isn't the first time you've misbehaved, though it's by far the most serious. You clearly need something more severe than impositions.' He flexed the cane again for effect and I winced.

'Lastly, there is the issue of your disrespect to Mr Taylor on being caught. He says you were insolent when confronted. Is that correct?'

My throat felt stuffed with cotton. I could barely speak. He'd set the scene up well. There was no way I could deny it without calling my housemaster a liar.

'Yes, sir,' I whispered.

'Very well, then. Normally a pupil would receive only two or three strokes for any one infraction. But your catalogue of misconduct demands that I make an example of you.'

The anticipation was excruciating and I felt dizzy as I waited for my sentence, though there was no mystery about the implement he proposed to use. My heart was throbbing in my ears and I stared in horror at the cane as a bead of cold sweat trickled down between my shoulder blades.

'Six of the best, Harker.'

Of course. I'd known it couldn't be any less. But actually hearing the words made my stomach swoop.

'When I give the order, you will bend and touch your toes. You will stay in that position throughout your caning. And when I have finished you will remain in position until I tell you to stand up. Is that understood?'

'Yes, sir.'

His belittling words made me want to shrink inside myself. The suspense was unbearable, but so was the thought of what was coming. I was terrified I wouldn't be able to take it. I reminded myself that a real schoolgirl wouldn't have a choice.

'Right. Touch your toes.'

I did as I was told, feeling the hem of my skirt rise up as I bent. I blushed, pressing my fingertips against the tops of my shoes.

Mr Markworthy laid the cane on the desk. Then I felt his hands at the hem of my skirt. He took his time raising it high up over my back while I stared at the polished rattan before me. I had to lock my knees to still the trembling in my legs.

My shirttail was next. He tucked it well up, clearing the target area. My face burnt as he made his preparations.

'I usually prefer to cane a girl over her knickers, Harker,' he said. 'But in cases of insolence I find that the added embarrassment of exposure can be salutary.'

He hooked his hands in the waistband of my white cotton knickers and pulled them slowly down over my bottom. I blushed and bent forwards a little more.

'Hmmm, it looks as though you've been punished recently.' He traced the welts with his finger, making me jump. 'But I'm afraid I'm not prepared to be lenient because of that. It's none of my affair if you've got on the wrong side of one of the prefects.'

I held my breath, as much to slow my ragged breathing as to prepare myself. But Mr Markworthy was in no hurry. He laid the cool length of rattan against my bare bottom, tapping it gently. I gave an exaggerated flinch at each tap, expecting the first stroke.

'Now then, Harker,' he said in a firm businesslike tone. 'I expect you know the protocol. You're to count each stroke and thank me.'

'Yes, sir,' I said, my voice a pitiful rasp.

The cane tapped again, addressing where it would strike. Once. Twice. Then it lifted away and I heard the awful sound as it sliced back down through the air and into my bottom. There was a disorienting delay and for a second I wasn't sure he'd actually hit me. First there was a slight tingle. Then the thin red line began to burn and flare. It spread from the point of impact to encompass my entire bottom. It took several seconds for the full effect to take hold. The stinging agony intensified until I couldn't help bending my knees.

'Stay in position, girl,' he growled.

I straightened my legs, hissing through my teeth at the astonishing power of the cane. A full minute must have passed before the pain began to subside to a dull pulsating ache. And that was just the first stroke.

I felt the cane tapping brusquely. Several seconds passed. At last he said, 'I'm waiting.'

I suddenly remembered. 'One,' I choked out. 'Thank you, sir.'

He laid the rattan against my bottom again and I held my breath as it drew back again to strike.

This time the pain followed the impact much faster, but it didn't hurt any less. My hands left my shoes and wavered in the air, desperate to clutch my sore cheeks and soothe away the sting. But I managed to resist, fearing extra punishment. I curled my toes tightly, uncomfortably, inside my shoes, trying to focus on anything but the searing parallel lines across my poor bottom.

'Two. Thank you, sir.' This time I remembered on my own, but the added humiliation of having to count and thank him seemed to make the stripes throb even more furiously.

The third stroke landed exactly on top of the previous one and I leapt up with a howl of pain, grabbing my sore bottom. Mr Markworthy frowned, but didn't say a word. I struggled to resume the position, but the burn was too intense. I gasped and panted for nearly a minute before I was able to touch my toes again. With the patience of a gourmet savouring his food, he straightened my skirt and replaced my shirttail over my back.

'If you break position again,' he said coolly. 'The stroke won't count.'

'Yes, sir. Three. Thank you, sir,' I panted, deliriously grateful he wasn't adding to the punishment this time.

I took the fourth stroke with only a guttural groan. And I didn't get out of position even though my legs were shaking from the effort of keeping my knees locked. I gritted my teeth until the worst of the blossoming pain was over. Then I counted the stroke.

Stroke number five found its mark between three and four and I yelped loudly. I managed to stay in position, though it took every ounce of my willpower. I forced myself to breathe slowly and deeply, letting the sensation wash over me. I counted.

Squeezing my eyes shut tight, I listened as the cane swished through the air one last time. It struck my tender bottom with a meaty whack, forcing the air from my lungs in a strangled cry. The pain was blinding. Tears shimmered in my eyes.

'Six,' I said at last, my voice a dazed breathless murmur. 'Thank you, sir.'

I stayed in position, breathing hard, blinking back the tears. Tiny starbursts twinkled behind my eyes and I had to open them so as not to lose my balance. I felt light-headed.

'Stand up.'

Shakily, I straightened up, wincing as the change in position aggravated the pain. My skirt slid back down and even its flimsy material felt like sandpaper against my backside.

Mr Markworthy held the cane in both hands, parallel to the floor. 'Now, young lady,' he said sternly. 'You will stand in the corner with your hands on your head. You will think about your behaviour and how you were punished for it.'

I lowered my head in embarrassed resignation. He nodded towards the near right corner and I made my way there as though to the gallows. Obediently, I pressed my nose into the angle of the two walls, feeling far younger than sixteen.

'Hands on your head.'

I took a step back and assumed the position.

I heard Mr Markworthy behind me and he lifted my skirt back up, before tucking it into the waistband to hold it in place. I whimpered softly at the exposure. I could imagine the picture I presented: a naughty little girl stood in the corner with her sore punished bottom on display.

'While you are in the corner, Harker, you're to reflect on your behaviour and how you're going to improve it in future. Afterwards you will thank me for caring enough about your behaviour to correct you.'

His chair creaked as he sat down at his desk behind me. I didn't dare turn my head to see if he was watching me; I was certain he was. The sense of vulnerability was overpowering.

There was some solace that my punishment was over, at least for now. As humiliating as it was, I would have stood there forever to avoid any more. Mr Markworthy told me sharply once or twice to stop fidgeting and I did my best to stay still.

Though the door to the room was closed, I could hear the clock ticking on the other side of the wall. I closed my eyes, focusing on the burning pain in my bottom. My head was swimming with the intensity of the scene and I felt thoroughly humbled.

It felt like an hour before he told me I could come out. I lowered my arms, hissing at the ache as the blood flow returned to them.

Mr Markworthy stood in front of me. 'I trust this is a lesson we won't have to repeat.'

Disoriented, I nodded. 'Yes, sir.'

'Right. You may adjust your uniform.'

I whimpered as I pulled my knickers up over my burning flesh and smoothed my skirt back down.

Mr Markworthy directed me to his desk, where a leather-bound ledger lay open. 'Sign the punishment book and you may go.'

He held a pen out to me and I stared at the book before me. The left page was filled with columns containing several names, offences and the number of strokes administered for each. There were additional notes for some of the entries. The final entry on the right page was mine. 'Harker, Angela,' it said. 'Out of bounds, disrespect, endangering herself. Cane, six strokes.'

I signed my name with a still trembling hand and set the pen aside.

'Very well, Harker. You're dismissed.'

Outside, I sagged against the wall, unable for the moment to leave the alternate reality. Peter appeared and his stern demeanour vanished. In its place was a welcoming smile. I sank into his arms. It was like hugging a fantasy made flesh. A month earlier I would never have believed there could be anyone so perfectly in tune with my bizarre needs.

'Did you enjoy that?' he asked.

'Not a bit,' I said honestly, still delirious from the pain and humiliation. I touched my scorching stripes with a wince.

His smile grew wider. 'Good. Punishment is not meant to be enjoyed. At least not at the time. But once the initial sting begins to fade I think you'll find that you relish the memory of it.'

He was right. It was a delicious paradox – loving to hate it. 'I can't enjoy it unless I don't enjoy it,' I murmured.

It was something I'd never been able to articulate before. Something I had never consciously understood, but knew instinctively. Something I never imagined anyone else could possibly comprehend, let alone provide.

Nine

Peter Markworthy was a true connoisseur and the house was a veritable spanking museum. He had amassed an impressive collection of spanking literature and paraphernalia over the years. I no longer had to lament the loss of my own meagre video collection; he had all of them and more. And books – the library shelves were crammed with books on our favourite subject.

There were many works of obscure erotica, including several I'd always wanted to read. I couldn't help but laugh as I flicked through *The Rodiad*, an infamous epic poem about the joys of flogging schoolboys. I'd heard of it, but never actually seen it before. Flagellant poetry was in a class by itself and most of it was pretty dreadful.

The most famous flagellant poet of all, Algernon Charles Swinburne, was responsible for such classics as *The Flogging-Block* and 'Charlie Collingwood's Flogging'. He made no secret of his love of the rod, having often been birched himself at Eton. For years after leaving the school he pined for the block, begging a photograph of it from a friend to refresh his memory. Sure enough, Peter had his biography.

Swinburne was a frequent contributor to the flagellant correspondence columns. He wrote a particularly delightful letter to the pro-flogging *Morning Post*, extolling the virtues of corporal punishment and declaring himself all the better for his school experiences. He signed it 'One who has been well swished'.

Peter shared his collection with me like a proud curator, pointing out books and periodicals he knew I'd especially appreciate. I was thrilled at last to see original issues of my beloved *Family Herald*, elegantly bound and preserved.

'You're a modern Henry Spencer Ashbee,' I said admiringly.

Peter's eyes lit up and I saw that he appreciated the reference.

Ashbee was an eccentric book collector who published a vast survey of pornography in the late nineteenth century under the pseudonym Pisanus Fraxi. Much of his writing focused on flagellation. He was dissolute and arrogant in the extreme, and many believed him to be 'Walter', the author of the notorious memoir *My Secret Life*. Tedious and repetitive, the book chronicled hundreds of encounters with lower-class girls willing to do anything for money. While painfully monotonous, 'Walter's' escapades did appeal to my class-inequality kink. Peter had all eleven volumes.

'If you like the library,' he said casually, 'then I imagine you'll like the schoolroom.'

My eyes widened hungrily. 'Schoolroom?'

An antique blackboard dominated one wall and a teacher's desk stood off to the side. Another wall displayed ancient maps and old learning charts – heraldry, Latin declensions and the Periodic Table. In the centre of the room were four old-fashioned wooden school desks, complete with inkwells. I stroked the scarred surface of one desk, examining the names and graffiti etched into it. When I lifted the lid the musty odour of antiquarian books wafted out. Several slim Victorian volumes were stacked inside, along with various exercise books.

'I prefer the classics,' Peter explained. 'I find they challenge a girl more.'

I paged through a battered nineteenth-century Latin grammar, ponderously written and heavily reliant on quotations from Ovid and Caesar. Yes, this would be an eye-opener for any modern student. But it was the spelling book that really astounded me. Published in 1877, presumably for children, it contained words like erysipelas, cicatrice, phthisis, usquebaugh and bdellium.

'I've never even heard of half these words,' I said, baffled. 'I wouldn't know how to pronounce some of them, let alone spell them!'

Peter took the book from me and replaced it in the desk with a sly grin. 'Yes, I must give you a spelling test sometime. It will be most salutary.'

That was a truly frightening thought. But the idea that he'd done this before – taught lessons to nervous girls in this outdated schoolroom – thrilled me to the core.

Up on the wall behind the teacher's desk, I noticed a display of school canes and tawses. On the desk rested a paddle, along with a wicked-looking acrylic ruler. I wasn't keen to open the drawers; I was sure they contained yet more implements.

As I cast a final glance around the room, my eye fell on a familiar object. To the uninitiated it could have been a set of small library steps or a mounting block. But I recognised it at once. It was a birching block.

I stared at it in disbelief for several seconds. 'Where did you . . .?'

'I had a cabinet-maker friend construct it for me,' he said with a modest smile.

He was certainly no amateur.

'Would you like to see my masterpiece?' he asked.

The girl stood in front of the tree, her eyes fixed pensively on the switch. On the screen all that was visible of the man beside her was his shoulder and arm. In the next shot the girl was bending over the stone wall next to the tree, her cutoffs down around her ankles. The third picture was a closeup of the switch against her unmarked bottom and the fourth showed a thin pink stripe across her cheeks. The sequence was artistic and well composed, clearly the work of a professional.

But it was the second photoset that really shocked me. It showed a different girl, a lanky brunette with pale-olive skin and an impish smile, standing naked on a tourist overlook at what could only be the Grand Canyon. I gaped at the pictures as she posed and pouted for the camera, showing off her flexibility. A few shots later and she was upended over the knee of a faceless man, her bottom reddening noticeably as the sequence progressed.

The website was englishvice.net: 'a celebration of spanking al fresco'.

'These are incredible,' I said, clicking on another set of pictures. This one showed two girls bending over a railing with their bottoms bared. The white sails of the Sydney Opera House gleamed behind them.

'I'm rather proud of that set,' Peter said. 'The ferry terminal was swarming with tourists.'

I couldn't believe what I was seeing. Some of the photostories were in everyday outdoor settings, but most were in highly recognisable locations – Westminster Abbey, the Arc de Triomphe, Charles Bridge in Prague.

'So which one are you? The headless spanker or the photographer?'

'Usually the spanker. But some were sent in by other people. I buy the really interesting ones for the website, especially if there was clearly some risk involved in getting the shots. My customers like the iconic location shots best. It's what we've become known for.'

I scrolled through the thumbnails, marvelling at some of the images. 'Good heavens, is that Chatsworth?' I laughed.

'It's remarkable what you can get away with in a few seconds. Though you'd be surprised at how deserted these places can be. Sometimes you can only get a single shot.'

He stood up, offering me the chair. 'Here, why don't you sit down?'

'No thanks. I think I'll be more comfortable standing.'

His eyes glittered. 'Then I definitely want you to sit.'

With a wince I lowered myself into the chair, the hard wooden seat making my stripes throb. I hadn't changed out of my school uniform and the skirt was itchy and unkind to my tender skin. I could tell he enjoyed my reaction. 'Don't you have anything softer?' I complained, secretly loving the sensation.

'Sorry,' he said, not sorry a bit.

'Where did you get the idea for the site?'

'Well, I always enjoyed taking spanking pictures in interesting places. And I know a few girls willing to risk it. I travel a lot for work, you see.'

'One might suspect you use the university's travel opportunities to subsidise your pervy hobby,' I said archly.

'Quite. I've no doubt that's how my employer would view it. That's why I don't show my face. I can't afford to have some first-year with nothing to lose stumble on to the site and recognise me.'

'Scary thought.'

'Someone introduced me to a fetish photographer at a spanking party and we started the website together. His girlfriend has modelled for us a few times – Courtney.'

I turned back to the screen, admiring a photo of a girl in school uniform touching her toes in front of one of the New York Public Library's stone lions.

'Have you ever been caught?'

'Oh yes. A few times. But it's generally just some unsuspecting tourist who blunders on to the scene. They're usually too embarrassed to say anything. We did some nude pictures once in Yellowstone and a Japanese tour group just thought it was a glamour shoot. The men watched for a while and then started taking their own pictures.'

I could just imagine the scene and the stories the Japanese men would be telling back home. I suppose if it looked artistic rather than pornographic most Brits or Americans would let it take its course, and watch rather than report it.

'I've been asked to leave places too,' Peter continued. 'There was a pretty stroppy security guard at Downing Street with no sense of humour.'

I laughed. 'Does your photographer friend ever show his face?'

Peter clicked on a group of photos taken in a vineyard. 'That's him – Shaun.'

The man spanking the redheaded girl among the grapes

was in his mid-thirties, with mischievous blue eyes and dark-blond hair.

'You'll like the name of the wine,' Peter said, scrolling down to another picture, a closeup of a wine bottle.

I couldn't believe it. The label showed a boy bent over a man's knee, being spanked on the bare. The name read '*Kröver Nacktarsch*'. I blinked at it and looked at Peter for help.

'Bare bottom in *Kröv*,' he translated. 'Though some people claim it's a corruption of "nectar".'

I shook my head in amazement. 'How do you *find* these things?'

He stood behind me, so close I could feel his breath on the back of my neck. 'The same way I found you.' He reached around me and opened another set of pictures. On the screen a corsetted goth girl presented herself, knickers down, against a familiar ruined abbey.

'What – stalking?'

He kept his right hand on the mouse, scrolling through the images, his arm pressing into my side. The sleeve of his schoolmaster's gown hung nearly to the floor. 'No. Research.' He leant in close to me. 'Single-minded, meticulous research.'

It was as though he'd been out there all my life, tracking me, waiting for the right moment to catch me. The girl at the abbey arched her back as a hand connected with her bottom.

I closed my eyes as Peter's hand lifted from the mouse and settled on the nape of my neck. He slid his fingers up into my hair. I lowered my head, relaxing as his other hand moved around me to slip between the lapels of the blazer and squeeze my breast. I moaned a half-hearted protest and shifted in the chair. He fisted his hand in my hair and firmly pulled my head back.

'I wonder . . .' he mused, letting his other hand wander to my lap. 'What is it about authority that so pushes your buttons?'

He lowered his lips to my throat and kissed me softly, barely a touch. I shivered, but didn't resist.

'Is it the power an authority figure has over you?'

I arched my neck into a deeper kiss and felt his teeth graze the soft skin of my neck. Trying to control my breathing, I gripped the edges of the chair.

'Is it knowing you're completely at his mercy?'

His hand crawled over my thighs, slipping in between them. With a squeak I pressed my legs together, trapping the hand.

'Perhaps,' he continued, his lips travelling down to my shoulder, 'it's the security of being subject to discipline, of knowing that any naughtiness or disobedience will be punished. Severely, if need be.'

I sucked in a breath, feeling weaker with each trigger word.

'Part your legs,' he said.

After a moment's hesitation I inched them apart. His hand slid up along my inner thigh and stopped at the gusset of my knickers, barely touching the cotton.

My breathing sounded loud and laboured in my ears. He was right about the authority; I was helpless before it. I desperately wanted him to touch me, to take it further.

He drew little circles over the damp white cotton with his fingertips, making me jump and gasp at the stimulation. With my bottom still tingling from the cane, my sex was alive in a way it had never been before.

Peter released my hair and I bowed my head, inviting him. Both hands found their way into the blazer, peeling it open then pinning my arms with it halfway off. He dragged the crisp school shirt up out of the waistband of the skirt and began to unbutton it from the bottom. He was deliberate, exposing my skin with slow precision, inch by inch.

His gown whispered like a co-conspirator as he exposed me, leaving the top button fastened. My tie hung absurdly over my white bra.

'Of course,' he said, his voice low and sonorous in my ear. 'Not all authority figures are so honest.'

With deft hands he unhooked the front closure, releasing my breasts for him to play with.

‘There are some who might take advantage of an innocent girl. Or a not-so-innocent girl. A prison guard, perhaps. Or a warder in a reformatory. Or even just an unscrupulous schoolmaster.’

His fingers teased my nipples, plucking them into eager points.

‘A girl at the mercy of such a man might find herself across his knee for the slightest infraction. Or perhaps for no infraction at all. He might invent excuses. And he might take other liberties as well.’

I made a hoarse little sound – part protest, part encouragement.

Peter guided me up on to my feet and led me across to the bed. I sat down and sank back on to my elbows. I gazed up at the menacing schoolmaster standing over me.

‘Ah, yes,’ he said, his voice barely a whisper now. ‘I always wanted a girl of my own. To examine and explore. To play with and to punish.’

Self-consciously, I pulled my shirt closed around me.

The severe expression on his face chilled me and I looked away.

‘Now, now,’ he said in a tone of unsympathetic reproach. ‘I was told you were a good girl. An obedient girl. But you’re not being co-operative at all, are you?’

Blushing furiously, I released the folds of the shirt. They fell open, partly revealing one breast.

‘That’s better. But I think we’ll have it all the way open, girl. Unless, of course, you *want* a spanking.’

The shame was exquisite as I complied, displaying myself to him. I felt more exposed this way than if I were naked.

‘See? You can be a good girl when you try.’ Then, with a menacing smile, he began to unbuckle his belt. ‘And now we’ll have your knickers off.’

I gave him a pleading look. I wanted it. I was ready. But I didn’t want it to be consensual. I wanted him to force me. ‘Please, no,’ I whispered.

Holding it by the buckle, he drew the belt slithering through the loops. It slapped free and he dangled it threateningly above me. 'Knickers *off*, girl,' he growled. 'Unless you want a dose of this.'

I melted into helpless submission, my tremulous fingers barely able to accomplish the task. I slipped the soft white cotton down to my knees and hesitated. Peter raised his eyebrows and began to double the belt. Hurriedly, I kicked them off and stared up at him, fearful and exhilarated.

He unzipped his trousers and pushed them down, revealing his hard cock. With the loop of leather he gestured for me to move further back on to the bed. I complied, knowing I didn't want to feel the sting of his belt over the still-aching cane strokes. I lay back, staring wide eyed at my tormentor, the evil schoolmaster who was about to take me.

His lips curled in a cruel grin as he lifted my skirt and knelt above me. The gown fell about him like a cape and I felt trapped, as though in the thrall of a vampire. Peter nudged my legs apart with his knee and I opened myself to him, as I covered my face with my hands.

But he wasn't letting me off that easily. 'Hands above your head, girl.'

I obeyed the soft-spoken command, gripping the wrought-iron bars of the headboard. He never raised his voice.

He stared at the smooth pale skin above my sex with approval. Then, with surprising roughness, he thrust his hand between my legs, making me gasp. His fingers probed and explored me proprietarily and I was scarlet with shame at the copious wetness I couldn't hide.

'My, my,' he said. 'Such a dirty little girl.'

In a husky voice I barely recognised as my own I offered one last feeble protest.

But he merely laughed – a low throaty villainous laugh. He withdrew his hand and pressed the head of his cock against my sex. He kept it there, pushing gently, but not penetrating me. The tension was unbearable. And he knew it. He wanted to torture me. But not by making me ask for it.

I couldn't stand it any longer and I abandoned myself entirely to the fantasy.

'No, please,' I begged, pushing him away. 'Stop!'

He caught my wrists and pinned them down on either side of my head. I struggled, using all my strength to yank and pull. But he was too strong. The realisation made my sex throb with desperate excruciating need.

'Oh no,' he said in a gruff voice. 'You're not going anywhere.'

I strained against him to reassure myself of my defencelessness. He could do anything he wanted to me.

At last he plunged himself inside me, making me cry out. I continued to fight him, but I knew I could never escape.

He lowered his mouth to my ear and whispered threateningly as he thrust into me again and again.

'You're here to be punished, girl, and I'm going to see to it that you are. Severely. I have all the time in the world. And as soon as I've had my fun with you I'm going to put you over my knee and smack your bottom.'

I melted into aching compliance at his words.

'Or perhaps,' he continued. 'Another caning is what you need to teach you a lesson. Or a sound paddling. No, it's no good resisting. That's only going to earn you more punishment. You're going to be a good girl and do whatever I say. Unless you want to feel my cane across your tender little bottom.'

He moved inside me with rough slow strokes, and each deep thrust wrenched a gasp from me.

'I've heard stories about you, girl. Always trying to get special treatment. I think I'll throw a little party and let the guards take turns whipping you. And when your bottom and thighs are a nice shade of red we'll pass you around. You'll be our little plaything, to use as we want. And, if you're naughty and you disobey us, we'll punish you again. Oh yes, we'll teach you some discipline, my girl.'

I had never been so aroused in my life. The fantasy made the physical stimulation almost irrelevant. My breathing grew rapid and frantic as his thrusts became more violent. The hands that gripped my wrists were trembling with the effort of holding me down and my arm muscles were beginning to ache. I wrapped my legs around him tightly, urging him deeper, harder, rougher, until I felt the spasms inside me begin to grow and swell. The pleasure expanded until it consumed me and every nerve in my body was screaming for release. I clamped my legs tighter as the climax swept me under in a surging blissful wave and my body leapt and bucked beneath him.

His own climax followed mine and he emptied himself into me in sharp hot jets, panting and lowering his head to my heaving sweaty chest. I didn't think I would ever stop tingling.

I moved in the next week and he introduced me to Shaun and Courtney. Of course, I'd already met Courtney. In a way.

Ten

The North Carolina night was intolerably hot and sticky. It was definitely a night to be inside drinking and watching half-naked girls writhing on brass poles.

Courtney Somerville's ID claimed she was twenty-one, but she was only seventeen. The club would never have hired her if they'd known, but they were unlikely to find out until after she was legal. Her birthday was only a few days away, after all. What was the big deal? She couldn't wait to be an adult, to be free of the stifling rules and restrictions. All her friends had tried to talk her out of it, but Courtney had stuck to her guns. It was the nicest club in Durham and she would be perfectly safe. She'd have a blast and make some money and celebrate her birthday in style.

She checked her reflection for the hundredth time, fluffing her frothy mess of auburn hair and debating whether she needed more lipstick. She'd never worn so much makeup in her life and she couldn't be sure if she was overdoing it. She frowned at her chest and bent forwards, moulding her breasts into a more satisfactory cleavage. The red sequinned bustier was slightly too big for her and it kept slipping down. Probably no big deal, since she'd be taking it off soon enough. But she didn't want to fall out of it before it was time. The matching thong and hotpants were incredibly uncomfortable and she was sure she'd have a rash from all the scratchy sequins.

'You look fine, sugar,' Celeste said. 'Quit fussing already.'

'But I'm so nervous,' Courtney protested. 'Can't you get me a drink?'

Celeste sighed. 'It's just stage fright. You'll be fine once you're out there.'

'I know, but I need something *now*. Just a shot of tequila?'

'You don't want to go on stage drunk.'

'Oh, please, it takes more than one shot to get me drunk!'

Tutting to indicate that she was going against her better judgement, Celeste gave in. 'All right. But just one. That has to be the worst fake ID I've ever seen and there are a million other waitresses who can take my place if I get fired.'

'Oh, thank you!' Courtney gushed, throwing her arms around Celeste.

While she waited for her drink she listened to the pounding bass as Tori danced to Nine Inch Nails. Courtney peeked through the curtain to watch. This girl had obviously been dancing for years. Swinging around the brass pole, climbing it and clamping her thighs around it to hang upside down . . . Courtney wasn't going to attempt anything like that. Not until she got some experience anyway. Celeste had assured her that her youth and good looks were far more important than any artistic talent, but it was still a performance to Courtney and she wanted to do her best.

Celeste returned with her drink. 'Here you go, girl. It's a double, so go easy. Dan's in a good mood tonight.'

Courtney gratefully took the glass. Then she downed half of it, grimacing as the liquid fire scorched its way down her tender throat to smoulder in her stomach.

Celeste shook her head. 'Girl, if you kill yourself in those heels, don't come cryin' to me.'

'I won't,' Courtney said, rolling her eyes. The five-inch stilettos were a challenge, but she was used to dancing at nightclubs and parties.

'Well, good luck to you,' Celeste said, leaving the girl alone in the dressing room.

Tori came off the stage, her sleek toned body gleaming with sweat.

'You were amazing,' Courtney said. 'I wish I could dance like that.'

Tori grinned as she plucked dollar bills out of her thong. 'Thanks, kid. Be sure and play to the frat boys on the right side of the stage. They're wasted and feeling very generous.'

'Thanks!'

Suddenly the DJ poked his head into the room. 'You Courtney?' he asked.

'Yes.'

'You're up. You got a stage name?'

Courtney's green eyes widened and she looked at Tori in horror. 'No, I didn't even –'

'Call her Diamond,' Tori said smoothly, winking at Courtney. 'In the rough.'

'You got it!' He disappeared again.

'Diamond,' Courtney mused. 'I like that.'

Tori gave her a sisterly kiss on the cheek. 'Break a leg!'

'I probably will,' Courtney said ruefully, throwing the last of the tequila down her throat. She gasped for breath as she waited for the DJ to announce her.

'And now we've got a real treat for you, gentlemen,' he said. 'It's her first time on stage, so she's feeling a little nervous, but I'm sure you'll make her feel right at home. Her name's Diamond, but don't let that fool you – this girl likes it rough!'

Her heart leapt at hearing her new name and she stepped through the curtains as the Rolling Stones began to blare from the speakers. Mick Jagger was asking if he was hard enough or rough enough. It was easy to lose herself in the raunchy melody and she made her way to the pole, grinding her hips and bending over to give the guys in the club a view of her toned thighs and bottom.

A vast floor-to-ceiling mirror covered the wall to her left and she gained confidence as the sex kitten in the reflection rotated her hips alluringly. She sank to her knees and crawled towards the cheering frat party. Courtney felt glamorous and desirable under the lights. The stage transformed her into an exotic creature men had to pay for.

She wasn't meant to go topless until the second song, but she could feel the bustier slipping down again. Besides, she was ready now. The tequila had warmed away her nerves and the atmosphere was whipping her vanity into a frenzy.

She slowly unhooked the garment in the back, taking her time, enjoying the tease. Some of the rowdier frat boys began to pound on the table in gleeful anticipation. Courtney didn't keep them in suspense. She let the bustier slide to the floor, where she nimbly kicked it out of the way.

Her breasts were young and firm. A perfect handful, Tommy Cantrell had said admiringly. That night of adolescent fumbling seemed a million years ago now. She peeled the hotpants down, revealing the round pale cheeks of her bottom. With a wiggle she coaxed them down to her ankles and minced out of them.

Now wearing nothing but the glittering red sequinned thong, Courtney leant back against the pole, displaying herself to the club. She cupped her breasts coyly, then uncovered them again, gyrating and swaying to the bump-and-grind beat. The song ended far too quickly.

'All right, gentlemen,' the DJ said enthusiastically. 'Let's show Diamond some real Southern hospitality now. Here's a little ZZ Top to help loosen your grip on those dollar bills.'

'Legs' began to play and Courtney showed hers off obligingly, lying on her back and stretching out, posing like a pin-up queen. She pointed her toes, bending her knees slightly and arching her back to display the graceful lines.

The portly man standing at the left edge of the stage was waiting to tip her. She slithered over to him and sat down on the stage, her hands behind her on the floor. Then she raised her legs in the air, showing him the tight muscles of her thighs. She turned her toes out and scissored her legs apart 180 degrees, delighting in his appreciative gulp. What would her ballet teacher think if she could see Courtney now? He folded two dollar bills lengthwise and slipped them one at a time into her thong, one on each hip. She wiggled her fingers at him and returned to the pole.

The frat boys were getting noisier and she delighted in their catcalls. Three of them were waving money at her, trying to lure her over. She worked her way across the stage to them, crouching down so that they could reach her. She was completely in her element now, revelling in the moment. They pawed at her. She let them. They stuffed her thong full of dollar bills and they applauded wildly as she left the stage.

'Like a fish to water,' the DJ said with a knowing chuckle. 'Yes, that was our own rough little Diamond. And just think – one of you lucky guys will get to enjoy her very first table dance. Good luck, darlin'! Now let's hear it for Tiffany!'

A pneumatic blonde took the stage as Courtney reached the dressing room. She was beaming as she put the bustier and hotpants on again and made her way out to the party. She wouldn't be surprised if they all wanted a dance from her and, at twenty dollars a pop, she'd be able to buy that Dolce & Gabbana dress she'd been drooling over.

'Hey, guys,' she drawled. 'Who wants to be first?'

Buzzed from the tequila and high on the attention, Courtney didn't notice Derek until it was too late.

'What the hell are you doing here?' her brother demanded.

Courtney gasped, then regained her composure. 'I could ask you the same question.'

Derek glared at her and bundled his coat around her shoulders. 'Come on,' he said decisively. 'We're leaving.'

Outraged, Courtney shrugged the coat off. Her eyes flashed with a black fury that bordered on hatred. 'I'm not going anywhere!' she spat. 'I'm not your baby sister any more and you can't tell me what to do.'

He seized her arm. 'Oh, yes, I can, young lady. You just try me. You're not too old to be put over my knee.'

Derek's fraternity brothers shifted their eyes at one another in stunned silence.

Courtney's face burnt, but she tried desperately not to show her fear. She was horrified that he would say such a thing in front of the others. 'Let go of me,' she hissed.

But he only held her arm tighter.

The standoff was broken by Bob, the manager. 'There a problem here?'

'Yes,' Courtney said petulantly.

'I'm taking my sister home,' Derek said.

'No you're not!' she protested.

'You can't force the lady to leave if she doesn't want to go,' Bob explained calmly, spreading his hands. The patronising tone probably worked with drunks, but Derek was sober and determined.

He smiled. 'No, but I bet I can get her fired.'

Bob returned the smile, reptilian in its coldness. 'Oh?'

'I suggest you start by checking her ID.'

'We did,' said Bob, surprised. 'She's twenty-one.'

Derek snorted. 'Is she? That's news to me.'

Suddenly realising what her brother was playing at, Courtney nudged him. 'Shut up, Derek,' she said through her teeth.

But he continued loudly. 'Unless I've forgotten my own sister's birthday, she won't even be eighteen for another week.'

Now Bob looked worried. The courts wouldn't care if she'd be eighteen in five minutes, let alone five days. Not if he'd hired an underage stripper.

'OK, OK,' Courtney said hastily, keen to avoid the humiliation of being dismissed by the manager. 'I'll go with you.'

'Wise girl,' Derek said, giving her arm an admonitory squeeze before releasing her.

Her faced fixed in a sullen pout, she rubbed her arm as Derek addressed his friends. 'I'll need the house to myself for a couple of hours. I'm going to teach my sister a lesson she won't forget.'

Courtney turned scarlet and stared at the floor.

The boys nodded in silent agreement, good little soldiers every one. No one was willing to stick up for her.

The drive to the frat house was made in frigid silence. Along the way Courtney thought of all the clever comebacks she should have used and didn't. But that was how it always was, wasn't it? You never thought of the cool things to say until the moment had passed. She knew without a doubt that she'd never be able to face any of Derek's fraternity brothers again.

'Well? Do you have anything to say for yourself?'

Courtney was taken aback by his presumption. No sooner had he shut the front door than he was acting like her father. She told him so.

He laughed, a harsh chilling sound. 'And it's abundantly clear to me that you need some discipline. Ever since Dad left you've been out of control. And I haven't been around to take you in hand. I intend to remedy that tonight.'

The threat sounded obscene in his mannerly Southern accent. He was the family's golden child, on a full scholarship to Duke University. Courtney was the black sheep, still with no clear idea what she wanted to be when she grew up.

Derek had been a typically overbearing big brother all her life but, when their father had left, he had taken it upon himself to discipline her when he felt she needed it. Courtney resented it intensely and rebelled against him at every turn. This time was not going to be any different. 'If you think you're going to treat me like a child, you're out of your fucking mind,' she warned. 'I only came back with you so we could talk. You're not laying a finger on me.'

He shook his head, furrowing his brow. 'Such language,' he said coolly. 'I ought to wash your mouth out with soap.'

Courtney glared at him. 'Don't you dare,' she snarled. 'How many times do I have to say it? I'm not a child!'

'No, you're clearly not,' he said, indicating her red sequinned outfit. 'But you insist on acting like one. Did you enjoy flaunting yourself tonight? In front of all those sweaty strangers?'

She laughed. 'Yes, I did. Especially when I realised one of those sweaty strangers was my own brother. What do you think Daddy would say about that? The perfect son out slumming with the boys at a strip club?'

'I'm an adult,' he reminded her.

'And why did you wait so long to confront me?' she continued. 'Enjoying the show too much?'

Derek's expression hardened. 'I was in the restroom, as a matter of fact. Todd came in and said I had to check out this new girl, this "way hot chick who looks like your little sis in a porn flick".'

Courtney blinked. She was sure Derek intended the comment to offend her, but she refused to rise to the bait. Besides, she'd always thought Todd was cute. 'Wow,' she said. 'Tell him I said thanks!'

His eyes narrowed and he drew himself up. 'I've had enough of your attitude, young lady,' he said. Then he grabbed her by the wrist and dragged her into the bathroom.

Courtney yanked to get free, but his grip was like a vice. Derek slammed the door behind them and released his sister, standing between her and escape. He turned on the tap and soaked a washcloth under the stream. Then he grabbed the back of her head with one hand while he began scrubbing her face with the other.

Courtney cursed as she spluttered and struggled, but her words were muffled by the cloth.

'I won't have my little sister looking like a whore,' he said, scouring the makeup off her face.

When he finally stopped, her face felt like he'd rubbed it with sandpaper.

'That hurt,' she pouted.

'You're going to be hurting a lot more before this evening is over,' he said severely, as he took her by the arm and hauled her out of the bathroom.

She went without protest, frightened of what he intended to do. She hadn't really thought he was serious. Surely he was just trying to scare her.

When they reached the living room, he released her and stood in front of the fireplace, his arms crossed. 'You have a choice,' he said solemnly. 'I can tell Mom what you've been up to . . .' He let his words hang in the air. 'Or you can take your licks from me.'

Courtney stared at him in stunned dismay. She knew exactly what he was insinuating, but she couldn't stop the indignant question. 'What do you mean?'

With a small tight smile, Derek glanced over at the fireplace and then back at his sister. 'I think you know perfectly well what I'm talking about.'

His words fell like a death sentence and Courtney struggled not to react. She couldn't let him know how worried she really was. Their father was miles away and Courtney really didn't care what he thought. But their mother would be devastated. She wasn't about to let him blackmail her, though. She had to preserve her dignity. 'Fine. Tell her. See if I care.'

'I suppose there's another option,' Derek said, speculating. 'I could call the police.'

'What?'

'I don't know if they'd arrest you, but you'd likely be put on probation. And since it would take more than a week to go to court, you'd be eighteen then. Old enough to be charged with a crime.'

Courtney felt her heart begin to flutter like a frightened bird.

'You wouldn't dare.'

'Possession of a fake ID. Underage drinking. Public lewdness.' He shook his head. 'The law is pretty clear.'

She knew better than to call his bluff.

'What's it going to be, Courtney?'

He knew she had no choice. Grinding her teeth in fury, she glared at him, her silence all the answer she would give him.

'Very well.'

He strode to the mantel and her eyes widened in mounting horror as he took the large wooden frat paddle down from its place of honour. Made of polished walnut, it was nearly two feet long and well over half an inch thick. Its smooth surface was elegantly embossed with Greek letters and the name of the college. It looked more like a decorative souvenir than something actually intended for use.

Derek smacked the paddle against his palm. He'd swatted Courtney with it once before, in play. It was just after he'd been accepted into the fraternity. He'd even proudly displayed for her the bruises from his own initiation. There was an implicit message: if he could take it, so could she.

'I'm sure you know the position, Courtney.'

The longer she waited, the more frightened he would think she was. And she wasn't about to let him think he'd mastered her. With a venomous accusing stare, Courtney put her hands on her bent knees, leaning forwards to brace herself. It was the position they used at school.

'Pull your pants down.'

She gasped. But, again, she had too much pride to show how scared she really was. She slipped the itchy hotpants down and they dropped to the floor, puddling round her ankles.

Derek held the paddle with two hands, like a baseball bat and placed it against her bottom. As the cool varnished wood touched her skin, Courtney gritted her teeth. She told herself it couldn't be worse than being paddled at school. That was a rite of passage and students bragged about getting whacked. But at school it was never on the bare.

The paddle lifted away and then it connected with a sharp crack. Her backside flared with pain, but Courtney refused to give Derek the satisfaction of yelping. The polished expanse of the paddle tapped her again and she held her breath as it drew back. The second stroke fell, painting a wide swathe of fire across both cheeks. She stumbled with the force of the blow, gasping a little. But she forced herself to get back into position immediately.

Another stroke fell and she couldn't restrain a little whimper as she fought to maintain her balance. As the paddle met her cheeks again, she wondered how many he intended to give her. Her bottom must be a bright-red beacon by now. She was certainly feeling it and it was all she could do to resist reaching behind to clutch her aching cheeks.

But Derek had said he was going to teach her a lesson she wouldn't forget. It was already memorable, but she didn't dare tell him that.

Another savage crack of wood against flesh. This time she couldn't help it: she yelped. Tears sprang to her eyes and she fought them with anger. There was nothing in the world more important than getting up from this paddling with her eyes dry and her spirit intact.

But as the next stroke fell she realised that was not going to happen. She staggered forwards and her hands flew from her knees. They were halfway to her hips when Derek stopped her.

'Back in position,' he ordered.

Courtney obeyed instantly, squeezing her eyes shut and waiting for the next awful blow.

It came, brightening the fire in her bottom and making her cry out. The next stroke knocked her off balance again and, as soon as she resumed her position, the final one broke her.

She sank to her knees and covered her face with her hands, tears of pain and humiliation streaming down her face. Oddly enough, she was no longer angry with Derek. But she was furious with herself. And she fought hard to restrain the torrent of emotion threatening to burst free.

She felt the touch of his hand on her shoulder and she weakened even more. When she didn't rebuff him, he gave her an affectionate squeeze. It was too much. She crumbled. Courtney couldn't remember crying so hard since her cat had run away when she was five. Their father had held her and rocked her while she cried and cried as though her little heart would break. She felt like that five-year-old child again as she sobbed in her brother's arms.

'Shh, it's all right, sis,' he said gently.

Courtney clung to him, baring her soul completely, vulnerable as she'd only ever been with their father. Derek held her securely, his arms big and warm around her. She knew she could trust him with her tears, and that allowed her to cry even harder. The physical pain was the last thing on her mind.

When her crying finally subsided, he tilted her tear-streaked face up to his. Courtney sniffled and gathered her wits, wiping her eyes.

'I'm sorry, Courtney,' Derek said. 'But I had to do it. You understand, don't you?'

She nodded reluctantly.

'You don't belong in a sleazy place like that,' he said.

He was no longer the tyrannical disciplinarian. He was just her overprotective big brother, intimidating her boy-friends and looking out for her.

With a long shuddering sigh, she agreed. 'I know. I just wanted to have some fun.'

He grinned. 'Was it worth it?'

Courtney went into the bathroom to have a look. Derek followed her. The mirror showed her two flaming-red cheeks, punctuated in the centre by large round bullseye bruises. She winced. Dancing was clearly not going to be an option for at least another week.

She reached behind to touch the scorched flesh. 'No,' she admitted.

'That was almost ten years ago,' Courtney said wonderingly. 'It still seems like yesterday.'

My eyes were like dinner plates. 'What an amazing story,' I said. 'It's exactly the sort of thing I always fantasised about. I always wished I'd had a big brother.'

Courtney tossed her red hair proudly. 'I blame him entirely for my frat paddle fetish.'

'And you should see our collection,' Shaun broke in.

Peter nodded in confirmation. 'It's impressive. More wine?'

Courtney held out her glass while he filled it. 'Sometimes I wonder what Derek would think if he knew what I was into these days. Shaun says we should invite him to a play party if he visits.'

Play parties! I couldn't keep up with this new reality. Just the idea of having like-minded friends to talk with about it, to conspire with . . . It was staggering. For years these things had been my dirty little secret.

'So Peter said he showed you the site,' said Shaun, inflecting it as a question.

'Yes, it's absolutely stunning.' I turned to face Courtney. 'I recognised you, of course. You got me into so much trouble. I still can't believe you managed to shove those knickers into my pocket without my knowing it.'

Courtney laughed, a high musical sound. 'Oh, that was easy,' she said in her sultry Southern drawl. 'I shoplifted a bit when I was a kid. I was good at slipping things into my pockets, so Peter knew who to recruit for the job.'

'I'm never stuck for an excuse with this one,' Shaun said, rolling his eyes.

'Don't some of those shots just blow your mind?' Courtney asked, ignoring him. 'I mean, that Japanese girl naked in the snow?' She affected an elaborate shudder. 'No way could I do that!'

'It's quite something,' I agreed.

'And they're so much fun to pose for too,' she said. Then her face brightened. 'You'll love it.'

Shaun agreed and I looked down, abashed. It was one thing to play privately, with a trusted partner. But to flaunt it for everyone on the Net?

'Oh, I don't know,' I said. 'I'm still just a newbie.'

'Hey, no pressure,' Courtney assured me. 'Just let me know when you're ready . . .'

I smiled into my glass at that. She was so cocky and confident. And I had to admit the idea was alluring.

'What would be your hottest fantasy location?' Peter asked.

Oddly enough, that question hadn't occurred to me when he'd shown me the site. 'I don't know,' I said, thinking. 'I suppose maybe . . . Well, I could see myself being smacked in some old Victorian schoolroom. Or Dartmoor Prison. No, better yet – how about *HMS Victory*?'

Peter rubbed his chin thoughtfully. '*Victory* might be problematical. But how about the *Cutty Sark*? Or the *Grand Turk*? She's moored in Whitby.'

I grinned. 'Hornblower's ship. How fitting.'

Peter didn't miss a step. 'Mr Wellard, you mean. One of the best canings in mainstream film,' he said.

Shaun laughed delightedly. 'I could be up for shooting that one,' he said.

Shaun was thirty-six and a native Londoner. He didn't have Peter's fine education or his accent, but Courtney clearly liked her bit of rough. They made an odd pair – the fetish photographer and the delinquent Southern belle.

'Where'd you two meet?' I asked, curious.

Shaun nodded towards Peter. 'Same place you did. Courtney was posting to the forum as "Little Miss Naughty", just begging to be taken in hand.'

Courtney sniggered at that. 'My brother would certainly agree. But he thinks we met at the Tate Gallery.'

'Very civilised,' Peter said approvingly.

I turned to Shaun. 'What about you? Have you always been into this?'

He grinned at Peter. 'Full of 'satiable curtiosity, isn't she?' he asked.

I blushed. 'The Elephant's Child' had been one of my favourite stories growing up. But if my mother was curious why I always insisted on her reading that one over all the others, she never asked.

'I didn't have any single defining episode like Courtney,' he said. 'I sort of found my way here through S&M. I had to search and refine what it was that worked for me until I arrived at spanking. For the longest time I thought *Story of O* was as close as I'd get to my own fantasies. There were some hot elements there, but it still wasn't quite right.'

'Not enough punishment,' I agreed.

'Well, it wasn't that,' Shaun said. 'There just wasn't any spanking. I don't mind if a girl enjoys it. I certainly enjoy it when I'm on the other end.'

I blinked. 'Oh, are you a switch? I hadn't realised.'

'He's a slut,' Courtney corrected. 'I'm the switch.'

Now I was really intrigued. I'd never had girl-girl spanking fantasies. But I could certainly see Courtney as a top.

'I can't even imagine spanking anyone,' I said, shaking my head. 'I only ever fantasise about being spanked myself.'

Courtney nodded. 'Yep. That's how I used to be. Then one day I just got curious. And I had a more than willing guinea pig.' She squeezed Shaun's knee.

Shaun turned to me. 'And you? How'd you fall into this?'

'I've been fascinated by it for as long as I can remember. Though of course I didn't understand it when I was little. I just knew that there were certain scenes in books and movies that made me feel funny. I didn't know they were sexual feelings.'

'Psychosexual,' Peter corrected.

'Yes. The focus wasn't on sex or sexuality, but control. It's hard to describe. There was something oddly reassuring about those idealised discipline scenarios. There was no ambiguity in what was expected of you. You did what you were told or you got punished. Then you were forgiven. That was it. The simplicity was comforting.'

'Someone to watch over you,' Peter said.

'Quite. The worst that ever happened was that you got a sore bottom. But you were always taken care of.'

Courtney absently wound a lock of hair around one finger, considering. 'Though perhaps not always so lovingly,' she said at last.

I understood completely and I smiled. 'No. Not always.'

'Sometimes mistreatment can be hot.' She crossed her legs and folded her hands coyly on her lap, pretending to be embarrassed by the admission.

'I know what you mean,' Shaun agreed. 'Something sort of clicked for me in a secondary school literature class when we read "Galloping Foxley" – you know, Roald Dahl. In a rather different mode than *Charlie and the Chocolate Factory*.'

'Oh, I loved that story!' I cried. 'I read it at school too and was so afraid everyone could tell I was reacting to it.'

Peter grinned knowingly beside me. 'Me too. I remember resenting having to read it to begin with. I thought it was a children's story. But the first mention of caning got my attention. I must have read it a hundred times.'

'That was the first time I pictured myself as a boy,' I confessed dreamily.

Courtney raised her eyebrows to me. 'Oh, really? Do tell.'

I blushed. 'Well, in so many girls' school stories . . . the girls have it easy. Lots of times they didn't even get told off. I got sick of reading girls' school stories where there was no punishment. I felt cheated. But boys got treated differently.'

'Too right they did!' Shaun laughed. 'That's certainly how it was at my school. The girls got it on the hand while we had to bend over for it. We had to take cold showers too – stand there in the glacial spray with our teeth chattering for sixty seconds.'

I felt cold just thinking about it. 'Bloody hell!'

'Oh, you'd be numb after that,' he continued. 'There was also a sadistic gym master – Kendrick. He loved to line up a row of us and whack us with an arrow. Nothing like that ever happened to the girls.'

'Mmmm,' Courtney purred. 'Across those tight white schoolboy gym shorts. That must have smarted.'

I giggled, enjoying the image.

'Well, there was no discrimination at my school,' Peter said sadly. 'There weren't any girls.'

Shaun looked at him with mock sympathy, but I squirmed in my seat, remembering what he'd told me about his school days.

Peter continued. 'My housemaster, Mr Carew, was rather fond of the slipper, especially at bedtime. So were the prefects. They weren't allowed to use the cane, so they made sure a slippering was no small punishment.'

'And you Brits think the paddle is crude,' Courtney said, laughing. 'Whacking boys' bottoms with a gym shoe – really! Well, if it makes you feel any better, I sure as hell wasn't spared. I got sent to the principal a few times. And my cheerleader coach didn't spare the paddle either.'

'You were a cheerleader?' I asked.

'Yep. Still have the uniform.' She and Shaun exchanged a meaningful grin.

'So . . . what was it like?'

'Well, for starters it's nothing like as formal. Americans don't go in for all the ritual, I guess. No uniforms, none of this "sir" and "miss" stuff. When you get paddled you just bend over and grab your knees and they give you a couple of swats. When I was in school it was a mark of distinction to get whacked. Practically a fashion statement.'

'But it must have hurt!'

She gave me a conspiratorial wink. 'Let's just say that if you were lucky you were wearing jeans when you got busted.'

'But if you were unlucky,' Shaun interjected, 'you got caught misbehaving in your cheerleader uniform.'

Her cheeks flushed and she reached for her wineglass. 'Well, I guess I knew I'd have a kinky English boyfriend someday, now didn't I?'

'There are some American rituals,' said Peter thoughtfully. 'There's the woodshed.'

'Oh, right,' Courtney said, laughing again. 'Them was the good ol' days when your pa used to take you out to the woodshed for a whipping with the razor strop. Or send you into the woods to cut a switch.'

The conversation was making me feel light-headed. 'That's heavy stuff,' I said, remembering *Tom Sawyer*.

'But it's not ancient history,' she added. 'There are schools in the States that still use corporal punishment today. Mostly in the South, of course.'

I shook my head, mystified. I felt for those unfortunate miscreants, but I couldn't help wondering how many of them were future spankos just like us. Were they being created? Or just awakened?

My bottom is served up to him for discipline and I clench my cheeks in anticipation, waiting for the first stroke. It's always the hardest one to take. The birch is familiar to me now, but that doesn't lessen its bite.

I stare at the spill of shadows on the floor. The rod draws back to strike and I watch, transfixed, as the shadow-man raises his arm. My thighs quiver with the effort of holding still and I watch the arm swing down sharply in an arc.

The birch whistles through the air with a ferocious hiss and strikes my bottom in a burst of fire. It's nothing like the cane. The bite of the birch is instantaneous and agonising. All my nerve endings come wildly, shockingly alive. But, with my weight on my hands on the floor in front of me, all I can do is arch my back into it. Surf the pain.

'One,' I gasp at last. 'Thank you, sir.'

It's how he always expects me to count. It's become second nature to me.

He waits a few seconds for the rise and fall of the pain. Then the arm lifts up again.

This time I squeeze my eyes shut and hold my breath. The second stroke covers the first, the flexible switches lashing round and into every unprotected bit of flesh. I can't restrain my scream. My legs kick impotently in the aftershock as I gasp for breath, twisting as though I can escape the relentless rising sting. I climb with it to a place where I can absorb it and, when I've found my voice again, I count.

'Two. Thank you, sir.'

I've a long way to go yet. The only comfort lies in knowing how many strokes I'm getting. There's no way to mitigate the pain. It just has to be endured.

Eleven

Discipline (noun)
1. Training intended to guide development, especially to produce behavioural improvement.
2. Punishment intended to train or correct.

'How are you getting on with your thesis, Angie?'

'Erm . . .'

Peter looked surprised.

I wasn't sure what to say. We hadn't talked about my thesis since the night I'd first told him about it – when I'd met him at dinner.

'Have you done any work at all on it this past week?'

'Well, not exactly, I –'

'Not exactly? What is that supposed to mean? I want a straight answer, young lady.'

I was caught. Equivocating wasn't going to save me. I blushed and looked down at my feet. 'I'm sorry,' I murmured.

'I'm sorry what?'

My face burnt as the blood rushed to my cheeks. 'Sir. I'm sorry, sir.'

'I expect that you are, but I want to hear what you're sorry *for*.'

Feeling like a schoolgirl again, I stammered out what he wanted to hear. 'Sorry for not doing my work, sir.'

'Look at me, Angie.'

I lifted my head to meet his eyes.

'I realise you're settling into a new life,' he began patiently. 'And that it's very exciting. I'm willing to make reasonable allowances for that, but it's no excuse for neglecting your responsibilities.'

I squirmed a little at his words.

'I've been giving this some thought over the past few days, and it's clear that you need some encouragement. I need to push you. I am therefore instituting a new schedule for you. Come with me.'

Apprehensive, I followed him up the stairs and into the schoolroom. He indicated one of the desks and I sat obediently.

Peter leant back against the teacher's desk, his arms crossed. 'You're a very bright girl,' he said. 'But you lack application. You lack discipline.'

I sucked my lower lip as he scolded me. This would be hot in a roleplay, I thought. But this wasn't a roleplay.

'With proper guidance and encouragement you could have achieved far more than you did in school. I think you'd have responded well to corporal punishment, properly administered. And it's not too late. I know what you're capable of and I intend to see that you achieve it.'

He reached behind him and retrieved a sheet of paper from the desk. I wondered when he had decided all this.

'Every weekday morning you're to put on your school uniform and report here at eight sharp. I will inspect your uniform and if I am satisfied you may start work on your thesis.'

'In here?' I asked sheepishly.

'Yes. I think you will work better in an old-fashioned school environment, where you are subject to punishment for not following the rules.'

My stomach tightened into knots as I registered this new turn of events. This was the true consequence of my rash honesty over the Net. In my desperate eagerness I'd revealed myself entirely without even considering where it could lead. This man knew exactly how to humble and dominate me. More than that: he knew exactly what I needed and even secretly wanted, yet still dreaded.

'When I come home from work I'll check what you've done that day. If I feel you haven't applied yourself, I will punish you. If it's a minor infraction, I will put you over my knee and spank you. I may also set you impositions. However, if I feel you've been culpably neglectful, then the punishment will be rather more severe.'

My heart gave a little flutter.

'I've drafted a schedule for you,' he said, holding the paper out to me.

I took it with trembling hands and read over it. I was allowed a break for lunch, and short breaks for tea, but the rest of the time he expected me to be working. The goal was five hundred words a day, or notes as evidence of seven hours' work.

Peter removed his glasses and polished them nonchalantly while I read. His utter confidence was both comforting and unnerving.

'I'm not unreasonable,' he said. 'Nor will I look for excuses to punish you. On the contrary, I hope you will make me proud. However, I won't hesitate to be strict if I feel you need it. Do you understand?'

'Yes, sir.' I felt belittled and frightened, but there was an undeniable frisson of arousal.

'Very good. Now, in a little while I'm going to spank you. This is less a punishment than a reminder. I have something else in mind for formal punishments. For severe infractions you will be birched.' He paused to let that sink in before dropping the real bombshell. 'Do you remember that *Family Herald* letter that intrigued you so much? The one about the ritualised discipline in the school in Edinburgh?'

I nodded, suddenly very worried. He took something else from the desk and held it out to me. It was a folded white garment. I took it with uncertain hands.

'Unfold it.'

I shook it out and held it up. It looked like a hospital gown – closed in the front, with strings to tie it closed in the middle of the back. If I bent forwards in it, the flaps would fall to either side, baring my bottom.

'You are to keep this punishment gown in your desk. When you are due a severe punishment, I will send you out to cut switches to make a proper birch rod. Once I have approved it, I will send you up here to change. You will put on the gown and stand in the corner to wait for me, hands on your head. I expect the rod to be sitting on your desk when I come up to deal with you.'

My heart was throbbing so hard it was almost painful.

He nodded at the birching block against the wall. 'When I'm ready you will place the block in the centre of the room and kneel on it, presenting yourself for punishment. Do you understand?'

'Yes, sir,' I breathed.

'I take your education very seriously, Angie. I want you to take full advantage of your opportunities. And I won't be satisfied with work I feel is beneath your abilities.'

I swallowed. 'No, sir.'

He nodded solemnly. 'Very well, then. Stand up.'

I got shakily to my feet, clasping my hands behind my back. Peter took the austere straight-backed chair from behind the desk and set it down. He unbuttoned his jacket and slipped it off, arranging it carefully over the back of the chair. Then he began rolling up his right sleeve.

In stories the ritual had always been my favourite part. The spanking itself was often anticlimactic. The telling off and anticipation were what really set my pulse racing. Then the careful positioning, raising of the skirt, taking down of the knickers . . . There was an art to it. It was a dance with precise choreography. And the moments leading up to the spanking were like the predatory circling before the tango.

Facing a genuine punishment was an entirely different matter. I could neither avoid it nor hurry it along. Mired in ambivalence, I didn't know whether it was worse to postpone it or get it over with. The preparations heightened my anxiety – a punishment in itself. I could do nothing but wait while he made ready to punish me.

At last he was satisfied and he sat down. 'Right, young lady,' he said sternly. 'Over my knee.'

Though the distance was tiny, I could barely cross it on my trembling legs. Standing powerless beside him, I implored him with my eyes. But I had no choice. I draped myself across his lap.

Without a word he lifted my tartan skirt to reveal my bottom, demurely covered by a pair of powder-blue boyshorts. Instead of taking them down, he smoothed them out over the curves of my unblemished cheeks, carefully arranging them so that they were trim and taut. I knew without being told that the next time this happened I would be in school uniform. White cotton panties would replace my boyshorts and French knickers. And my array of tartan skirts would hang like lonely orphans in the wardrobe, forsaken for the plain navy-blue pleated school skirt he favoured.

Peter lifted his right knee, raising my bottom a little more. My sense of shame increased and I whimpered, wrapping my hands around his leg.

I expected another scolding – his palm describing languid circles over my nervously clenching cheeks while he lectured me further on my negligence. But he didn't waste any time getting straight to business. He spanked me briskly and vigorously and I squealed and struggled right from the start.

'I know it hurts,' he said, not without affection. 'It needs to hurt if it's to do any good. And I'm not going to stop until you've learnt a lesson.'

Peter's hands were beguilingly smooth, almost the hands of an artist. It was hard to believe he was capable of the exceptionally hard spankings he could deliver. His arm was tireless and he slapped each tender cheek in turn with a rigorous cadence that made it impossible to hold still. But he didn't let that deter him. He simply held me down and wrapped his right leg around the backs of my knees, pinning me in position. The spanking continued in earnest and I couldn't even kick. Gasping for breath, I made my usual frenetic promises that I would be good, that I would work hard and not slack off.

At last his rhythm began to slow and I could breathe again, thinking it was almost over. He stopped and placed his hand alternately on each cheek, feeling the warmth. Then he tugged my knickers down to my knees.

Tears welled in my eyes as I braced myself for another onslaught. His hand descended in a steady torrent of slaps that echoed and rebounded in the room, making my ears ring. I was crying long before he was done.

Finally, he let me up and I stumbled to my feet, wiping my tear-streaked face. Peter stood up and folded me in a tight hug. I clung to him, sniffling piteously.

'I don't enjoy having to do this,' he said sincerely. 'I'd rather roleplay a scene with an imagined offence. But I won't hesitate to discipline you when you need it. Caring punishment can be very effective in the right context and I think you will respond well to it. But remember – this is just a warning. A reminder of what is expected. Serious offences will warrant stricter punishments.'

My eyes strayed fearfully to the birching block and I couldn't suppress the shudder as a surge of cold fear went through me.

In bed that night, I replayed the scene over and over, caught between dread and arousal. I knew that I would never be able to live up to his exacting standards, however hard I tried. A slide was inevitable. It only heightened my arousal.

Twelve

'You'll never guess what we did,' Courtney sang.

'You're probably right,' said Peter drily. 'So you'll just have to tell us.'

The waiter had taken our orders and the four of us had relative privacy in our corner of the restaurant. Courtney dug in her handbag and I was surprised when she came up with a handful of phone-box cards.

On the way to dinner she'd been giggling at every phone box we passed.

'Was it that one?' she'd asked Shaun at one point.

He shook his head. 'No, the one in front of Starbucks. On the corner.'

Peter and I just looked at each other quizzically. I guessed that, since she was American, the novelty of tart cards hadn't worn off yet. She'd only been in London a couple of years.

Courtney spread the cards out across the table like a blackjack dealer. We looked at the cards, then at Courtney and Shaun.

'Well, go on, pick one,' Shaun said, enjoying the game as much as Courtney.

Peter and I perused the cards. Some of them were, admittedly, enticing. But most were just silly. There was an implausibly gorgeous Scandinavian blonde named Astrid. She was bending over with her skirt up, revealing what Peter would call a very spankable bottom. 'Spanking and –' I peered closer at the typo '– Canning. An odd pair of services.'

Peter smirked at another one. 'I can't imagine this is the actual girl at the end of the phone line,' he said. 'This is some Brazilian supermodel clipped out of *Vogue*.'

We leafed through the cards, chuckling at each unbelievable girl. If they were truly the girls in the pictures they belonged in Hollywood, not turning tricks in a sleazy London brothel.

There was a Young Oriental Beauty with strategically placed stars covering her nipples. Her ad declared she was 'hot and spicy', offering 'unhurried services'. There was an Italian Stunner who did lesbian shows. A Sexy American Transsexual who was New In Town was eager to offer All Services. One girl, calling herself simply New Blonde, specialised in Bubble Baths.

But the corniest one of all said, 'Czech me out.' Peter and I groaned in unison at the odious pun. The picture showed a fresh-faced Eastern European girl with a shy smile and dark hair cut in a bob. 'Lenka. Petite Student from Prague.' There had to be some pervy joke that Shaun and Courtney wanted us to find.

I had always enjoyed the kinky cards. Some of them even showed girls in school uniform advertising my kind of play. Wide-eyed girls in gymslips, claiming they'd been ever so naughty . . . I'd once entertained a silly fantasy of making my own card and sticking it in a phone box. But the prospect of sex with a sweaty stranger when all I wanted was a smacked bottom was just too squicky.

When we'd looked at all the cards, I shrugged. 'OK, I give up. What's the story?'

Shaun picked out the corny Czech one and handed it to Peter. He blinked at it, turning it over. There was an address written on the back, but nothing illuminating.

He shrugged. 'Sorry, mate,' he said. 'What are we missing?'

Shaun and Courtney exchanged conspiratorial grins.

Suddenly, we understood.

'You didn't,' I breathed, gaping at the card.

Courtney shrieked with laughter and the other diners in the restaurant frowned at us, startled and annoyed.

Peter handed the cards back to Shaun, shaking his head. 'OK, this sounds like a good story,' he said, 'Let's hear it.'

'Well,' Shaun said, 'it started out just as a laugh. We never thought we'd actually go through with it.'

For several nights they had been collecting phone-box cards, looking for just the right girl. But neither of them was into vacuous blondes or exotic foreigners. They wanted a girl-next-door who didn't look like a pro.

'Let's keep trying,' Shaun said. 'I still don't think any of these are quite right.'

They had been up and down Tottenham Court Road and around Russell Square. Now they wandered along Bloomsbury Street, past the British Museum. They peeked into all the phone boxes along the way, finding more of the same cards.

At last Courtney entered a phone box and stopped. 'Got her,' she said, holding the card out to Shaun.

'Czech me out,' said the card. Lenka was exactly what they were looking for.

Shaun grinned. 'Oh yes,' he said. 'Definitely.'

Nervously he picked up the receiver and sent the coins rattling into the slot. He gave Courtney a lopsided grin. 'I don't know what I'm going to say.'

Courtney shrugged and waited, bursting with subversive excitement. Shaun's expression changed and she knew someone had answered.

'Hello,' Shaun said cheerily. 'I'm calling for Lenka.' He listened for a moment, then replied to the person on the other end. 'I found her card in a phone box. Is that really her in the photo?'

There was a pause.

'In photo,' he said slowly. 'That is really Lenka?'

Courtney giggled. She could only hear Shaun's side of the conversation, but she was able to fill in some of the gaps.

'It is? OK. And who are you?' Another pause. His brow furrowed. 'The maid?'

They blinked at each other. Maid?

'Well, can you tell me what her rates are?' he asked, then simplified his wording. 'How much?'

A tinny voice buzzed in response, but Courtney couldn't make out what it was saying. She pressed her head close to the receiver and Shaun held it away from his ear for her. When she still couldn't make it out, she gave up.

'Sixty pounds for half an hour,' Shaun repeated for her. 'What about spanking?' He winced slightly at the lengthy answer that followed. He made two rude gestures, miming what must be a graphic list of everything Lenka was willing to do. 'OK. Well, listen, I have a couple of questions. I'm here with my girlfriend.'

At that Courtney giggled again and Shaun nudged her with his foot to be quiet.

'No, I don't want to *be* spanked. I want a girl I can spank. Will Lenka do that? Let me spank her? Good. And my girlfriend will be with me. To watch. No sex. Just spanking.'

There was another long pause as the maid was clearly laying out the rules for Shaun. He nodded distractedly, squinting and rolling his eyes at various things. At last he said, 'That sounds fine. Where are you? Upper Montagu Street? All right. Hold on, let me write it down.'

He gestured to Courtney and she handed him a pen. He wrote the address on the back of the card.

'What Tube station? Baker Street? OK. So we call when we get there and you'll let us in? Fine. We'll be there in about half an hour. OK. See you then. Ta.'

He hung up and Courtney bounced up and down like a puppy, begging him to share it with her.

'She'll let me spank her. But not too hard. No marks.'

'Fair enough.'

'And it's sixty quid.'

She let out a low whistle. 'Holy shit, I'm in the wrong line of work!' She laughed.

It was a dark street of peeling Victorian houses and they found the address easily. They were both apprehensive as they stood outside the nondescript building, trying to get up the courage to call.

'Are we really going to do this?' Shaun asked.

Courtney played with her hair, agonising. 'I don't know. Do you think it's safe?'

He shrugged and looked up at the darkened windows. 'I've no idea. It's not like I've ever done this before.'

They were silent for a long time. Finally, Courtney spoke. 'If we chicken out now we'll regret it forever and we'll never have the guts to go through with it again.'

Nodding, Shaun murmured agreement. He took a deep breath and hit the redial number on his mobile.

'Hi,' he said. 'I called a little while ago about Lenka. We're outside the building. OK, we will.'

He rang off and looked to Courtney for courage as his finger hesitated on the button to the right of the door. With a bright flash of a smile, Courtney pushed his finger on to the button and they both gave a little jump when the buzzer sounded to let them in. Neither of them had any idea what to expect. In the back of their minds was the worry that they'd be arrested or roughed up by gangsters.

But a small older Eastern European woman with a weathered face and bright orange hair let them in and introduced herself as the maid. She beckoned Shaun and Courtney up the stairs. The house was cluttered, but clean. At the top of the stairs was a small bedroom, where she asked them to wait. She offered them tea, but they declined politely.

Shaun reminded the maid what they were there for and she gave them a friendly smile and nodded as if it was a perfectly normal request she got all the time. Perhaps it was.

'Lenka is busy now. But soon she is ready.'

'How soon?' Shaun asked.

The maid shrugged. 'Fifteen minutes? Is hard to say.'

'What is she wearing?' Shaun asked.

'Wearing?'

'What clothes? How is she dressed?'

The maid seemed surprised by the question. Presumably most of her customers didn't care what she was wearing, as they'd want it off as soon as possible.

'Blue dress,' the maid said slowly.

'What about her underwear?' When the maid laughed, Shaun explained, 'I don't want her wearing a thong. I like panties that cover her bottom.'

Puzzled, the maid shook her head. 'I do not understand.'

'Courtney, stand up,' he said.

Shaun turned Courtney around and bent her over, raising her skirt so that the maid could see her panties. They were soft and pink and covered her bottom fully.

'Like these.'

The maid gave another laugh. 'Oh, I understand! Yes, she will wear.'

'Thank you.'

'You wait, please. I bring Lenka.' With that she left, closing the door behind her.

Courtney eyed the small sagging bed. 'You could have *me* while we wait,' she suggested impishly.

'You're incorrigible.'

'You don't have enough money for two girls anyway.'

'Yes, but I don't have to pay you to redden your backside, do I?'

She giggled.

While they waited they listened to the sounds of the brothel. The phone rang almost constantly and they could hear the low voice of the maid as she chattered away to the callers. There was the intermittent squeal of pipes and the sound of a toilet flushing, then a torrential shower, which seemed to run forever. At one point the lights went out and they froze, fearing a police raid. But then the maid was arguing with someone, a man, in Czech. After some energetic banging, the lights went back on.

'It's a madhouse,' Courtney said, laughing.

They strained to hear any sounds of sex, but couldn't. Once, they heard what they thought were smacking noises. They both pricked up, listening, but the sounds were not repeated.

It was nearly an hour before the maid returned. 'OK,' she panted, slightly out of breath. 'Lenka is here.'

She stood aside and the girl from the photo came into the room. Lenka looked about twenty and her hair had grown an inch since the picture was taken. It was a little shaggy and tousled, but that only added to her appeal. She had dark eyes, high Slavic cheekbones and a girlish smile. The simple denim dress she wore enhanced her student image; she could have come straight from class.

'Hello,' she said.

Shaun stood up and greeted her with a smile.

The maid said something to Lenka and Lenka responded with a rapid burst of Czech.

'I explain to Lenka,' the maid said to Shaun. 'Spanking, no sex.'

'That's right,' said Shaun. 'You said sixty pounds on the phone.'

'Yes. Come. I show you room.'

The maid led Shaun and Courtney into a larger room that was decorated with garish floral wallpaper and smelt strongly of cinnamon. The double bed was freshly made with pastel-green sheets. The place could have been a homely B&B anywhere in the country, but Courtney was amused by the little details that confirmed it was not. The bottles of lotion and lubricant next to the bed. The boxes of tissues stacked chest-high against the far wall. The baby wipes and condoms side by side on the rickety dressing-table.

'You pay now,' the maid said decisively, holding out her hand.

Shaun obliged and, when the maid didn't withdraw her hand, Shaun added a tenner for a tip. She seemed satisfied and said something else to Lenka in Czech, who nodded. Then she left, closing the door behind her.

Lenka smiled shyly at Shaun. Waiting.

Ready to play voyeur, Courtney sank quietly into a chair by the window.

'So you're a student?'

Lenka nodded. 'Yes. I study the English,' she said proudly.

'What about the English vice?' Shaun asked, his eyes glinting.

Courtney grinned. There was no way the girl would know what that meant.

Sure enough, Lenka looked puzzled. 'Please?'

'Spanking,' Shaun said.

She blushed. 'Oh, yes. I know spanking.'

'Have you ever been spanked?'

'I am spanked one time by American tourist,' she said brightly.

Shaun and Courtney exchanged a look of surprise.

'Hard?' Shaun asked.

Lenka shook her head.

'Are you a good student?'

Lenka glanced at Courtney, then began to smile. She gave Shaun a kittenish look. 'No,' she said. 'I am very – what is word? Naughty? Very naughty student.'

'Oh?'

'Yes,' she continued, sidling up to him and unbuttoning the top button of her dress. 'I am having sex with my teacher for high marks.'

Shaun shook his head at her with mock disapproval. 'You wouldn't get away with that in my school, young lady,' he said sternly. 'Naughty girls in my school take their punishment.'

Lenka pouted. Courtney was delighted by her natural reactions. She had been expecting a slick professional who would be skilled, but predictable and uninteresting. This girl seemed almost shy, but she also seemed to be enjoying herself. Courtney could see Shaun's body responding. He stiffened slightly and the bulge in his pants began to grow.

'Do you know what happens to bad girls?' Shaun asked her.

The Czech girl twisted her hands together, shifting back and forth apprehensively. 'They are spanked?'

He nodded seriously.

Lenka bit her lip. Her reactions were so authentic that Courtney was almost convinced she genuinely dreaded it. But the twinkle in Lenka's eye when she glanced over at Courtney gave her away.

Shaun sat on the corner of the bed. The springs squeaked slightly under his weight, the sound magnified in the silent room. He crooked his finger and beckoned to Lenka.

She lowered her head, pouting endearingly, as she slowly made her way to the bed to stand in front of him.

Shaun patted his knee in an affectionate avuncular fashion. Lenka hesitated a moment, chewing on her knuckle, looking up at him from under her wide dark eyes as if to ask whether she absolutely had to. Her unspoken question was answered by a slow nod of his head, as though he regretted that it had come to this.

Courtney felt herself getting very warm – and wet. Her hands, folded demurely in her lap, pressed down into her crotch.

Lenka submitted and bent slowly over Shaun's lap. His position on the corner of the bed meant that her arms and legs hung down to the floor on either side. She placed her hands on the floor and held herself up, looking over at Courtney.

Courtney blushed and instantly tried to disguise her actions. But Lenka had seen. The Czech girl gave her a mischievous smile and lifted her head smugly. *I saw you*, she seemed to be saying.

Sheepishly, Courtney turned her gaze to Lenka's other end.

Shaun caressed the girl's bottom over the denim dress. He scolded her in a low soft voice. 'Now then,' he said, resting his hand on Lenka's backside. 'Girls who try to bribe their teachers deserve to be punished, don't they?'

Lenka whispered, 'Yes.'

'Yes, *sir*,' he prompted.

'Yes, sir.'

Shaun nodded his approval. 'Nothing teaches a naughty girl a firm lesson like an old-fashioned over-the-knee spanking on her bare bottom.'

Courtney sighed. The heat between her legs was becoming insistent, unbearable.

'But I think we'll work our way up to that.'

With that, he brought his hand down on Lenka's skirt-covered backside. First one cheek and then the other. Lenka made sharp little inhalations of breath, but no more. Shaun was being very gentle. They were little more than love taps. And she could hardly be feeling it over the denim.

He spanked her for a little while and then he stroked the backs of her thighs, making her shiver.

'I think that's enough of a warm-up,' he said at last. 'It's time to have your skirt up, my girl.'

He slowly raised the hem of her skirt until it was high over her bottom, exposing most of her lower back as well. It was a trim tight little bottom and Lenka was wearing a pair of girlish panties with daisies on. Courtney knew Shaun would approve. Sure enough, he could hardly wait to start smacking her over them, punctuating his smacks with more loving scolding. Lenka lifted her hips obligingly to meet his palm.

Courtney curled her right leg up under her, pressing her heel into her sex. Even through her skirt and panties she could feel how wet she was. And, as soon as she adjusted herself to provide the right amount of stimulation, Lenka looked over at her again. This time Courtney didn't stop. She met the girl's eyes and smiled.

Shaun's strokes were starting to sting and Lenka winced, then forced a cheeky smile for Courtney, blatantly flirting while Shaun smacked her bottom. Courtney delighted in the little gasps and yelps Lenka made.

Shaun stopped and caressed the girl's bottom again, running his fingers up and down the insides of her thighs, eliciting low soft moans from her. If the Czech girl wasn't truly enjoying herself it was the most believable performance Courtney had ever seen.

'But I did say on the bare, young lady,' he told her. 'A proper lesson can only be taught on a girl's naked backside. So we'll have these down.'

Lenka shuddered delightfully as he dragged down her flowered panties, revealing the pale inverted triangle of a bikini line that only enhanced the illusion of innocence. The girl's bottom was perfect. Ripe and rounded. Made for spanking. Her cheeks were slightly pink, emphasised by the paler skin. It was like a canvas waiting to be painted. Courtney shifted her weight again, pushing her heel even harder against her sex. Shaun smiled as he exposed the target area, running his hands over the pink flesh and squeezing her gently.

He shifted his knees, lowering his left and lifting his right. It raised Lenka's bottom up higher, presenting it splendidly for punishment. Courtney felt a wave of heat wash over her as she watched him fondle Lenka's bottom. There was no more perfect position for a spanking. Skirt up, panties down, bottom raised up invitingly. There was something very vulnerable about only having the bottom exposed. It enhanced the childish nature of the punishment.

As he stroked Lenka's bottom, Shaun's hand slipped down to her thighs again. He patted them gently, urging them apart. Lenka obliged at once. Courtney knew that if she looked she would see dew glistening between the girl's legs.

Shaun raised his hand and brought it down with a crisp smack. He found his rhythm and spanked first one cheek, then the other. Again and again.

Now Lenka was beginning to kick and struggle, whimpering and wincing. But when Courtney caught her eye again she could see the pleasure behind the pain. The girl seemed to sense each time Courtney was watching her face. Sublime in her sweet suffering, Lenka made her enjoyment plain. She gasped out little staccato protests in Czech and Courtney met Shaun's eyes, delighted. The words needed no translation.

Encouraged by Lenka's obvious pleasure, Courtney abandoned her pretence of modesty. She slipped her hand down inside her skirt, inside her panties, and touched the slick little button, stroking it softly with her fingertip until she felt it harden slightly under her hand.

Shaun saw her and smiled. His wanton little slut who just couldn't help herself.

Lenka's bottom was reddening nicely under Shaun's palm. And Lenka was wriggling over his lap, squirming and grinding against his knee. Every time she pleasured herself with a surreptitious rub he smacked her harder, making her gasp and cry out. Finally, she couldn't take it any more and threw her hands back, covering her bottom.

Shaun calmly gathered her wrists in his hand and pinned them in the small of her back. Courtney rubbed herself harder. Faster. Lenka looked up at her and then closed her eyes in ecstasy as Shaun intensified the spanking. She kicked her legs and one of her shoes came off, leaving her to paw at the floor helplessly with her bare foot.

At last Shaun began to slow his strokes. Lenka was moaning with unconcealed desire and her innocent face was transformed into a mask of salacious greed. She looked hungrily at Courtney.

Shaun released Lenka's hands and she continued to squirm over his lap, pressing her sex into his knee and spreading her legs. Her body language was unmistakable. Shaun obligingly slipped his hand between her legs and she uttered a long shuddering sigh.

Courtney's fingers worked enthusiastically in her own wetness as she watched Shaun fondle the Czech girl. His hand disappeared under the soft mound of her red punished cheeks. Lenka was grinding on his hand, her eyes closed and her head thrown back. Her lips were parted in unself-conscious euphoria. And, as her cries grew louder and more urgent, Courtney recognised Lenka for what she was. She wasn't a prostitute; she was a true libertine. And her screaming orgasm was something no one would fake. Looking at Lenka's face was like looking in a mirror.

Spent, the Czech girl collapsed over Shaun's knee, her head hanging down. She panted for breath while the aftershock of her climax battered her again and again. Then she raised her head.

Courtney's hand was still inside her panties; she hadn't finished yet. Lenka offered her a naughty grin and got to her feet. She sat on Shaun's lap and cupped her hands round his ear. Eyeing Courtney wickedly, she whispered something to him.

'What an excellent idea,' he said, smiling. 'Courtney, come here.'

She obeyed, looking warily at Lenka. What had she said to him?

Lenka got to her feet, kicking off her other shoe. She grinned slyly and stood to the side, her skirt still up around her waist and her panties at her ankles.

Shaun patted his lap. The same invitation he'd made to Lenka. Courtney looked meekly at the floor and assumed the position. His thighs were very warm from Lenka's body and she could feel the damp patch on his right knee where the girl had tried to pleasure herself.

Courtney's sex was throbbing with the need to come. Shaun placed one hand on the back of her neck and stroked her hair with the other. She sighed and strained against his leg, asking for the same treatment he'd given Lenka.

Courtney felt her skirt lifted to expose her bottom. Then the feeling of cool hands inside the waistband of her panties. With a start she realised that Shaun's hands hadn't moved. It was Lenka who was baring her. She shuddered at the delicious thrill. The girl's soft hands smacked Courtney's bottom delicately, teasing her.

She felt Shaun's right hand draw itself down along the length of her spine, before stopping to rest on her bottom. She wriggled, offering him an invitation. The warmth of his hand left her for a moment and then he brought his palm down sharply, eliciting a squeak of pain from her. Then another smack. Then another.

Where was Lenka? Was it her turn to watch? Was that what she had said? Courtney felt dizzy as Shaun spanked her. Much harder than he had spanked Lenka.

Suddenly she felt the Czech girl's gentle fingers on her inner thighs. She gasped. Shaun's hand didn't stop.

Lenka's fingers urged her legs apart and Courtney melted into submissive obedience, desperate for release. Teasing herself during Lenka's punishment had intensified her need.

Shaun held Courtney down with his free hand while he spanked her hard and fast, making her yelp and cry out. Lenka's gentle probing hands explored her with the care of a new lover. Finding the spots that elicited the best reactions. Exploiting every weakness discovered.

Shaun shifted his knees again so that her bottom was delivered up to his palm and Lenka's questing fingers beneath. Lenka insinuated a hand between Courtney's pelvis and Shaun's knee, raising her up even further. Then she stroked the smooth ribbon of flesh, drawing her fingers over the little knot of Courtney's clit. Courtney was lost in the maze of sensations, delirious between pleasure and pain.

With skilled fingers, Lenka rolled Courtney's clit between her thumb and forefinger, sending sparks through her body. The effect was incredible. Her body jumped with each jolt of stimulation. Her legs inched closer together as Lenka applied pressure. But Shaun scolded her and ordered her legs back apart, delivering a sharp volley of extra hard smacks to the backs of her thighs.

Whimpering with pain, Courtney parted her thighs for Lenka, who cupped her palm over Courtney's sex, moving it up and down in a slow sensual motion. Again, the stimulation was almost too much. Courtney heard herself as if from under water, pleading, begging for them both to stop. But Shaun knew her too well.

Suddenly Lenka increased the pressure, rubbing Courtney's sex very roughly, forcing the fingers in and out with feminine violence. And all the while Shaun continued to spank her, turning her soft white bottom a bright hot red.

Lenka squeezed the little button one last time and Courtney plunged into a climax that made her want to scream. She gritted her teeth instead, making a low growling animal noise. As the orgasm engulfed her, Lenka's fingers continued to stroke her softly.

Thirteen

There is nothing more distressing than witnessing a young lady who should know better behaving in an unseemly fashion.

Even the pressure of the pen against the tender skin of my palm was acutely painful and I cursed my long fingernails as they dug into the raw skin at the base of my thumb. By the time I'd written the line fifty times I could barely move my hand.

I agonised over sharing my latest fascination. I'd told Courtney, of course; she and I were as close as sisters. But I was too embarrassed to tell Peter.

I wanted to be a boy.

Unable to get the story about Peter's school days out of my head, I'd created a persona for the spanking chat room. His moniker was 'Eton lad' and his name was Martin. It was a naughty little thrill. No one knew I was a girl. Of course, it was common enough for guys to pretend to be girls in chat rooms, but I hadn't met anyone else who did it the other way round.

Martin was often summoned to cyber-studies to be caned or slippered. Always the perfect young gentleman, he would submit bravely to whatever punishment his headmasters and prefects saw fit to administer. Cyberplay was dull and unexciting when you had the real thing. But it was my only outlet for play as a boy.

Most of the men Martin submitted to were straightforward CP players who wanted pure school discipline scenes and nothing more. They often shared their own 'authentic' school experiences with me – highly fetishised accounts I knew had no basis in reality, but which I enjoyed just the same. Occasionally, however, I had been astonished by just how crude guys could be with one another. I'd had some nasty propositions as a girl, but they couldn't compare to some of the things these men said.

One day Courtney was reading over my shoulder while I played a scene online with a top who called himself Hdmstr4boy. He wasn't very convincing; his spelling was deplorable and he kept hitting the caps lock key, which looked to me like constant shouting.

'One-handed typist,' Courtney said, sniggering.

When the scene was over, the 'headmaster' asked Martin how big his cock was. Courtney was in hysterics. I responded calmly that I had never measured it.

'That ought to make him envious.' Courtney laughed. 'A boy who's so supremely confident he's never measured!'

Another time I played online with a man in the southern USA. He was very taken with Martin's upper-class accent and impeccable manners, which I managed to convey in pure text. He said the American boys would tease Martin about it and bully him.

'Then I would kick them in the shins,' I wrote, enjoying the image.

'That would be ungentlemanly, young man,' he responded. 'I have much higher standards for a well-bred English boy like you and that kind of behaviour will earn you a trip to the woodshed.'

The words made me writhe and I couldn't remember having been so aroused by a chat session since . . . well, since meeting Peter. The American described in great detail how he'd love to introduce an English boy to the sting of the paddle, to teach him how effective American discipline could be. I was so lost in the role that I quite forgot I was a girl.

I tried to limit my online time and stick to the timetable Peter had laid out for me. But the temptation was impossible to resist. I couldn't even justify it as research.

While it was an interesting experiment, the girl-disguised-as-boy theme had no place in my thesis.

Naturally, I was allowed to play if I'd met my writing quota for the day. But some days the words just wouldn't come. And it could get lonely sitting in the schoolroom at the hard wooden desk, staring out of the window or at the walls. I'd memorised the heraldry chart. Soon I'd be able to recite the Periodic Table as well. But, as a displacement activity, there was nothing to compete with cyber.

I shook myself out of a distracting fantasy and stared at the page in front of me. I had run out of things to say about the pro-birch offerings in the *Englishwoman's Domestic Magazine* and my thighs were going numb from inactivity.

I heard the music-box tinkle of my mobile phone, playing 'Tubular Bells' and I dug in my bag for it. 'Hello?'

'Hey, Angie, it's Courtney.'

'Oh, hi.'

'You sound bored. Getting any work done?'

'No,' I sighed. 'The muse of Victorian porn has deserted me.'

'Just as well, then. You're coming with me. I was just calling to invite you to lunch. There's a new Thai restaurant in Soho and I thought we could go cruise Wardour Street and Old Compton Street afterwards.'

Ever since the episode with Lenka, Courtney and Shaun had been frequenting the adult emporia, expanding their collection of toys and CP literature. Peter had every issue of *Blushes* that had ever been published, but Shaun preferred *Janus*. Courtney wasn't especially keen on either one; she just enjoyed hanging around the shops and getting chatted up by the occasional bold punter. She also got a charge out of asking for implements and CP videos in the vanilla shops. The proprietors weren't easily abashed, but she'd succeeded on more than one occasion.

'I'd love to,' I said. 'But I'm on thin ice. I've got to finish this chapter today or I'm in trouble.'

'He can't keep you prisoner,' she protested hotly. 'I won't let him.'

With a laugh I assured her that I was usually a very happy and willing prisoner.

'Well, I know you're allowed to eat. It's not the chat room this time. And, anyway, so what if you do get spanked? What's the big deal?'

'It's not quite like that. We're not talking about a fun little roleplay.'

'Oh, God,' Courtney moaned. 'Don't tell me you've gone vanilla on me!'

I couldn't help but smile. She could always wear me down. And I was stuck in a rut anyway. I was starting to worry that my thesis had lost its spark. What conclusions could I make? That the Victorians were a pervy lot? That they were repressed and deviant? That wasn't news to anyone. A diversion was just what I needed. The seedy side of London beckoned.

'OK, OK, I'll go with you. Just let me get out of this uniform.'

It wasn't until evening that I decided to phone Peter and realised I'd forgotten my mobile. And his dinner plans.

'And just where have you been, young lady?'

Peter and Shaun met us in the entrance hall like fathers who'd stayed up to catch their daughters sneaking back in.

I looked at Courtney and then down at the floor. 'Soho,' I murmured.

'It was all my fault,' Courtney began valiantly. 'Really, I was –'

'I didn't ask you,' Peter said, eyeing her severely. 'I asked Angie. But you'll be explaining yourself as well in a minute.'

'Yes,' Shaun agreed. 'You certainly will.'

'We went out for lunch,' I said. 'And then we went to the shops.'

'Which shops?'

I blushed, though there was no reason to be embarrassed. We'd all been there before. 'The adult shops.'

'I see. So, while I was sitting at the restaurant with my colleagues, waiting for you to turn up and getting more and more concerned, phoning you and getting no response . . .'

I flinched in misery. 'I'm really sorry. I don't know what to say. I just – forgot.'

'You're sorry and you forgot? That is hardly adequate, is it, young lady?'

He was cross, but still in complete control. His low measured tone was even more unsettling than shouting and raving might have been. But calling me 'young lady' reassured me a little; it meant the issue could be dealt with and I would be forgiven. I knew he was going to punish me and I knew it would be severe. I flashed back to the rules he'd laid out and I gave a little shudder as I thought of the birch. I was struck again by the curious paradox and I wondered fleetingly if it was unique to spankos. It seemed absurd that a spanking fetishist could be punished with spanking. And yet at that moment I couldn't think of anything more desirable than getting out of it.

I glanced over at Shaun, but didn't really expect to find sympathy there. His usually boyish face was darkened with disapproval. He was just as annoyed with Courtney for leading me astray.

'I trust,' Peter continued, 'that you at least met your work quota for the day before you went out.'

Now I truly wanted to die. My vision grew blurry as my eyes shimmered with tears. 'No.'

Peter's eyebrows lifted expectantly.

'No, sir,' I said. 'I'm sorry, sir.'

There was a long silence, awful in its implication. 'Yes,' he agreed at last. 'You will be.'

He gestured to Shaun that he should take over. It was Courtney's turn to be reprimanded.

'Do you realise,' Shaun said, 'that you've landed your friend in serious trouble?'

'Yes, sir.' She glanced over at me and mouthed, 'Sorry.'

Shaun shook his head sadly. 'I'm very disappointed in you, Courtney.' He turned to Peter. 'I think perhaps they should be punished together.'

Courtney and I looked at each other mournfully.

Peter was nodding thoughtfully. 'Yes. I think that might be a very effective lesson. Girls, wait for us in the library, please.'

Courtney grabbed my hand and we scuttled down the hall. Inside the library, we fell into each other's arms.

'I'm so sorry,' she said, squeezing me in a tight hug. 'I didn't mean to get you into this much trouble. I had no idea you had these dinner plans or that –'

'Hey, I don't blame you. I'm the one who forgot about dinner. *And* I forgot my phone. To be honest, I'm kind of glad you'll be here with me.'

She offered me a brave little smile. 'Me too.'

They kept us waiting for several minutes. I put my ear to the door once and could just make out the low hum of male voices down the hall, in the living room. But I couldn't hear what they were saying. Neither of us could sit down. We paced and fidgeted and gazed out the window at the darkened garden. Distorted by the crown glass, the dim hulks of shrubs and trees morphed into sinister crouching figures. Silent voyeurs that peered in at us, eager to witness our disgrace.

Finally, we heard footsteps coming towards the library and we jumped as though we'd been shot. We looked at each other fearfully and retreated hand-in-hand to the corner furthest from the door.

Shaun opened the door and joined us inside. Outside, Peter's footsteps continued on up the stairs and we listened to the creak of the floorboards as they crossed the landing and faded into the upstairs hall.

'Well, girls,' Shaun said, sounding like the good cop in the canonical pairing. 'You're not going to like what we've decided, but Peter and I both feel it's deserved.'

I swallowed hard. Overhead, Peter's footsteps began moving back in the direction of the stairs and before long he reappeared. When I saw he had the Lochgelly tawse I nearly fainted. He'd shown it to me before, but never used it – at least not on me. I knew what it was capable of, though.

The dense leather was about three-eighths of an inch thick, split down the middle of one end into two tails.

'John J Dick, Maker, Lochgelly' was stamped into the leather midway down, along with a large 'XH' at the end of the handle. It was an implement intended to impart a short but memorable lesson with no lasting damage. The dreaded 'strap' or 'belt' of Scottish schools had delivered many a savage bite to the palms of errant schoolchildren. This one was well worn.

From the corner of my eye I saw Courtney grimace. My fingers clutched the hem of my skirt, trying to still the tremors.

'Hands flat against your sides,' Peter said. 'They'll be smarting soon enough.'

'Please . . .' Courtney began.

Peter silenced her with a look. 'Do you want double?'

She shook her head emphatically and stepped back, avoiding eye contact with everyone.

Peter flexed the strap. 'You've never had your hands strapped before, have you, Angie?'

There was a plunging sensation in the pit of my stomach and I felt the colour drain from my face.

'No, sir.'

'Then perhaps,' he said, addressing Shaun, 'Courtney should have hers first, so that Angie can watch.'

Shaun nodded agreement and leant back against the wall, his arms crossed. I was surprised he wasn't going to punish Courtney himself. But then, of the two, Peter was much more the disciplinarian.

'Courtney, come here.'

She obeyed, looking timidly round the room. She stood before Peter, her hands behind her back.

'I'm going to give both of you two strokes on each hand for the embarrassment you caused me by ruining my dinner plans. If you don't take it properly, the stroke will be repeated. Now then – hold out your hands, please, Courtney. Right hand on top. Palm up.'

I watched fearfully as she stretched out both arms to chest height, resting the right one on top of the left. She gritted her teeth as Peter measured the stroke. He gave her a meaningful look that told her not to move. He raised his arm at the elbow so that the tawse rested on his shoulder. Then he brought it down lengthwise on her palm with a sharp crack. Courtney yelped in pain, immediately yanking her hand away.

Peter allowed her to writhe for a few moments before clearing his throat softly.

Courtney instantly resumed the position and I could see a ferocious red stripe blossoming along her palm.

'No. Swap hands,' Peter said.

She offered him her left and he addressed it carefully. Then the strap flashed down again, eliciting another cry of pain from her. Hissing through her teeth, Courtney extended her trembling arms again, her sore right palm open for another attack. The tawse found its mark and she howled in agony. Tears shone in her eyes and I held my breath for her as she switched hands for the final stroke. It was harder than the previous three and Courtney shrieked in pain, dancing in place and cradling her hands to her chest.

Peter was unmoved by her display. He fixed his stern gaze on me and I crept over to him, my hands already tingling with anticipated pain. Courtney gave me a sympathetic look and went to stand by the window, where I had been. Somehow the idea that she would be watching gave me a small crumb of comfort. I felt closer to her for what I'd witnessed.

'Right,' he said. 'You saw what's expected. Cross your hands.'

I lifted my arms, alarmed at how much they were shaking. I could barely hold them still. Peter arranged my hands so that my right palm was supported by my left and my fingers stretched straight out. He held both wrists in his hand for a few seconds until the shaking was reduced to a slight tremble.

He laid the tawse across my palm and then raised it up behind his shoulder. I held my breath and closed my eyes.

'No, you're going to watch,' he said impassively.

With great reluctance, I did as I was told, squinting my eyes like a child desperate to hide from a scene in a scary movie. I watched in detached slow motion as the heavy leather swung down in an arc, then connected sharply with my vulnerable palm. I yelped as Courtney had at the searing pain, writhing away and clutching the injured hand as though I'd just pulled it from a fire.

I looked pleadingly up at Peter, but there was no mercy to be found there. 'Swap hands.'

I surrendered my left palm to the Lochgelly, astonished by the scorching rhythmic throbbing in my right. Again the leather slashed down with a crack like a stick snapped in two. All I saw was a dark-brown blur as my hand came alive with agony. I cried out and both hands instinctively flew to my underarms.

Halfway there, I told myself. At Peter's expectant look, I put my hands up again. As terrible as it was, it was only four strokes.

The tawse tore into my raw aching palm a second time. Tears spilt down my face as I tried to cope with the brutal numbing pain. I shook my hands limply and made myself present my left palm for the last stroke.

It fell with a loud leathery crack and I was so blinded by the pain I couldn't even cry out. I staggered back, gasping, until the throbbing fire began to fade to something slightly more tolerable. I stared at my hands. Both palms bore livid scarlet stripes – like the worst sunburn I'd ever seen. And they felt as burnt as they looked.

Peter set the tawse down on the table and motioned me to stand beside Courtney. She was blowing on her hands, trying to ease the sting. I gingerly pressed my palms together and winced. Of all the implements in Peter's arsenal, the tawse was the one I had underestimated the most. The lingering ache of the dense leather was past enduring. It was almost enough to cure a girl of the kink entirely.

'What do you have to say for yourselves?'

Dazed and a little shell-shocked, I looked forlornly at my hands. The redness showed no sign of fading and the throbbing only seemed to be getting worse. 'I'm sorry, sir,' I said. 'I won't let it happen again.'

Peter acknowledged my apology with a nod and turned to Courtney.

'I'm sorry too,' she said at once, her words thick in her throat and clearly heartfelt. 'I honestly didn't mean any harm.'

'I expect Shaun will deal with you himself when you get home.'

'Yes, sir,' she said, darting a glance at her boyfriend.

'Don't worry,' Shaun said. 'I fully intend to.'

'As for you,' Peter said, returning to me. 'You can go up to the schoolroom and wait for me. I think I shall set you an imposition. It's very effective for a girl to write lines after she's had her hands strapped.'

I winced in dismay. Holding a pen would be a harrowing ordeal.

'In the morning we will go out to the woods. I'm going to show you how to make a proper birch rod.'

'Ten. Thank you, sir.'

The fresh agony of each new stroke builds on the one before it, driving me steadily towards remorse. My knees ache from the hard wood of the block and all I can think about is getting through the punishment. In the moment I honestly believe I will never slack off again.

So it continues for several interminable minutes. The birch slashes relentlessly, pitilessly, into my bottom and I shriek with pain. Then I count the stroke and gather myself for the onslaught of the next. I desperately want to reach round and clutch my blazing cheeks, but I don't dare.

My tears and frantic contortions are received with all the compassion of a hanging judge. This isn't a game. I have made promises and broken them.

I know the punishment is just and I accept it. I need it. To be effective it must take me to my limits and push me just beyond them. It's a profound dangerous intimacy. I crave it and fear it and I am incomplete without it.

With each stroke, the ends of the switches break and fly off. By the time he is finished, the birch will be shredded and bits of it will litter the floor. Weeks from now we'll still be finding the pieces.

Finally, there are only two strokes left. I brace myself, pressing my hands into the floor as though I can push right through it. I hold my breath and wait.

Fourteen

Unable to find a comfortable position at the school desk, I shifted my weight and winced with pain. I didn't think the birch stripes would ever stop stinging. There was also an underlying itchy sensation beneath the sting that was just as unpleasant.

I could not fathom Swinburne's infatuation with the rod. It did no lasting damage, but it caused excruciating pain when it was applied. And yet that was part of its deadly genius. A caning or a strapping could leave deep penetrating bruises that needed a week or more to heal fully. But a birch could be applied again very soon after a first dose. No wonder the tyrannical Dr Keate and his ilk were so enamoured of it.

I sighed and looked up from the page. The tattered remains of the rod caught my eye, sitting complacently in front of me on Peter's desk. I could almost believe it *wanted* me to slack off so it could taste the delicate skin of my backside again. I made a face at it and felt a surge of superstitious fear, like a child taunting an object that might come to life and attack. It was nothing but a handful of broken twigs now – eighteen inches of impotent threat. But all Peter had to do was send me outside with the secateurs and I could be thrashed again.

I had been working steadily all morning, not even tempted by lunch. My only excursions out of the schoolroom were to the library, for legitimate research material. Peter had called to ask how I was and I assured him that

I was uncomfortable, but surviving. And working very hard. Indeed, I had never been more productive. The combination of my thesis topic and the methods used to encourage its writing struck me as so twistedly stimulating that I felt inspired again.

I wrote twice the amount I was expected to and I glared triumphantly at what was left of the rod, as I slammed Swinburne's biography shut with a dusty thump. Now I had the rest of the day and all of the next to play. eBay awaited. But first I called Courtney to check on her.

'Are you sitting comfortably?' I asked.

'Ha ha.'

'I'm not either if it's any consolation.'

'It's not, actually,' she said, her voice tinged with sadness. 'I still feel guilty.'

'Don't be silly. It was my fault and I'm perfectly willing to take responsibility for my own screwups. And I paid for it this morning.'

'Poor thing. You must have been up all night, fretting.'

'I was, rather.'

A long silence followed and at last I asked what she knew I wanted to know. 'So what did Shaun do when you got home?'

Her dismissive laugh was full of bravado. 'Oh, not much,' she said. 'Just reminded me how hard a frat paddle can be used.'

'Ouch.'

'That,' she said with a snort, 'is the understatement of the century.'

I couldn't resist a little barb. 'Aren't you the one who said it was no big deal? "So what if you get spanked?" I think those were your words.'

She groaned. 'Don't remind me.'

When she didn't volunteer anything else I pressed her. 'Well? How many strokes was it?'

She tried to sound unconcerned. 'Oh, it really wasn't too bad. It was only ten.'

'*Only* ten?' Having seen her collection, I could scarcely imagine such an implement being used with force. At least not on a girl's bottom.

‘I have some awesome bullseyes, though. I’ll show you next time I see you. I don’t think they’re going away any time soon.’

Her pluck was reassuring. ‘The Thai was good though, huh?’ I offered lamely.

This time her laugh was genuine. ‘Yeah. And Shaun thoroughly approves of my new toy, even if it is a bit noisy for my tastes.’

‘Discipline as foreplay,’ I mused. ‘Surreal. I’m amazed you were able to operate heavy machinery after what Peter did to our hands.’

‘I didn’t use it on myself, silly,’ she said, giggling. ‘That’s what boyfriends are for.’

‘Ah. Yes. Silly me indeed.’

‘I’m just relieved there are no hard feelings.’

‘None at all.’

I could sense her working herself up to the question, so I didn’t make her ask it. Knowing she’d never been birched before, I described in detail the nerve-racking process of going into the woods with Peter to cut switches. Tying them together with twine, fashioning the very implement I was to be whipped with. Putting on the humiliating punishment gown and waiting in the corner for him to come up to the schoolroom. The torment of the strokes and the bliss of comfort and forgiveness afterwards.

When her stunned silence began to get awkward I reassured her. ‘Don’t worry, I’m still kinky.’

‘I hope so.’

‘And my knees look like I’ve been deep in prayer for days.’

‘I’ll be deep in prayer that I never have to experience a real birching,’ she said. ‘I’m not sure *my* kinkiness would survive.’

When she rang off, I went to have a look at my marks in the cheval mirror in the bedroom. The angry red had faded to a pink blush. Thin ridged lines snaked across my sore round cheeks, punctuated by tiny swollen spots where the buds had struck. My upper thighs also sported lines where the switches had splayed out as they landed.

Peter was uncompromisingly strict, but always fair. I wasn't proud of myself for needing punishment, but I was proud for taking it. I had thought the Lochgelly tawse was more than I could stand, but the birch was a step beyond even that.

Courtney hadn't got off lightly either. Ten strokes with a paddle, well laid on, would weaken anyone's knees. Peter didn't care for the paddle. He thought it unrefined and so he rarely used it. When he did, he made it a very childish punishment indeed and preferred to administer it over the knee. The belittling nature of it was almost harder to bear than the acute sting of its impact.

I felt myself growing hot as I remembered one of my earliest fantasies: the spanking machine. It was the ultimate impartial punishment. And until I discovered the spanko community I couldn't have known how common a fantasy it was.

My version was an elaborate ritual of objectification, set in a futuristic reformatory. I had been disrespectful to one of the instructors – a serious offence. My name was called over an intercom system and everyone listened as I was summoned to the disciplinary wing of the compound. It was called simply 'The Centre'.

A bookish man in a pristine lab coat led me into the room where the punishment was to be administered. The room resembled a sterile operating theatre and above the floor was a large gallery where several seated figures observed the proceedings with disinterested solemnity.

The doctor betrayed no emotion at all as he consulted his clipboard and explained to me that the reformatory governors were introducing a new form of discipline. Because of my persistent want of respect, I had been chosen as the first experimental subject. His function was simply to operate the machine and take notes on the results.

There was no need for any telling off. Indeed, once the system was perfected, there would be no need for any human interaction at all. The machine would ensure that instructors and administrators were not swayed by manipulative tears and pleas for lenience. Absolutely fair and impartial, it would simply perform its function and the offender would soon learn that it was no use fighting the system. Resistance would be punished swiftly and severely and the machine was incapable of pity.

An adjustable padded stool stood in the centre of a large platform. Two sturdy legs angled out in either direction away from the seat. A wide leather strap hung from the seat and there were smaller straps at the base of each leg. Behind the stool stood a large hooked arm with a complicated network of chains, cogs and springs. At the end of the arm, suspended above the seat, was a thin wooden paddle.

The doctor measured the distance from my feet to my waist and set about preparing the machine. I watched with a mixture of awe and dread as he raised the seat to a satisfactory height and tilted it forwards, so that it sloped downwards and away from the paddle.

'Come here,' he said. When I hesitated he added brusquely, 'Do as you're told, girl.'

There was a murmur of disapproval from the gallery and the doctor nodded and made a notation on his clipboard.

Had I earned extra strokes for not co-operating? I was too scared to ask. I moved towards him fearfully and he guided me into position over the seat, securing the strap tightly around my waist and effectively pinning me down. The slope of the seat forced my back to arch invitingly, making a prominent target of my bottom.

My legs hung down so that the tips of my toes just reached the platform. The doctor fastened the straps round my ankles and buckled them tightly. My arms were next. I struggled a little in protest, but he merely smacked my hand. I couldn't move.

The doctor set aside his clipboard and without a word he lifted my skirt. Then with a brisk businesslike motion he tugged my knickers down to my knees. I moaned a little and darted a glance up at the gallery. A chair creaked from there, but I couldn't make out any faces. Behind me the doctor was making some final adjustments to the arm of the machine.

At last he retrieved his clipboard and stood to one side. 'Ready, gentlemen,' he said.

A booming voice from the gallery responded, 'Begin.'

The doctor moved into my peripheral vision and there was a whirring noise as he switched on the machine. I heard the clicking of gears and the paddle drew back, striking my vulnerable bottom smartly, immediately.

I recoiled and strained away from the arm, but I was held fast. Before I could begin to process the sensation, the paddle struck again. I yelped, struggling feebly in my bonds. Another sharp swat; another yelp. The unremitting paddle rose and fell, brutal in its unstoppable cadence.

Tears were soon streaming down my face, but the machine did not relent. I had no idea how long it was programmed to spank me and my helpless cheeks burnt as the unfeeling machine performed its simple function, impervious to my distress.

Over the humming of the machine I heard the scratch of the doctor's pen as he jotted down his observations. The men in the gallery looked on silently as I cried out at each swat.

I was so lost in the pain and misery that I barely registered when the paddle stopped. Relief washed over me and I went limp, panting for breath. I hung my head and saw the doctor behind me, examining my bottom. I winced as he placed his hand on each cheek in turn, gauging its warmth and tenderness. Again his pen scratched and he addressed the gallery with satisfaction. '38.2 degrees.'

My objectification was complete and total.

I drifted out of the fantasy to discover that my hand had strayed inside my knickers. Flushed and excited, I indulged myself, turning on to my stomach on the bed. Shoving a pillow under my hips, I raised my skirt and pushed my knickers down below my bottom as I pictured myself strapped down to the spanking machine.

The cool air on my bottom enhanced the sense of exposure and I reached behind to squeeze my sore cheeks, rekindling the pain from the birching. Gasping, I ran the fantasy through my mind again. This time, however, I was made to wait in a queue, watching with increasing anxiety as each girl ahead of me had her bottom smacked by the unrelenting automaton. Before each punishment the doctor read out her offence and the length of time she was to be paddled.

By the time it was my turn I was ready to explode. The machine had barely begun to redden my bottom when I felt the first quivering spasms. Within seconds they overwhelmed me and I drowned myself in a flood of images.

Fifteen

'I've had enough of your insolence, young lady. And your excuses. It's clear you don't take my authority seriously, so I have no choice but to show you that I mean business.'

Without another word, the governess seated herself primly in one of the straight-backed wooden chairs against the wall. I stared at her lap, watching the way her skirt rose slightly and tautened against her long firm legs.

'Over my lap,' said Courtney.

'Wanna play?'

I blinked at her. 'What, just the two of us?

Her bright-green eyes sparkled with mischief. 'Of course. I've been dying to get my hands on your bottom since the night I got you into trouble at Selfridges.'

I smiled at the memory. The planning still blew my mind.

'I was dying to follow you and watch,' she said. 'But Peter wouldn't let me.'

'Yeah, I might have been a little suspicious if I'd seen you.' I laughed.

Peter was in York for the night and Shaun was working late, so Courtney had come over to have dinner and keep me company. She was a natural flirt, so I didn't take her hints as anything but her usual playful banter. But, after a few glasses of the spicy Barossa Valley Shiraz she'd brought, our conversation evolved into something more than sisterly intimacy and I realised she was serious.

'So . . .?' she promtped.

We'd been punished together only a few days before. Submitting to her after that would seem strange. I also had no idea what she was like as a top. Would she be as intimidating as Peter?

As though reading my mind, she said, 'Don't worry, I won't traumatise you. *Much.*'

I relaxed into a laugh, considering her offer. I had absolutely no idea what to expect. And, even though marks from the birching still criss-crossed my cheeks, the allure of power exchange was irresistible. 'All right,' I said finally. 'Let's play. What did you have in mind?'

'Oh, I didn't really have anything specific in mind,' she said with forced nonchalance, making it obvious that she did. 'But I do have this governess fantasy . . .'

I shifted in my seat, my face growing hot as I thought of the governess stories I'd read. Uncompromisingly strict, Victorian governesses. The idea of being a child under her control definitely appealed to me, but I was too embarrassed to admit to wanting it. I needed her to take the initiative.

Sensing my obvious interest through my hesitation, Courtney did just that. 'All right.' She lifted her head, lengthening her neck. The simple gesture made her appear formidably tall. 'Your father has decided that you're too wilful to be sent away to finishing school, so he has hired me to instruct you in manners and etiquette.'

I bit my lip.

'But you're a little rebel and you decide to embarrass him at a dinner party one night.'

My imagination ran with it: I could see the elegant Victorian dining room laid with fine china and the polished family silver. A seven-course meal served by footmen in vibrant livery. Pheasant. Fine claret. Plovers' eggs in aspic. My father and his stuffy friends in evening dress seated around the glossy table, politely and condescendingly making small talk for the sake of the ladies. Perhaps I had been told off earlier for speaking to a young man without a proper introduction. Perhaps I resented my governess for restricting my liberty. Perhaps I set out to get her sacked by displaying deliberately bad manners at this respectable gathering. I imagined my father's thunderous face as he sent me from the room.

'Oh, yes,' I said. I licked my fingers, smacking my lips as though devouring the last of the chocolate sauce from the sweet course.

Courtney grinned as though she could taste it too. 'Very well, then. You'd better go up to the schoolroom and wait for me.'

I smiled slyly and went upstairs. I sat down at one of the school desks, drumming my fingers to dissipate my nervous energy.

Courtney kept me waiting about ten minutes and I hardly recognised her when she came in. She was wearing a sombre ankle-length black dress and she'd pulled her hair back away from her face in a severe bun. The very picture of strictness and sophistication.

I couldn't suppress a smile. Despite her pretence that she'd thought of the scene on the spur of the moment, she'd come to the house well prepared.

'There's nothing to smile about, young lady,' she snapped, closing the door behind with her a sharp bang.

I jumped.

'Stand up, young lady,' she snapped.

I got shakily to my feet.

'Your father tells me that your manners at the dinner party last night were deplorable. He says you embarrassed him in front of his guests and that I am to straighten you out.'

Her velvety Southern voice was made for scolding. She had definitely missed her calling.

'Your lapses in etiquette make you look bad, young lady, but they make me look worse. You know this very well, so I'm forced to assume it's deliberate.'

A nervous laugh fluttered at the back of my throat and I fought to swallow it down.

She saw the struggle in my face. 'There's nothing to smile about,' she said coldly and waited for me to get myself under control. 'Do you have anything to say for yourself?'

'Erm . . .'

'Don't mumble! And look at me when I'm speaking to you.'

I straightened up. 'I . . . suppose I just . . . forgot myself,' I said. 'Miss.'

Courtney arched one eyebrow. 'You forgot? I see. So you need a reminder, do you?'

'No, miss.'

'Oh, but clearly you do if you're forgetting my etiquette lessons so completely.'

'I didn't forget, I just . . .'

She gave me an icy smile. 'Just chose to disregard my teaching so as to embarrass your father, is that it?'

I protested again, but she cut me off. 'Your father employed me because you didn't have the discipline to be allowed to go away to finishing school. He expects me to instil that discipline, and your behaviour last night shows how much you need it.'

'But I –'

Courtney raised one slender finger and I shut my mouth instantly.

'Over my lap.'

'But miss, it's so undignified,' I protested.

'Punishment isn't meant to be dignified. If you had behaved you would have retained your dignity. But when you act like a petulant child you will be treated like a petulant child. Now if you don't place yourself over my lap you will suffer the further indignity of being hauled across it.'

Suddenly, the stuffy schoolroom felt like a meat locker as the chill of erotic fear overwhelmed me. I stepped to her side and stretched out across her shapely thighs. I gazed at the grain in the floorboards, pressing my fingertips to them. Her lap was soft and yielding, so unlike a man's.

Courtney's hand rested lightly on my bottom and gave it a gentle pat. Then she flipped up my tartan skirt. She slipped my knickers down and a delicious shiver ran down the stepping-stones of my spine.

'Naughty little girls,' she purred, 'need to be taught how to behave, don't they?'

'Yes, miss,' I whispered.

Her cool hand descended on my bare bottom, caressing it in slow circles, savouring its smooth whiteness.

'When girls act in vulgar ways, they disgrace not only themselves, but also their families.'

Her mellifluous words were so eloquent and proper. And I knew without being told that they were words she'd heard before, probably from some Southern belle governess of her own. The authenticity made me blush and I surrendered to her firm ladylike admonition.

'I'm sorry that it's come to this,' she said and I could almost believe the wistful tone in her voice. 'But you've brought it on yourself. You've had this spanking coming for a long time and now you're going to take it.'

'Yes, miss,' I said, my voice so soft I doubted whether she even heard me.

'What a sweet little bottom you have,' she murmured. 'So round and delicate.'

The soft hand lifted from my skin and seemed to hang suspended in the air forever before coming down on my bottom with a loud smack. I gave a small mouselike squeak. Another smack, another little yip. Another and another and another. It didn't hurt, but that made it even harder to endure. She was treating me like a very little girl indeed. The embarrassment warmed me like a fever as she smacked me briskly and thoroughly. Her soft hands didn't neglect the tops of my thighs, either, and I kicked feebly at the low smacks.

'Blatant disobedience,' she chided affectionately. 'And what has it earned you, young lady? A good sound spanking.' A harder volley of swats punctuated her words and I began to yelp in earnest.

I imagined my bottom growing pink under her ministrations. Pink and then red. Now it was starting to hurt. It was nothing like as hard as Peter spanked me, but her words were exquisitely humbling.

At last she stopped and I whimpered softly, wriggling a little over her lap. The warm glow in my backside was slightly comforting, matching the flush in my throat and face. She urged me up with a sharp swat and I struggled gracelessly to my feet, too embarrassed to look at her. I stood before her, rubbing my bottom. When I reached down to pull my knickers up she stopped me.

'No, leave them down. I'm not finished with you, little miss.'

I wilted.

'If you think that's all your little performance last night has earned you, you're sorely mistaken.'

Now I was really worried. I looked up at her fearfully.

'Your mother's hairbrush,' she said. 'The one on the dresser. Bring it here.'

For a second I was puzzled. Then I remembered. The antique ebony one on the dresser in the master bedroom.

'At once!'

I scurried to obey, my legs hobbled by the panties that clung round my knees. I couldn't bear the humiliation of shuffling down the corridor like that and I hesitated in the doorway and cast a pleading look back at her.

'I don't care if the servants do see you,' she said frostily. 'Now if you don't fetch it this minute I will call the parlour maid in to horse you on her back while I spank you.'

One couldn't help but admire her exquisite cruelty.

Out on the landing, I glanced around nervously as though the butler might appear at any moment and see me bare-bottomed. I hurried to the master bedroom, afraid to keep Courtney waiting too long.

I had seen the hairbrush lying there so many times, looking so innocent. Just another authentic prop in the eighteenth-century house. But as I picked it up I felt its heft. I smacked it against my palm, startled by its potency. It was a fearsome implement, belied by its Victorian gentility.

With shaky sweaty hands, I crept back into the schoolroom and presented it to my governess, nearly dropping it in my nervousness.

Courtney took it from me with the barest hint of a smile. She stood up and set the hairbrush down on the chair. 'I think we'll have a little deportment lesson while your bottom is still nice and pink. Then we can see about driving the message home with the hairbrush.'

'Yes, miss,' I groaned, not knowing what else to say.

She took a large book from the shelf and tested its weight in her open palm. Then she raised it above me and gently lowered it down on to my head.

Anticipating her, I adjusted my stance to keep my head level.

She let go of the book and I felt it wobble slightly. I reached up to steady it and she smacked the back of my wrist with a dainty flick of her fingers.

'Hands at your sides.' She circled me, inspecting my posture. 'Let's see that naughty red bottom,' she said, lifting up my skirt and tucking it into the waistband.

I bit my lip, turning scarlet at the feeing of exposure.

Satisfied at last, my beautiful tormentor nodded towards the far corner of the room. 'There and back,' she said.

I gulped. It seemed a mile. And having my skirt up and my knickers round my knees only enhanced my disgrace. I took one hesitant step, trying to hold my head perfectly still. So far, so good. Another step and I felt the book shift slightly to one side. I tilted my head so it wouldn't fall and had to fight to keep my hands away. But as I lifted my foot to take another step the book slid off and thudded heavily to the floor.

Courtney tutted and shook her head. She retrieved the book and placed it back on my head. 'Again.'

This time I made it halfway across the room before the book began to slide. I held my arms out like a tightrope walker, tilting my head at an absurd angle to avoid the inevitable. The pages flapped noisily as I tried to save the book from falling. But I fumbled it and it fell to the floor in an undignified heap.

I raised my eyes to my governess. She merely shook her head, her lips pursed. 'Disgraceful.'

I stared forlornly at the book.

'It's no use sulking, young lady,' she said with supreme disdain. 'You've brought this on yourself. It's little wonder you behave like a barbarian at the dinner table when you haven't even learnt to walk as a lady should.'

Her belittling tone made me feel like a spoilt child and I scowled at the floor.

She picked up the hairbrush and stroked its glossy back. 'But I intend to correct that. Now you will ask me if I will be pleased to give you the spanking you deserve.'

'Nooo!' I wailed. I couldn't help it; she'd regressed me to a childlike state and it was impossible to react like an adult.

An oppressive silence followed my outburst. 'Angela,' she said, twisting the knife.

I stiffened on hearing my full name. Then I stamped my foot. 'No,' I insisted with a pout.

Courtney crossed her arms over her chest and looked at me. 'I'm very disappointed in you,' she said. 'Now I'll have to tell your father that you threw a temper tantrum. I expect he'll put you over his knee himself and redden your little bottom and put you to bed without any supper. Then, when you're ready to accept your discipline, you can come to me and ask me politely to punish you.'

I burnt with shame and dropped my eyes to the floor. Her words were an auger, skewering my dignity and shaming me beyond endurance. Desperate to stop her honeyed torture, I gave in.

I took a long shuddering breath. 'Please, miss,' I began.

'Look at me.'

Reluctantly, I lifted my head. 'Please, miss. Please give me a spanking.'

'The spanking you deserve,' she corrected.

I shaped my mouth around the words and somehow managed to speak them. 'Yes, miss. Please give me the spanking I deserve, miss.'

She smacked the brush against her hand, harder than I had done. I winced. 'Good girl. Back over my lap, then.'

I practically collapsed into position.

She pressed the cool wood against my burning skin and I closed my eyes, bracing myself. Smoothing it over my bottom, she continued to rebuke me, speaking in a stern but gentle voice that was maddening in its kindness.

The first stroke fell at last and I arched wildly on her lap, crying out at the pain. This was no soft ladylike palm. She gave me no time to recover before giving me the next one. Scolding me all the while, she peppered my bottom smartly with brisk little smacks. The startling density of the hairbrush elicited unseemly howls and cries from me as I kicked and writhed in vain.

I found myself pleading like a naughty child. 'Oh! I'm sorry, miss, I'm – oww! – really sorry! I promise I won't – oh! I won't do it again, miss! Please . . .'

But she ignored my pleas and spanked me harder, covering every inch of my backside with sure strokes. My knickers inched their way down my legs as I struggled. I tried to keep them from slipping off, but the hairbrush was too intense. I couldn't focus on anything but the pain and before I knew it they were dangling from one ankle and then they were off entirely.

By the time Courtney slowed her rhythm and stopped I was willing to promise her anything. I sagged with relief. It felt like she'd taken off a layer of skin.

'There, now,' she cooed. 'Have we learnt not to be a naughty girl?'

Her words were almost more painful than the hairbrush had been, but I nodded frantically. 'Yes, miss.'

Courtney leant down to her left to place the hairbrush on the floor beside my hands. I stared at it, amazed at its power. I would never underestimate it again. Then, wickedly, she trailed her fingertips over my punished bottom. She pressed her manicured nails into my flesh and drew them down over my rounded cheeks, making me squeal.

I heard her soft laughter and felt even more humbled.

'Up with you,' she said at last, urging me up with a mild smack.

I scrambled to my feet. My hands, chilled from pressing into the floorboards, felt heavenly against the scorching glow of my bottom.

'Now you'll show me a nice curtsey and thank me for your punishment,' she prompted.

Shifting my weight from foot to foot in humiliation, I made myself meet her eyes. With my knickers before me on the floor like evidence of my naughtiness, I dropped an awkward curtsey. But she stopped me before I could speak the awful words.

'Oh, dear me,' she said, shaking her head sadly. 'We haven't even learnt how to curtsey properly.'

I pleaded with my eyes for her to stop the torment, though every little reproach made me squirm in delicious misery.

'How do you ever expect to be presented at court if you don't trouble yourself to practise what I teach you? Watch.' Gathering her skirt, Courtney placed one foot behind her with the grace of a ballerina. She lowered her head demurely and dipped her body in a sweeping *grande reverence* until she was almost kneeling. She stood up again and gestured that it was my turn.

I tried to copy what she had done, but I lost my balance and faltered.

My governess was unimpressed. She wore her displeasure like a sovereign's mantle and I imagined the horror of stumbling like that at the feet of Queen Victoria.

Blushing furiously, I tried again, this time with more success if with little elegance.

'Better.'

At her expectant look I forced the hateful words out. 'Thank you, miss, for punishing me.' Then I squeezed my eyes shut and bowed my head, praying the lesson was over.

'Very good,' Courtney drawled, sounding genuinely pleased. 'Then I expect to see your manners much improved.'

'Yes, miss.'

She gazed at me, her sternness dissipating. I blushed, uncertain whether the roleplay was over or not. I desperately wanted my knickers back now. I felt so exposed. Mostly because I could feel how wet I was and I feared she would see it.

'Is it very sore?' she asked with a playful grin.

'Uh-huh' was all I could manage.

'Let's see.'

I turned around so she could examine her handiwork. Her long fingers traced the redness, making me shiver. They trailed over my tender backside and along my thighs, slipping down to the delicate undercurve. My legs tensed as her thumbs crept further in and she parted my cheeks with gentle pressure. I gasped, but I remained absolutely still, unwilling to do anything to break the moment.

Encouraged by my stillness, Courtney leant forwards and my skin prickled as she pressed her lips to the burning flesh, kissing first one cheek, then the other.

A soft hand found the small of my back and exerted easy force until I obliged her by bending forwards. I braced my hands on the desk in front of me as her other hand slid between my legs. My breathing quickened and I relaxed my thighs to allow it.

I had never been with another girl. I'd fantasised about spanking, certainly, but nothing beyond that. It was uncharted territory and I didn't know if it was allowed. But at that moment I didn't care.

Her hand strayed slowly upwards, to where it must feel the heat emanating from my damp little slit. My sex was throbbing with a need that was becoming painful and I willed her to continue. Just half an inch.

When her fingertips grazed my lips I shuddered, bending further forwards in compliance. Encouraged by my invitation, her hand advanced more boldly until the palm rested right against my sex. I rose on tiptoe and she increased the pressure, pushing against me and stroking her other hand down over my punished bottom.

I drew a long shuddering breath and heard her laugh softly. She released me and beckoned me to follow her through the door, unbuttoning her dress as she backed away along the hallway.

We reached the master bedroom and Courtney slithered out of her dress. It pooled at her feet and she stepped out of it, never taking her eyes off me. Her hands moved to her hair and unpinned it, releasing it from its bondage and shaking it loose like a 1950s pinup girl. She sat on the edge of the bed – a vision in a red satin bra and matching panties. Nervous and uncertain, I stood watching her with longing and apprehension.

She kicked off her shoes and regarded me with a catlike grin. Her glittering green eyes urged me closer and she untucked my shirt, tugging it up to expose my midriff. I raised my arms and allowed her to pull it off over my head.

Then she unzipped my skirt and it slid to the floor. I was curious and eager, but still hesitant. I didn't know what to do with my hands. But my shyness only seemed to excite Courtney, who was glad to take the lead. She pulled me towards her until I had to move on to the mattress. I knelt there passively while she stroked my face, sliding her fingers through my short hair and tugging it in mock roughness.

I closed my eyes as she continued down along my throat, making me quiver as though chilled. But her hands were warm. Very warm. And when she stroked them lightly over the lace of my bra I gave a little moan. She slid a hand inside one of the cups, giving me a gentle squeeze. I felt the nipple respond immediately, stiffening to her touch.

Her arms encircled me and unhooked my bra, freeing my small breasts. Suddenly embarrassed, I covered myself with my hands. But she took my wrists and peeled them away, placing them, crossed, behind my back. I surrendered as she caressed me, teasing my nipples into stiff little peaks and lazily circling her fingertips round them.

My breathing grew deeper, heavier, as she awakened my body. I pressed myself down on my heels to rekindle the sting in my bottom just as her lips closed over one erect nipple. A soft kiss, barely there, but then the tip of her tongue began to circle it as her fingers had done, swirling around and across it, stimulating me almost to the point of suffering.

I felt her teeth then, closing just enough to touch without biting. I forced myself to stay absolutely still, expecting a jolt of pain. But with a final kiss she moved to the other breast, meeting my frightened eyes with a wicked smile. With her palm she covered the nipple she had been teasing, insulating it from the sudden chill of the air on the damp flesh. I trembled at the tiny act of kindness.

Her tongue continued its keen exploration of the other nipple, subjecting it to the same treatment. I relaxed into the sensation, my wrists still crossed behind me – a good little submissive.

As she flicked her tongue back and forth across my nipple, her hand crept down over my chest and belly, down to my wet and eager sex. I arched my back, an invitation. She obliged me and slid her fingers down along the slick crease, before drawing them back up again with unbearable deliberation. There was a deep ache welling inside me and I knew she was going to release it. I wanted her to. When I sensed she was watching me, my eyes fluttered open.

She stopped her ministrations and guided my hands to her bra. I unhooked it obediently, eager to discover what made her gasp and shudder. Confronted with the soft round fullness of her breasts, I felt a moment's hesitation. But she'd shown me exactly what to do. Her pink nipples stood out like hard little knots and I pressed my lips to each in turn, tasting her, sucking her, devouring her.

I enjoyed her responsiveness. She was noisier than me, crying out shrilly at each little surge of pleasure. Anyone hearing her responses would have had trouble telling whether she was experiencing pleasure or pain and I was delighted to be the one making her react.

Without warning she fisted a hand in my hair and pulled me up forcefully. Then she guided me down on my back and straddled me, her long hair cascading down on either side of her neck, tickling my chest. She gazed at me, her eyes roaming over my face until she leant down and kissed me.

Her lips were soft and pillowy, not at all like a man's. I plunged my hands into the mass of her auburn hair as her tongue pushed its way inside my mouth. She tasted rich and wanton, like stolen wine. Her tongue swirled around inside my mouth and I clutched her hair, letting go only to grab another handful.

She relaxed on top of me, the beautiful smooth warm weight of her body pressing into mine. I let go of her hair and stroked my fingers along the xylophone of her arched spine, running my nails up and down the length of her. I ran my tongue along the edge of her teeth and she nipped it gently. She withdrew and kissed my lower lip, sucking it into her mouth then releasing it again.

I could have stayed there forever, kissing her, but Courtney wanted more. She wanted everything. Her lips travelled down to my neck, where she nibbled me playfully before moving on. She kissed each breast as she crept further down, heightening the suspense. I knew exactly what she would do next, but her languorous pace was whipping me into a frenzy. It was all I could do not to grab her head and shove her down there.

She curled between my legs, spreading them apart and drawing her fingers along the moist folds. I was a little embarrassed at how wet I was, but it only seemed to excite her. With the flat of her hand she gave me a delicate little smack that made me jump. But it sent a jolt of ecstasy through my body. Clearly enjoying my response, she did it again. And again.

Then she let her long hair fall across my breasts and moved her head slowly from side to side, brushing it over my skin. The sublime softness of it contrasted deliriously with what she was doing with her hands and my sensations didn't know how to keep up. I alternated between sighs and squeals.

At last, she swept her hair over one shoulder and, with a last flicker of a grin, lowered her mouth to me. Her lips were gentle, just as they had been with my breasts. And when I felt her soft tongue begin to probe the outer folds of my sex I clutched the headboard, suddenly wishing she'd tied me up.

Her tongue moved expertly up and along the sides and over my clit, stimulating me with almost intolerable pleasure. When I thought I wouldn't be able to take any more she spread me open further and dipped first one, then two fingers inside. Her tongue never ceased its relentless caress and it wasn't long before I felt the demanding ache inside me begin to intensify. It rose wildly, building and swelling until it consumed me completely. I threw my head back with a breathless gasp as my vision went black and the devastating climax threatened to render me unconscious.

When the spasms began to dissipate I lay helpless, trembling and weak. My body had never felt more alive and I blinked away the startled tears that sprang to my eyes, blurring my vision.

Courtney sat up, staring at me with something like wonderment. Or was it envy? All I knew was that I was desperate to experience giving her the same pleasure she'd just given me. It took me nearly a minute to find the strength to get up, but when I did she stopped me, suddenly looking slightly sheepish.

'You don't have to –'

'Shh. I want to.'

I realised with some surprise that she hadn't taken off her knickers. And as I pushed her down on her back I saw that they were drenched. She lifted her hips as I eased the sodden scrap of red satin down, revealing a soft downy strip of slightly reddish hair. Smoothing it with my thumb, I slid her knickers down her long legs. I paused to admire her shapely feet and expertly pedicured toes. The nails were varnished in a sleek lustrous red and I couldn't resist kissing them.

She shuddered and made a low purring sound. Encouraged, I took her big toe in my mouth as I would a cock, sliding my lips up and down the short length of it. Her foot was pleasantly musky and I let my lips travel down further, to the soft flesh of her sole. Courtney writhed on the bed, somehow managing to hold her leg still for me. I trailed my tongue over the bottom of her foot as though licking cream from a bowl. At last I gave the toes a final kiss and moved up between her legs.

She clamped her legs around my wrist when I touched her, pinning my hand against her. I moved my fingers as much as I could, playing with her until she relaxed her grip and her legs opened, inviting me. I smiled, then lowered my head to her. The scent of her arousal was intoxicating – a sharp piquant aroma that made me even more impatient to taste her.

Like a picture frame, the trimmed fluff of hair exhibited the little slit below it, drawing my gaze there and holding it. It looked so delicate and inoffensive, so much less explicit than a man's cock. Fascinated, I traced my finger along the line of soft creases, enjoying the way she arched her back at my touch.

Her silky folds reminded me of the curved closed shell of a fortune cookie concealing a secret. I splayed her open, touching her as I touched myself. Watching her respond was like watching myself and I badly wanted to see her come.

I pressed my mouth against the hot little hollow and lapped eagerly, savouring the damp silky feel and creamy taste of her. She raised up to meet me, pushing herself against my mouth, grinding her hips hungrily. I knew it wouldn't take her long.

And, as her moans and cries grew louder and more demanding, she bucked wildly, clutching the duvet so violently I thought she would tear it. She squeezed her legs against either side of my head until the waves subsided and she drifted back down to earth. We lay entwined, sweaty and sated, and with a sigh of exhaustion she threw a limp arm over me.

'Holy shit,' she breathed, and it was so unrefined and out of character that she caught herself and laughed.

'Did they teach you all of that at finishing school?' I couldn't resist asking.

She smiled serenely and stroked my face. 'No, but I think your governess might make it part of your plan of study.'

I hid my face in her waves of hair. 'Yes, miss,' I whispered.

Courtney turned up unannounced the next day looking ever so coy.

‘Oh no,’ I said, immediately suspicious. ‘What have you done?’

She gave me her best Southern belle simper. ‘I felt really dirty when I thought about what we did last night. I mean, seducing my best friend and all . . .’

I blinked in confusion.

‘Only very bad girls do dirty things like that,’ she continued. ‘And – well, I just felt so guilty I had to get it off my chest.’

I realised where this was leading and I covered my face with my hands. ‘You didn’t,’ I groaned, peering out at her from between my fingers. ‘Tell me you didn’t.’

Courtney beamed with perverse delight. ‘I did. Father Michael thought it was most unnatural indeed. Wanna see the marks?’

Sixteen

Courtney couldn't decide whether she was relieved or disappointed by the men's reaction to our little escapade. Peter's knowing smile told us he wasn't a bit surprised. Shaun lamented that he hadn't been there to take pictures. That was hardly unexpected, given what had happened with Lenka. I was just relieved to know we hadn't overstepped any boundaries or broken tacit rules.

'While we're on the subject of pictures,' Peter said, 'I think it's time you and your red bottom graced the pages of englishvice.net.'

'Who, me?' I asked stupidly.

'Of course, you!' Courtney broke in. 'You have to. You know you want to.'

I peered round the circle of expectant faces. It was true that the exhibitionist in me wanted to come out to play, but the possibility of getting caught filled me with terror.

Shaun spoke up. 'Courtney and I are shooting Lenka in Cornwall next month. There are standing stones all over Bodmin Moor and around the Land's End peninsula. The sites won't be crawling with tourists at this time of year. Why not join us and we'll make a road trip of it?'

Courtney looked at me with puppyish expectation.

'It sounds great,' Peter said. 'But I have a different location in mind for Angie's debut.' At my startled expression he gave my hand a comforting avuncular pat. 'Trust me. You'll love it.'

I thought back to the first time we'd discussed the site. I'd mentioned Dartmoor Prison and *HMS Victory* and he'd suggested the *Grand Turk*. He had to be joking. Megalithic sites in Cornwall were one thing, but prisons and national monuments were never deserted.

I gave him a pleading, searching look and he relented.

'There's a nineteenth-century prison up in Scotland,' he said. 'Perfectly preserved.'

'Go on.'

'Visitors can go into the cells and lie in the hammocks, turn the crank machine or be locked up in the airing yards.'

I felt myself being won over.

He paused before adding the clincher. 'Scene of many floggings.'

I was there.

It should have been an uneventful journey. A short flight from London to Glasgow and a drive along the shores of Loch Fyne to the historic town of Inveraray. But enhanced security measures at Heathrow turned the boarding procedure into a nightmare. For me, anyway.

'Excuse me, sir, but could you tell me what these items are?'

Peter and I peered round at the monitor. The x-ray screen showed the inside of his holdall with several objects conspicuously visible. The security guard pointed to the most obvious ones and eyed us expectantly.

'That's a school cane,' Peter said offhandedly. 'And that one's a paddle.'

I turned away, my face blazing.

The guard wasn't fazed. 'Would you mind opening the bag for me to have a look, please?'

'Certainly.'

Peter unzipped the case completely and revealed its contents. His schoolmaster's gown lay folded neatly on top. I inched away from the table.

He reached beneath the gown, unbending the rattan cane and drawing it out with a flourish. He set it carefully on the inspection table while the guard watched. Then he fished around and brought out the Lochgelly tawse. I gasped and hung my head as the guard peered at me.

'We *are* going to Scotland,' Peter explained, as though it were a requirement for anyone travelling there. 'Suppose you misbehave at the B&B.'

Blushing furiously, I bit my lip and resigned myself to the total humiliation.

Several passengers passed through security behind us as Peter continued to search in his bag with a shameless lack of concern. People stared, blinking in surprise at the exhibition. I stared fixedly at the floor, darting my eyes up only to see what new horror Peter had uncovered. I'd had no idea he'd packed so many implements and I had to wonder if this cruel little comedy had been planned.

Next came the ebony hairbrush, which hadn't been pointed out on the x-ray screen. As though to leave no doubt to anyone of its purpose, Peter smacked it against his palm before laying it beside the cane and the strap. The sound drew the attention of two smartly dressed businessmen who didn't hide their amusement as they looked from me to the toys and back at me again.

I stared in mute chagrin as a pair of handcuffs joined the array. I'd never seen them before.

'I'm sorry,' Peter said with an amiable smile. 'It's in here somewhere.'

'Take your time, sir,' the guard said calmly. 'Take your time.'

They could have been two gentlemen discussing the weather over afternoon tea.

At last he found the paddle. 'Here it is,' he said. He held it up ostentatiously as he removed it from the case and passed it to the guard.

The unflappable man turned it over in his hands to examine it. He peered through his glasses at the inscription. *Experientia docet.* He aimed the unspoken question at Peter, who translated graciously. 'Experience teaches.'

'Ah, yes,' the guard said with a non-committal nod. Agreement? Appreciation? I was just thankful he wasn't looking at me. He stroked his finger along the fine oak grain of the paddle once more before returning it to Peter.

'Very good, sir. Thank you. That's quite in order.'

Peter smiled politely. 'You're welcome.'

I endured the scrutiny of more passengers as Peter took his time replacing the implements in the holdall. He flexed the cane into a C to make it fit and the guard raised his eyebrows with interest.

'Is there no danger of breaking it?' he asked.

'Oh no. Canes are remarkably resilient if you take care of them. I soak mine in brine. It keeps them supple.' Peter spoke with clear authority on the subject and the guard seemed impressed.

'I shall remember that.'

This time he did look at me and his eyes roamed up and down my body as though he could see through my clothes. I tugged at Peter's sleeve like a bashful child and my silent entreaty was finally granted.

'Bye, then,' Peter said as he led me away.

'Have a nice flight.'

I stared straight ahead and had to remind myself to put one foot in front of the other.

Inveraray was the seat of the Duke of Argyll. Its castle and gardens were probably more popular in the summer, but even in the bleak wet drizzle that greeted us we could see it was a lovely town. I buttoned my coat against the chill, already regretting my short red tartan skirt and black thigh-high socks. The exposed skin between them prickled with gooseflesh and I longed to be inside where it was warm.

We headed straight for the prison, happy to discover it was almost deserted. An elderly Chinese couple browsed the gift shop, but didn't seem to speak any English. Otherwise, it looked as though we had the place to ourselves.

We explored the old prison first, where women and children had been housed. There was nothing there to pique our offbeat interests, so we went back outside to investigate further. The leaden sky glowered down at us with condemnation as we crossed the small compound. On our way a warder in period uniform offered to lock Peter in one of the airing yards. Peter volunteered me instead.

Built to give prisoners a place to exercise in the open air, the airing yards were basically a pair of outdoor cages. Each one was roughly eight feet by ten feet – just enough room to pace like an animal in a zoo while the icy rain streamed down through the bars overhead.

'Prisoners were allowed oot here for an hoor each day,' the warder said. 'But they werenae allowed tae speak tae each other.'

I wrapped my hands round the bars of the gate while Peter took the necessary photograph and the warder told us about prison life in the 1800s. It sounded a dreary miserable existence. Even a stint in this frigid cage must have been a welcome change from the drudgery of picking oakum or climbing the treadmill. However, despite the grim reality painted by the warder, the experience of being locked behind bars was exhilarating. I was incorrigible.

I blushed as the warder turned the massive key in the lock and opened the door, releasing me from my too short confinement. We thanked him and went inside the new prison. To my dismay, there were voices on the floor above us. A group of rowdy students from the sound of it, talking and laughing loudly in incomprehensible Glaswegian. I shot Peter a worried glance, but he was undaunted.

'Ah, here we are,' he said, pushing open the door of one of the cells.

I followed him inside. A bulky pine table stood against one wall, with two large armholes cut into it near one end, spaced about a foot apart. My breath caught in my throat. 'Is that . . .?'

'It is,' Peter confirmed. 'The original whipping table.'

My eyes bulged and as I ran my hand along the polished surface I fancied I could hear the cuts of the judicial birch, chastening the delinquents who'd fallen foul of the law. I empathised with them across the years.

'Scottish courts were firm advocates of the judicial birch,' he said. 'And the regulations specified that a birching must be sufficiently severe to make the wrong-doers dread a repetition. I don't suppose there were many recidivists.'

On a podium beneath the barred window sat a large book with laminated pages of foolscap. The whipping register. Peter flipped through it with the delectation of a collector finding a rare specimen.

'Two shillings and sixpence per whipping,' he mused. 'Not a bad rate for 1874.'

Neatly lined columns listed the date, the offender's name and age, the number of strokes administered and the name of the punisher. I was disappointed that the actual offences weren't recorded, but the pages of graceful script were enough to tease and stimulate my imagination.

As I turned back to the table I saw it. A birch rod was hanging on the wall above the table, very like the ones I was accustomed to preparing. The ends were frayed, as though from recent and frequent use. But it was the sign that was truly noteworthy: 'Please try.'

I stared in incredulity. 'Do they really mean it?' I asked.

Peter beamed and raised the camera, removing the lens cap. 'That's why we're here, Angie.'

I blushed and bowed my head, trapped.

He patted the table. 'Right. Give me your coat. Up you get. Arms through the holes.'

'But those yobs upstairs –'

'Are still upstairs. They're making enough noise to give us ample warning.'

My pulse began to race, but I climbed obediently up on to the table. My arms fit perfectly through the holes, hanging straight down.

Peter took a few innocent shots of me and I affected a sullen pout for the camera.

'Very nice,' he said. 'These are brilliant. And the vanilla pictures will complement the kinky ones beautifully.'

He unzipped the back of my skirt and I offered a meek appeal.

'Don't make a fuss,' he chided. 'You know perfectly well that birchings are given on the bare bottom.'

I put my forehead down on the table as he slipped off the skirt and peeled down the school knickers he'd insisted I wear for the occasion. He took the rod from its place on the wall and balanced it across my cheeks. I heard the camera beep and click as he took several more pictures.

'Head up, now,' he urged. 'That's good. No, don't smile. Imagine you were caught picking the pockets of the local gentry and you've been sent here to be punished.'

Colouring deeply at the fantasy he was spinning, I quite forgot that there was anyone else in the building. The boisterous echoes were deceptive in the stone corridors and by the time I realised how close the voices were it was too late.

Two male figures appeared in the doorway and froze, staring in silent amazement at the sight before them. I tried to scramble up out of the armholes, but there was nothing to brace against. Peter put a firm hand on my shoulder and held me in place.

'I didn't say you could get up.'

My eyes widened, a desperate grovelling plea. I couldn't bear to look towards the doorway, but I caught the movement out of the corner of my eye; another figure had joined the ones already standing there. He too was silenced by the tableau before him.

I turned my head away from Peter, mumbling a pathetic 'Please' I knew he would ignore.

I heard him sigh and then he broke the ponderous silence. 'Do you want me to ask one of these lads to assist me?'

'No!' I cried before they could answer. Defeated, I lowered my face to the cold distressed wood.

I heard the soft clink of something metal. Looking to the side I saw Peter crouch down below the level of the table. I realised what he was doing, but by the time he'd snapped the handcuffs around my wrists it was too late to struggle. He ratcheted the cold steel tighter and there was a murmur of excitement from the watchers in the doorway.

'Standard procedure,' Peter told me. 'Though if you take this as bravely as your last birching they won't really be needed.'

My face positively ached with shame. I heard a comment from one of the boys – something like 'nice arse' – and I squeezed my eyes shut tight.

Peter addressed the group good-naturedly. 'Do come in if you'd like to watch. But close the door behind you, please.'

I looked up in horror.

There was an enthusiastic chorus of 'ayes' and the trio edged into the room, pulling the door shut behind them with a loud clang. This was so far beyond my simple fear of being caught. Unsuspecting vanillas I could have coped with. A church group. My parents. Anything but this coarse gang of neds. An innocent stumbling on to the scene would be just as embarrassed as I was. These boys were going to enjoy every minute of it.

'Now then,' said Peter. He held the camera out to them like an offering. 'Could someone take some pictures for me?'

A lean ginger-haired boy in a hoodie accepted the camera eagerly. 'Aye, pal, ah will. Ur ye gonny git yer legover?'

His friends laughed raucously and Peter ignored the question, the meaning of which I could guess.

'Just press the button,' said Peter. 'It'll beep once when it focuses, twice when it takes a shot. Thanks.'

The other two leered at me, their eyes shining with keen expectation. The ginger-haired boy raised the camera to his eye and I heard the tiny robotic sounds as he adjusted the lens, zooming in and out to frame the shot. There was a soft scrape as Peter picked up the rod from the table and I flinched. The camera clicked prematurely and I was momentarily blinded by the flash.

One of the other boys, a stocky specimen, gave a loud horsy laugh and punched the photographer hard in the shoulder. 'He hisnae even started yet, Iain!'

'Ah'll malkie ye in a minute, Billy, ye wee twat!' Iain glared at him and there was a burst of impenetrable Glaswegian slang from all three, most of it clearly rude. I was thankful I didn't understand.

Peter waited patiently for the little squabble to end and eventually the boys noticed the silence. 'Whenever you're ready, gentlemen,' Peter said with polite condescension.

'Well, git on wae it, then,' said the third one, a scruffy lad in a vintage Rolling Stones T-shirt and ripped jeans. He had a wiry angular physique that I could have found quite attractive if he'd been better dressed.

'Birchings were quite a spectator sport back in the nineteenth century,' Peter said. 'Some avaricious warders even charged admission when there was a pretty girl involved.'

This elicited a lively round of derisive laughter and I held my breath as Peter raised the birch. The camera beeped as he brought it down, though not with much force.

The camera beeped again and the one called Billy burst out with another obnoxious laugh. 'Haw, mister, gie it some wellie!'

Gritting my teeth, I waited for the next stroke. It landed considerably harder than the first and I gave a little yelp.

They cheered wildly, urging Peter on like spectators at a race. I was appalled to find myself moistening in response to the rich humiliation of their taunts. I squeezed my legs together, glad they couldn't see me from behind.

The scruffy lad was nearest me and he watched my face intently as Peter delivered a stroke that left me gasping.

'This is pure dead brilliant, man!' he enthused, practically frothing at the mouth.

As the cuts grew harder and harder, I was unable to restrain my cries. The room grew steadily still and quiet. The boys looked uncertainly from one to the other, their eyes growing wide as the whipping escalated and I twisted from side to side, crying out in pain. The only other sounds were the swish of the birch and the beep and click of the camera. Somehow the lull was harder to bear than their abuse had been.

I hardly noticed when Peter stopped. He caressed my bottom and I heard the camera beep dutifully as it recorded the moment.

'Look at the state o' her arse, man!' said Iain, lowering the camera. 'She's rid raw!'

'Gonny gie us a look at her fanny?' asked Billy. He was the crudest of the lot.

I felt my face colour and I averted my eyes.

'Oh, I don't see why not,' Peter said in a considering tone. 'It wasn't unusual for warders to take advantage of their prisoners.'

His hand slipped down between my legs and I drew a sharp breath, trying in vain to pull myself up out of the armholes. When he tried to separate my ankles I resisted and accidentally kicked him.

He tutted and gave me another stroke of the birch, this time across the tops of my thighs. The flash of searing pain forbade any further opposition and I simply prayed that Peter would tell them the show was over.

'But if the prisoner didn't co-operate,' he added, 'the spectators might be asked to hold her in position.'

The insinuation was luridly clear and it was the only signal the boys needed. The scruffy one jumped first, hauling the table out away from the wall and into the centre of the room. I squealed with surprise. Then Iain handed the camera to Billy and moved to the other side of the table to stand next to Peter.

Like sharks circling their prey, they closed on me. Billy was taking pictures now and I sensed things were about to get worse. I begged Peter with my eyes not to let them do it. His lips curled in a grin that was pure evil.

Hands pawed at me from both sides, groping clumsily, greedily. They hauled my legs apart and I strained against the handcuffs, but I was outmanoeuvred. My fruitless struggles only inflamed my tormentors further.

Iain snaked a hand down the front of my jumper and I tried to squirm away. I pushed myself against the table, squashing my breasts uncomfortably against the wood in an attempt to spare them his attentions. He was stronger, though, and his fingers wormed their way into my bra, roughly kneading the soft flesh at his mercy.

Billy repeated his request in a wheedling voice. 'Gie us a look at yer fanny, hen.' As if I had any control over what I exhibited.

The scruffy one laughed and Iain growled a mocking obscenity at him, still mauling my breasts with his cold callused hands.

But Peter leant down to whisper to me, 'It's only fair that paying customers should get their money's worth.' He unlocked my left wrist and hauled me up on to my knees. I reached back in a pitiful attempt to pull my knickers up and he slapped my hand away.

My jumper had a row of buttons down the front, but Iain ignored them, yanking it unceremoniously up over my head and pulling it off. Billy gave a crass gurgling laugh and clicked away at the scene. They stripped me and I let them.

Iain didn't bother unhooking my bra; he simply dragged my breasts out over the modest cups. 'Look at the pair on that,' he said, giving me a hard squeeze.

I debased myself further by responding to his unkind touch. My nipples puckered and tightened, betraying me.

It was horrible. Sordid and demeaning. Utterly obscene.

And yet . . .

I had never felt more alive than I did now at the mercy of such extravagant debauchery, such magnificent degradation. I was completely helpless. They could do anything they wanted and I was powerless to stop them.

Peter clicked the other cuff back on to my wrist and pushed me down on my back. I hissed as my tender bottom pressed into the hard table and Peter stretched my arms over my head, holding me down.

The scruffy lad worked at my knickers, dragging them down my legs so he could pull them off. Grinning, he held them out to Peter, who shook his head.

'Keep them,' he said.

The boys arranged me with my head to the window and my splayed legs open. At last Billy got his wish. The camera beeped and clicked hungrily, devouring every explicit image. They'd left my thigh-highs and shoes on, which only emphasised the other bits on display.

Their vulgar commentary continued, much of it like a foreign language to me. They raised my legs up over my head, holding them apart and flaunting my stripes and my sex for the camera. Then the scruffy one drew back his hand and smacked me hard across the fullest part of my bottom, making me yelp with pain.

‘Ach, haud yer wheest, hen, it’s no’ that sair!’

I blinked in bewilderment, but caught the gist. I tried to be quiet as he gave me several more solid whacks before lowering me back down. Then his hand was between my legs, searching along the dampening crease with frenzied determination. He spread me open with both hands, forcing two fingers roughly inside me. I gasped and writhed on the table as he described the state of me in gory detail for his friends.

Billy barked an instruction to the others and I arched in pain as I felt my nipples cruelly tweaked. Their graphic observations increasingly excluded me and I closed my eyes, losing myself in the rough treatment as countless hands fondled and molested me, forcing me closer and closer to the edge.

I fought it, but their determined fingers finally reached the limit of my endurance. My body convulsed in ecstatic unbearable pleasure as I succumbed to wave after wave of sensory overload, almost screaming at the intensity. With a long shuddering sigh, I wilted on the table.

The hands released me and all of a sudden the room was scarily quiet. Even the camera had stopped clicking. Panting, I raised myself up on to my elbows. And gaped at the ashen-faced Chinese couple standing in the open doorway, their mouths working soundlessly in horror-struck disbelief.

Seventeen

Seeing myself on the website seemed even more transgressive than the whipping had been. Of course, Peter had only posted the birching photos. The explicit ones were just for us. Encouraged by the elaborate nastiness Peter had orchestrated, I decided it was time to confess my secret fantasy to him. But in my own special way.

'I need your help, Courtney. I need you to plant something in a phone box for me.'

Courtney narrowed her eyes. 'What?'

I displayed the card with pride.

She looked at it and then exploded into laughter.

'I know, I know.' I blushed. 'But Peter will love it. He won't be expecting it.'

At the top of the card were the words 'Eton lad'. And beneath it was a picture of me, posing in my prize eBay acquisition – a vintage Eton suit, complete with bumfreezer jacket and topper. The only other text was my mobile number at the bottom.

'Handsome,' Courtney purred, tracing the outline of the hat. She put her arm around me and kissed me on the cheek. 'My little rent boy,' she said, grinning hugely. 'Oh, this will be fun. Sure, just tell me which phone box.'

That afternoon, I called Peter. 'Would you do me a favour?' I asked.

'Sure.'

'Remember the phone box where Shaun and Courtney said they found Lenka's card? Would you stop by on your way home and see if there's anything interesting?'

I could sense Peter's smile through the phone. 'Of course. You think it's our turn now, eh?'

'One never knows.'

Peter agreed and I hung up, barely able to suppress my excitement.

I went back to my own flat and took my time getting dressed. I knew it would take Peter a while to reach the phone box and call me. The suit was an amazing find. I'd never worn an authentic Eton collar before, though I'd read how uncomfortable and confining they were. The stiff starchy paper was like a posture collar that rubbed constantly against the neck.

Shopping for boys' underwear had been loads of fun as well. And wearing them was strangely erotic. They felt so foreign, so thick and unfeminine, covering more than a pair of knickers ever did.

The suit fitted as though it had been made for me, though the trousers needed a belt to sit on my girlish waist without falling down. The archaic top hat completed the image. I was tomboyish enough in girls' clothes, but dressed like this I could easily pass for a teenage boy.

I'd originally wanted a tailsuit, but my research showed me that that was for older boys. I needed to be a younger one, fagging for a prefect who would take full advantage of his authority and privilege.

When I was dressed and preening and posing in front of the mirror, 'Tubular Bells' began to play. I let the tune cycle three times before reaching for my mobile. I couldn't let Peter think I was sitting by the phone waiting for it to ring.

'Hello?'

'Eton, eh? What put you on the game, then? You lose all your money, you little dandy?'

I froze. It wasn't Peter. I pulled the phone away from my ear, gawking at it. Courtney had said she would watch the box until Peter showed up. She also said she'd dash in and grab the card if anyone reached it before he did. I tried to think of something to say.

'Erm, I, er . . .'

The man laughed and continued in his abrasive estuary accent. 'A posh education and that's all you can say?' His tone turned harsh. 'What'll you do for fifty quid?'

My heart felt battered with a sledgehammer. This was like some of the ruder encounters in the chat room. Worse than what the Glaswegian yobs had said, much of which had been unintelligible to me. But that had been different. Men could be so much cruder with one another. Even with such a delicate lad as Martin.

'Well . . .'

'I want to bugger you,' the man growled. 'Shove it up inside you so hard you cry like a girlie. Fuck you good and proper.'

In spite of the coarseness, I couldn't help but notice the insistent pulse between my legs. The idea of a total stranger happening on my card . . . Wanting to be so rough and nasty with sweet little Martin . . . It was intoxicating, like forbidden fruit.

I made a sound I hoped sounded like a murmur of interest, just to see what the caller would say.

'You gonna resist me, boy?' he asked. 'Because if you do I'll bend you over and strap your arse till it's raw. Then you'll take it like a choirboy.'

I thought I would faint.

'I'll shove my cock in you, make you take it all, every inch. I want to hear you beg for it, nancy boy. Beg me to fuck your raw sore little arse.'

Mortified, I wanted to respond, but I couldn't. Meeting the man was out of the question, of course. He thought he was talking to a *real* boy. But the thought was delirious and I squeezed my legs together, listening to the rustle of my pinstriped trousers.

The man chuckled. 'Don't have the guts, lad?' he said. 'No, I didn't think so. Go back to school, little boy. Go learn some proper lessons.' There was a click as he rang off.

I stared at the phone, bewildered. My legs were trembling and I sat down on the edge of the bed. What was I going to do now? The man had my card. Now Peter wouldn't find it when he went to the phone box.

'Tubular Bells' began to play again and I jumped, startled. I pressed the button to answer.

'Hello?' I asked tentatively.

'Did you enjoy that?'

My eyes widened. 'Courtney?'

I heard wild laughter, Courtney's and someone else's. Then Courtney came back on the line. 'Well, nancy boy? Did it get you all 'ot and bovvered?'

'Was that you?' I gaped.

'No, that was Shaun,' she choked out, struggling through her laughter. 'Wanna say hello?'

'I'm going to kill you!' I said, surrendering to my own laughter. 'And him! You two are pure evil!'

'Well, Martin needs to learn that if he sticks his card in phone boxes he's bound to get some nasty calls. They won't all be gentlemen. Besides, I thought it might help get you in the mood.'

Still shaking my head over the prank, I found myself thanking Courtney. It *had* got me in the mood. 'Where's Peter?' I asked.

'Don't worry. We'll see him long before he sees us. And we'll make sure no one else dodgy finds your card.'

There was a burst of male laughter in the background and Shaun said something I couldn't make out.

'What was that?'

'Shaun says unless you're into dodgy men, in which case he'll be your next customer.'

'Tell him he's a total perv,' I retorted.

'Will do,' Courtney chirped. 'Now get to work, boy. Or I'll tell your pimp you're holding out on him and he'll make you sorry you ever left the comforts of the birching block!'

'Yes, miss,' I said, a huge grin spreading across my features. I ended the call and lay back on the bed, revelling in the new game. I couldn't wait for Peter to call.

Half an hour later, the phone rang again. It was hard to force myself to wait, but I did it, again letting the tune play more than once before answering. It wouldn't do to appear too eager.

'Hello?' I said, pitching my voice lower.
'*Floreat Etona*,' said Peter.
I bit my lip.
'How much, lad?'
'Depends what you want to do,' I said, trying to sound casual.
Peter gave a sinister chuckle. 'I know what I'd *like* to do to a boy who uses the school's name in such a way. I think your headmaster might have something to say about it. I doubt he'd be pleased to hear about some little rent boy besmirching the name of the school like that. Do you?'
The stern tone was having its usual effect on me. 'No, sir,' I said.
'Right. Well, I think we can do business, *Eton lad*.' He emphasised the nickname. 'How does a hundred pounds sound?'
'Fine, sir.'
'When I was at Eton they had certain rules and traditions. You boys are all coddled nowadays. You've probably never even seen a school cane, have you?'
I sighed as I felt my female body begin to respond. 'No, sir,' I said softly.
'No, I didn't think so,' he said, a sneer in his voice. 'Well, we'll get that sorted. I hear they've abolished the fagging system too. It used to be a privilege for the younger boys to act as servants to their seniors. In exchange, they got protection from bullying by their peers. It was good for them. It was character building and they were grateful for it.'
I smiled at that. Grateful. About as grateful as they were to the headmaster for all those birchings.
'What's your name?'
'Martin,' I said.
'Your surname, boy,' Peter said impatiently.
I squirmed. 'Oh. Um, Shepherd.'
'I'm Carruthers. I was a prefect at Eton many years ago. I'm going to take you back in time, Shepherd. You're going to see what Eton College was like in my time. In the good old days.'

'Yes, Carruthers,' I said nervously. It sounded like Peter had something very specific in mind. Courtney's comment about the birching block had almost sent me over the edge. I couldn't guess what he was planning.

'I'll be home by seven,' he said. 'I'll expect to see you at half past. Don't be late, boy.'

'I won't, sir.'

Peter hung up and I closed my eyes in blissful dread. I didn't have much time and I didn't want to make matters worse than they were already. I knew this prefect would view any mistake as deliberate disobedience.

I took one last look at myself in the mirror and set off, reminding myself that I wasn't a girl disguised as a boy; I *was* a boy. This was going to be intense.

I'd never get to Peter's house in time on the Tube, so I treated myself to a cab. The driver didn't even bat an eye as I got into the taxi and gave him the address. I was a bit disappointed, but I supposed he was used to fancy dress. He'd probably seen a lot stranger things than me.

It took me several seconds to get up the courage to knock and it seemed an age before I heard the slow deliberate footsteps increasing in volume as he neared the door. There were a few more agonising seconds of silence and then the door swung open. Peter stood there, dressed immaculately in tails. He gave me a sardonic smile, then made a big show of looking at his watch.

'You're late, Shepherd,' he said icily.

I gasped. 'But I'm –' His look silenced me at once. He didn't need to say it. If Carruthers said Martin was late, then he was late.

Peter stood to one side, a silent command.

I obeyed, stepping inside as though for the first time.

He shut the door and strode purposefully down the length of the hall and headed up the stairs. I hesitated at the bottom, not sure whether I was meant to follow or not. But he looked down at me and waved his arm impatiently. 'Well, come on, snotty,' he snapped.

I flushed at the name. It was what they called midshipmen too. My anxiety began to grow as I followed him into the master bedroom. Standing in front of the window, Peter crossed his arms, scorn and disapproval written across his face. 'You've done it this time, boy,' he said, shaking his head. 'And get that hat off! Anyone would think you were never taught proper manners.'

I hurriedly removed my topper, clutching it in front of me like a shield.

'I want to know what you've been doing all day, boy. Did I not tell you to clean my study?'

I opened my mouth to protest, but I didn't know what to say.

'Well? Speak up!'

'I – I thought I did clean it, Carruthers,' I mumbled.

With a cold smile, Peter ran his finger along the windowsill and looked at his fingertip, just like Galloping Foxley. He tutted and crossed the room, holding his finger right up to my face. In my mind he was wearing Foxley's white glove.

'You call this clean, oik?'

I could clearly see the line of dust on Peter's fingertip. I didn't know how to respond.

'So that's yet another offence,' Peter said. 'Albeit a minor one compared with telling tales.' He glared at me.

'Telling tales?'

'Yes, boy. Whining about your treatment. Complaining about deserved punishments. Ring any bells?'

I shook my head slowly.

'Fleming seems to think I've been bullying you. Why would he think that, Shepherd?'

I could see where the roleplay was going. And now I was genuinely frightened. This was going to be intense. I looked pleadingly at Peter, then followed where he had led me. 'But Fleming asked and I didn't know how much he already knew. I couldn't lie to him!'

'You couldn't lie,' Peter repeated mockingly. 'No. It doesn't work like that, boy. That sort of thing is not done at this school. Not done at all. We're not little cry-babies here. We don't go running to masters when life gets a little rigorous.'

'But he asked . . .'

'And you told.'

'What was I supposed to say?'

'Don't answer me back, snotty. You need to learn some respect. You're the lowest of the low. A little rat. You're here to do what you're told, when you're told. And to take your medicine when your elders and betters think you deserve it. Got that?'

His words were making me feel smaller and smaller. 'Yes, Carruthers,' I said meekly.

Peter drew himself up indignantly. 'The thrashing I gave you last time doesn't seem to have taught you anything at all, Shepherd. So I think I shall have to make sure this one is more instructive.' He paused to let his words sink in.

I looked at the floor.

'I think it's time for you to find out what a Pop tanning is like.'

I blinked. I didn't know what he meant, but it didn't sound pleasant. I shook my head slowly in baffled ignorance.

Peter's mouth spread in a slow predatory smile. He walked to the table near the window. On it was a cane. But it wasn't the usual kind of cane. It was shorter, thicker and knobbly. Malacca? Peter picked it up and flexed it slightly to demonstrate how little it would bend.

I took a step back. Where in the world had he got that? Had he been hiding it from me, waiting for the perfect scene to use it in?

'Pop was the club of senior boys who ran the school,' Peter explained in a silky voice, relishing every word. 'When a boy had done something particularly reprehensible he was summoned to their common room. He wasn't told what was going to happen, though. Oh, no. The note merely said he was to present himself wearing a pair of old trousers.'

Eyeing the cane fearfully, I swallowed.

Peter was standing by the window now. He beckoned me closer.

'The boy had to put his head out the sash window. Then

they lowered the window on to his neck like the blade of the guillotine.'

As he spoke I was visualising the scene. I peered through the window, down at the drive. I tried to imagine being trapped like that, my bottom helplessly served up to those inside, my cries audible to everyone outside.

'It is said that boys feared a Pop tanning far more than a birching from the headmaster,' Peter said, caressing the length of the cane. 'And, as you can see, a Pop cane is much nastier than an ordinary prefect's cane.'

The knuckles in the malacca looked savage. They would leave deep bruises where they struck.

'The president of Pop administered the caning while the others watched. Naturally, a boy would try to be brave and keep his composure but, after two or three dozen good hard strokes, the seat of his trousers – not to mention his dignity – would be in tatters.'

My mouth drifted open in silent horror. Two or three dozen strokes? He couldn't possibly be intending to subject poor little Martin to that! I would never be able to suppress my screams and the police would be banging on the door within minutes.

Peter raised the cane and brought it down with a ferocious swipe. It cleaved the air with a deep full-throated carving sound that made me jump.

With a dangerous smile, he laid the cane on the table and raised the window. My eyes bugged.

'Head out, boy,' he said.

I was terrified. My knees turned to water and I made my way to the window as though in a dream. I kept looking back at him, hoping he'd laugh and tell me he was just trying to scare me.

I realised I was still holding the topper and I blinked at it in surprise.

Peter gave me a withering look. 'You may set it on the desk,' he said, as though speaking to a feeble-minded child.

With trembling hands, I placed the hat on the desk and turned back to the window. I had to bend my knees to get my head down low enough to rest it over the windowsill. I felt like Anne Boleyn stretching her head out on the block. I caught the pungent scent of wood smoke from a chimney near by and I looked across at the houses on the other side of the village green. Lights shone in several windows. There was traffic noise in the distance and the voices of people talking not too far away. Anyone going for a stroll past the old vicarage would hear me.

Without a word Peter lowered the window down. It rested loosely enough on the back of my neck, but it would hold me in position. My chin pressed uncomfortably into the sill. The difference in temperature was disorienting. Outside, the air was bitterly cold, isolating me from the warmth of the room inside. I placed my hands on the edge of the windowsill for balance. At least he hadn't made me take my trousers down.

Then I heard the muffled swish of the cane as he sliced it through the air again. I flinched and gave a little yelp of fear, but the cane didn't strike. I was shaking all over, in utter terror over what he had described.

I turned my head as far to the left as I could and I could just make out his arm, raising the cane to strike. I knew it would be a real stroke this time and I held my breath and squeezed my eyes shut tightly, digging my nails into the windowsill.

The cane slashed through the air and into my bottom with astonishing force and I couldn't hold back the breathless cry of pain as my body tried to process the unusual sensation of the Pop cane. It had the penetrating thud of a much heavier implement, and the knuckles in the wood made the impact even worse.

The pain began to swell and crest until I thought I couldn't bear it. I bounced on my heels, trying to will the sting away. My nails gouged into the windowsill and I gritted my teeth, reminding myself that I was a boy.

Boys don't cry, I thought, desperately needing courage. I repeated it in my head like a mantra. *Boys don't cry, boys don't cry, boysdon'tcrydon'tcrydon'tcry . . .*

There was no placement tap, so I wasn't prepared for the next stroke. My right foot flew up behind me, shielding my bottom. The struggle to keep silent took all my willpower. In my mind the shadowy village dissolved and I was looking out over School Yard at Eton College. It bustled with activity as the other boys went about their business, oblivious to my disgrace. If I made a sound they would look up and see me. I couldn't shame myself by yelping after only one or two strokes.

'Get those feet out of the way, oik,' said Peter scornfully. 'I can't cane you if you're writhing like a cut worm. If you can't take it properly, it's likely to become a very much longer caning.'

I instantly stamped my foot back into place on the floor. The position was ingenious. It was impossible for me to straighten my legs and lock them into place. Nor could I simply lie across the sill and surrender to the beating. I held my breath, flinching in anticipation.

Again, there was no warning tap before the cane attacked again, knocking the wind out of me. I struggled as much as the position would allow, holding my foot up behind me to deflect further attack until my tormentor snapped at me to remove it.

I tried to be stoic, but the next stroke wrenched a howl of agony from me.

'Your behaviour is unseemly,' Peter said. 'Don't disgrace yourself further by putting on a display for the whole school.'

My face burnt with shame and my breathing grew fast and shallow as I awaited the next stroke. I couldn't un-see the image Peter had painted in my mind. A boy's trousers shredded by the relentless slashing Pop cane, his face stained with tears of pain and humiliation. He wouldn't be showing off those marks as proudly as he would a simple six of the best from the headmaster.

The next one was the hardest of the lot, but somehow I managed to gut it out without yelping. The well-aimed stroke fell just at the tender crease where the bottom and thighs meet. I clawed at the windowsill, scraping flecks of paint loose as the scorching line flared and intensified until I thought I would faint.

I gasped for breath as it burnt and throbbed, hissing through my teeth and tensing for another whack. The suspense lengthened and my fear intensified with every second I was made to wait.

But then I felt Peter's hand by my throat and he raised the window. 'In you come,' he said gruffly.

I scrambled to my feet instantly.

'Not pleasant, is it, boy?'

'No,' I panted.

He smiled and slammed the window. It thunked shut like the chopper's axe burying itself in the block.

'That's just a little taste. That's what you can expect the next time you go crying to Fleming like a girl.'

I melted with relief and genuine gratitude. I wanted to kiss his feet for sparing me. I could scarcely conceive of taking any more and yet boys had taken dozens of such strokes through the years. The idea made me dizzy. 'Thank you, Carruthers,' I said.

He snorted. 'I hope you don't think that was your punishment, oik. No, that was just a warning for next time.'

My heart sank. He was a sadistic one, this Carruthers.

'You're due a bloody good hiding, Shepherd. And you'll get one. But first I'll address your laziness and indolence in neglecting to clean my study.' Peter pointed to the centre of the room. 'Stand there.'

With weak legs, I did as I was told. Peter rummaged in the wardrobe while I fidgeted, straightening my jacket and shifting my feet back and forth. I didn't dare rub my bottom.

Peter found what he was looking for very quickly. It was a slipper – a heavy battered plimsoll. He smacked it imperiously against his palm.

I told myself to be thankful I wasn't getting the full Pop tanning. The slipper would have a wicked bite, but it couldn't be anything like the malacca cane.

'Touch your toes.'

I bit back a whimper. I hated that position. It tautened the flesh of my bottom, making the punishment sharper and even more painful. But I bent down and placed my fingertips on the tops of my smartly polished shoes.

'Bend over properly, boy. Grab your ankles.'

I took hold of my ankles, gritting my teeth. I felt so exposed and vulnerable.

Peter tapped the slipper against my bottom. It was extremely tender from the cruel treatment at the window and I cringed like a beaten dog at each little slap. I took a deep breath, bracing myself.

The slipper exploded against my bottom with a loud meaty whack. I choked back a cry and kept my legs straight. The rubber sole of the shoe imparted a brutal sting, but I resisted the urge to grab my bottom.

The next three strokes came in rapid succession, hurting terribly. With each stroke I bent my knees a little more, until I was quite out of position.

'Back in place, snotty,' Peter growled. 'Right down. Come on, show some pluck.'

I turned scarlet as I straightened my legs and clutched my trousers. The taunts and scathing tone of his Carruthers persona were so unfamiliar to me. He'd never played a bully before. It was humiliating and frightening, but in an exhilarating edgy way. I didn't fully understand it, but somehow I knew that I could endure more of this as a boy than I ever could as a girl. Peter seemed to know it too.

Again Peter applied the slipper. He allowed very little time between strokes, which made it harder to take. I straightened my legs when he barked at me to do so, but there was no way I could maintain the position for long.

'Feeling these, are we, boy?'

'Yes, Carruthers,' I whimpered.

'Good. Then I may be getting through to you.'

The onslaught continued until I had lost count of the number of strokes. Again and again the slipper descended, painting its distinctive imprint on my cheeks.

By the end I was yelping with total abandon, not caring if I sounded like a girl or not. I clung to my dignity as a boy, not breaking position too badly and not reaching back to shield my bottom. I didn't beg him to stop, either. And I didn't cry.

Finally, Peter stopped.

Thinking it was over at last, I stood up, stumbling a little.

'What do you think you're doing? I told you that was for failing to clean my study properly. I'm not finished with you yet.'

I lowered my head.

Peter's face was a mask of cruel glee as he fetched a rattan school cane from the wardrobe. It was long and dense, but at least it wasn't the Pop cane.

'Back in position,' he ordered.

With a soft moan, I resumed the position.

'This time you can drop your trousers, boy,' he said. 'And your underpants.'

I gasped.

'You heard me. You're a cry-baby, Shepherd. And cry-babies are punished on the bare. Now take them down.'

'But, Carruthers –'

'Now, boy. I want to see those baby-cheeks. Drop your trousers or I'll do it for you.'

I blushed so hard my scalp tingled. But I wasn't about to disobey. With a mournful sigh I bent to the task, unbuckling my belt and unfastening my trousers. I held them up for a moment before letting them slip down to the floor. They puddled around my feet and I stood before him in my boy's underpants. Putting them on earlier had felt sexy and transgressive, but now I was self-conscious. I knew Peter was thoroughly enjoying my discomfort and I hesitated only another few seconds before hooking my thumbs into the elastic and pushing the cotton underwear down my thighs.

'Feet apart.'

I managed to shuffle my feet away from each other until they were about twelve inches apart. Then I felt the cane tapping against my backside. I winced. I already felt well and truly beaten. My bottom burnt and tingled from the assault of the Pop cane and the slipper. The school cane would be excruciating after that. And I knew he would use it hard. After all, he wasn't punishing *me*; he was punishing a boy who had broken the schoolboy code by telling tales. No matter how much you were bullied, no matter what was done to you, you *did not* squeal. As always, he had set me up nicely.

'Six strokes,' Peter pronounced. 'Stay in position. You know I'll repeat strokes if you give me an excuse. Don't you, you little worm?'

'Yes, Carruthers,' I whispered.

'This is for running to Fleming. Before each stroke you're going to say, "Please teach me not to be a cry-baby".'

I moaned with shame. Oh, God, this was torture! I swallowed and plucked up my courage. I could do this.

'Please teach me not to be a cry-baby,' I said.

The cane sliced into me instantly, painting a line of fire across my already sore backside. I gritted my teeth, grimly determined not to make a sound. The words I had to speak were degrading enough; I didn't need the added dishonour of blubbing.

'Again,' Peter directed.

'Please teach me – not to be a cry-baby.'

Another savage stroke met my aching flesh, but I kept my legs straight and my cries to myself. I swallowed and spoke my line again.

The third stroke made me hiss, but I forced my legs to stay rooted to the floor. My fingers were gripping my trousers so hard they were shaking. I felt tears pricking my eyes and I willed them away.

The final three strokes steadily increased in intensity and I knew he was trying to break me. But I stuck to my resolve, gasping and biting back my yelps of pain. I spoke the awful phrase six times, feeling as though I was being brainwashed. By the time it was over I was a trembling mess.

'Very good, Shepherd,' Peter said, a trace of pride in his voice. 'Get up. Get dressed.'

I hurriedly adjusted my clothing, eager to let poor Martin escape the evil clutches of Carruthers. I stood before him, my eyes on the floor.

'Right, boy,' he said. 'This time if Fleming asks you about the state of your girlish little backside you'll tell him how much you deserved it, won't you?'

'Yes, Carruthers.'

'Excellent. And I expect to find my study habitable tomorrow.'

'Yes, Carruthers.'

I turned to go, but a lift of his eyebrows summoned me back.

'Isn't there something you're forgetting, boy?'

I looked up, confused and worried that there was more to come.

He raised his eyebrows.

Suddenly understanding, I lowered my head again. 'Thank you, Carruthers,' I murmured.

He smiled. 'You're welcome, boy. Now, off with you.'

I headed for the door, snatching up my hat as I went. I scampered down the stairs, eager to get out of my tormentor's sight, and sank back against the wall outside the study. I felt drunk. Drowning in that confusing cocktail of embarrassment, arousal and shame. I covered my face with my hands. It was so flushed it felt feverish. I knew my bottom was bright red and I couldn't wait to look at it in the mirror.

I heard Peter's footsteps on the stairs and I braced myself for the encounter. When I peeled my hands away from my face he was standing by the clock, grinning cheerfully at me.

'You OK?'

I buried my face again. 'Oh, God,' I moaned. 'I don't know if I can face you again!'

'Oh? That's a shame. Because, while that little roleplay may be over, you still have your customer to deal with. Rent boy.'

I didn't think it was possible to blush any harder. My face felt scorched.

He opened the door to the library. 'Inside,' he said, beaming wickedly.

I obeyed, a lamb to the slaughter.

'Now then, my lad,' he said, his tone different. 'That's as far as I ever got in school. With you, I can go much further.'

I recalled some of the things Shaun had said in his mock obscene call. I hid my face again, horrified.

Peter was positively revelling in my embarrassment. 'Yes, that's exactly right,' he teased, as though reading my thoughts. 'Trousers down.'

With nervous fingers, I unbuttoned my trousers again and let them slide down my legs.

'Over the arm of the sofa.'

I shuffled to the spot he indicated and bent down over it. I grabbed a cushion and shoved my face into it.

Behind me, I heard Peter chuckle. Then I felt his hands in the waistband of my underpants. He pulled them down slowly over my punished bottom, making me wince at the pain.

'Very nice,' he commented, running a finger along the tramlines. 'I do like a lad who can take a proper caning.'

At the sound of his zip, I realised just how wet I was. Endorphins were pinging around in my head and my sex was screaming for release. I was desperate for him to touch me, to take me.

I heard the soft pop of a plastic top coming off a pot and then there was a cold oily sensation between my cheeks. He eased them apart with his thumbs, exposing me completely. His finger sought the little rosebud of my anus and I whimpered into the cushion as he swirled his finger around the puckered ring, probing. Coaxing it open. I couldn't stop myself clenching at the intrusive sensation. But the determined finger pushed inside, up where no one had ever been. It must have been obvious to Peter that I was a virgin there.

'Rent boys get buggered, lad. Ever done it before?'

I moaned something I hoped he would take for 'No', clutching the edges of the cushion at his soft laughter.

He withdrew his finger and positioned himself behind me. 'Come on, legs apart,' he said, gently smacking the insides of my thighs.

I wanted it. But I also wanted the floor to open up and swallow me. I spread my legs obediently, as much as the trousers around my ankles would allow.

His cock pressed against the tiny opening and I tightened up involuntarily.

'Relax,' he said, placing a warm hand on my lower back to hold me down. 'Don't clench.'

I forced myself to do as he said, whimpering at the intrusive pressure. He pushed cautiously, with soft little thrusts, until at last the head was inside. I cried out, more out of fear than pain.

'That's it,' he said, pleased at my surrender.

I dug my fingers into the cushion, shuddering as he slid the length of his cock up inside the virgin passageway. The sensation was completely alien to me and impossible to process. I couldn't decide if it was pleasure or pain or both. I trembled with shame and exhilaration at the invasion.

He thrust himself in up to the hilt, his pelvis smacking against my welted backside. I yelped as he began to fuck me in earnest.

I tried to imagine having a cock, feeling it rub against the arm of the sofa as he thrust himself in and out of me. Would he reach round and grab it? Squeeze it and fondle it to bring his little rent boy off as well?

Peter wasn't tender at all. He twisted a hand roughly in my hair, shoving my face down even further into the cushion. 'Dirty boy,' he said with perverse affection. 'So tight inside.'

I was grateful for the position, as I would have died had he made me face him. My bottom stung with each thrust, as his skin met my skin. I cried out at the pain, but they mutated into muffled animal sounds through the cushion.

He slid in and out of me with ease, pounding against my punished flesh. Over and over. The friction against the sofa was stimulating me as well and I adjusted myself to get the maximum benefit from it. But Peter sensed my movement and he reached round with his hand to pleasure me himself, all the while talking to me as a boy.

At last I felt the spasm of his climax and he clutched at my sex. Within seconds, he forced me to my own shattering orgasm. Spasm after spasm battered me from within and for a moment it seemed like the pleasure would overwhelm me. It was almost more than I could take. I screamed into the cushion, liberated by the primal release.

I sagged over the arm of the sofa, panting and spent, unable to move.

Peter withdrew himself and I heard him doing up his trousers. I lifted my face from the cushion, but I still couldn't get up. Dazed, I stared at the stitching in the upholstery of the sofa.

I reached around and gingerly touched my bottom. 'Oww,' I groaned.

Peter was still standing over me and eventually I lifted my eyes from the cushion to look at him. He placed a handful of twenty-pound notes on the sofa in front of me.

'Worth every penny,' he said.

Eighteen

Dear Angela,
I understand that Dr Morrison has become increasingly concerned about the progress of your research, and that despite repeated requests you have failed to provide satisfactory evidence of the data that you have gathered for at least three months.

As you know, your supervisor is required to make regular progress reports to the funding body, and the present situation jeopardises both your own project and the Department's prospects of securing funding for other students in future. At this point in your research, you should be collecting your results into final form for presentation in your thesis. If you are to remain in good standing, we need you to present drafts of at least two chapters of your thesis within the next four weeks.

This letter is the final warning stage before we will need to report your lack of progress to the Dean for disciplinary action.
Yours sincerely,
Prof. Richard Chalcroft
Head of Department

I folded the letter with trembling hands and slid it back inside the torn envelope. I felt an awful sinking sensation in the pit of my stomach. Thank God Peter hadn't intercepted the letter. It was incontrovertible evidence of a crime, laying out my guilt in cold impersonal writing. Like a bad report card you knew that you would have to show your parents eventually. The longer you put it off, the more worked up you got and the worse you knew it would be. And as the anxiety began to spiral out of control you had to ask yourself whether it wouldn't be better just to face the music and have it done.

Lowering myself into the nearest chair, I considered my options.

Over the past few weeks I'd had a succession of concerned emails from Dr Morrison and I'd filed them away, promising myself I'd respond to them later. I never did. It wasn't as if I hadn't been working at all. I stuck to my schedule. Well, more or less. Naturally, I had lapses and I bore the cost when they caught up with me. Stroke by stroke. Ah, the stories that birching block could tell . . .

I winced at a phantom cut of the birch and made my decision. I couldn't show the letter to Peter. I would have to reply to it; that went without saying. But Peter didn't have to know about it.

Except that he *would* know about it. He didn't keep such a close eye on me any more; he trusted me now to be honest. I couldn't lie to him. But was it really lying? A lie of omission, perhaps, but not a complete falsehood. Where was the line?

I knew that, in not sharing the situation with Peter, I'd be excluding my most powerful ally. He was a professor himself, though at a different university. He knew how these things worked and could give the best advice. He could possibly even plead on my behalf. But would he? I wavered between an awful choice and its awful alternative.

What could I possibly say to the department head? That my computer had died? My dog ate my homework? He was bound to have heard every lame excuse a student could concoct. All I could do was admit I'd wasted my time and everyone else's and promise to deliver the drafts of my thesis as soon as possible. It was a substantial document, but it was riddled with holes. There were plenty of chapters, just none that were finished. None that were in any way ready for presentation. It would be a hard letter to write.

The situation wasn't hopeless. It would be unpleasant and embarrassing, but a sincere apology should mollify my supervisor and the department head. I could dust myself off, pull my socks up and get to work with a will. It was Peter I was in agony over. I paced the house, vacillating between telling him and not. I knew I had to decide before he got home from work.

Several times I found myself hovering by the phone, on the brink of calling Courtney for advice. But I didn't want to make her an accomplice. I had no one to turn to and I was beginning to feel wretchedly, crushingly alone when the solution came to me like a breath of cool air on a sweltering day. There was a compromise. I would hide the letter for now and make my apologies to the funding body. I would apply myself and submit the required drafts and once I was out of the woods I would show the letter to Peter. He would be cross and I didn't doubt that he would punish me. But by then I would be out of academic danger. Surely that would be mitigating.

I took the letter out and read it again. 'Final warning stage before disciplinary action.' In spite of the sickening dread it triggered, the key phrase still made my stomach swoop with excitement. My face felt hot and for one crazy moment I entertained the idea of going to Professor Chalcroft and making not-so-subtle innuendos about 'disciplinary action' I'd accept in exchange for more time.

Shaking my head, I slipped the letter into a drawer of the nightstand. Then I went to the schoolroom with my laptop and spent an hour staring at the cursor as it blinked and blinked and blinked.

Nineteen

'I have a surprise for you,' said Peter. He was wearing a white shirt and tie, looking very smart.

I smiled warily. I didn't know if it was the kind of surprise that was a treat for him or for me. 'What is it?'

'It's a surprise,' he repeated, as though that explained everything. But he wasn't smiling. 'First I want you to put on a school shirt and school knickers. Nothing else.'

'OK,' I said, puzzled and a little apprehensive.

When I'd done that he told me to close my eyes. His arms reached around me and I felt him fastening a skirt around my waist. The tie was next. Then the blazer. He guided me a few paces to where I knew the mirror was and told me I could open my eyes.

My breath caught in my throat. Staring back at me from the mirror was the girl I'd been at Ravenscroft. Nostalgia closed my throat as I looked at the uniform I'd worn for so many years. I stepped closer, admiring the green striped tie and school crest.

I stroked the badge fondly, tracing the soft embroidery with my finger. A green shield with two black ravens in profile in a silver circle. A silver scroll unfurled beneath, displaying the Latin motto. My finger stopped its caress abruptly.

Initium sapientiae timor poenae. Fear of punishment is the beginning of wisdom. The last word had been changed from the original. It should have been *ignorantiae*, not *poenae*. Ignorance not punishment.

Peter straightened my lapels, brushing me off. 'It was a nice enough motto, but I think this one is more fitting, don't you?' He said it so solemnly that I felt my skin prickle. His demeanour unsettled me. What was he playing at?

'Are we going somewhere?'

'I'm taking you to school.'

Though I knew the answer, I had to ask. 'To Ravenscroft?'

His cryptic expression told me all I needed to know.

'It's the holidays,' I reminded him. 'There won't be anyone there.'

'No one who'll look askance at the uniform, at any rate. Now come on.'

As I realised he was serious I began to get nervous. 'Please,' I begged, my face colouring. 'I can't go out dressed like this!'

His eyes narrowed. 'Would you prefer to go with a sore bottom?'

I bit my lip. 'No, sir,' I said, succumbing to his authoritarian tone.

He held my hand as we crossed the street to the Tube station. It made me feel like an overprotected child and the atmosphere of disquiet intensified. The uniform wasn't a light-hearted gift; there was something else going on. I glanced around with the paranoid certainty that everyone was watching me. And when we got to the crowded platform I couldn't stand still.

Not wanting any of the other passengers to see, I crossed my arms over my chest, trying to hide the blazer badge. With its altered motto it felt like a flashing neon pin that screamed, 'Pervert!'

In front of us an old man with outdated sideburns leant heavily on a walking stick, staring off into space. Next to him a stout woman with a prematurely aged face was trying to mediate a dispute between her two squabbling sticky-fingered children. An attractive young couple behind us chattered animatedly in French. None of them was paying me any attention, but Peter fixed that.

'Stand up straight, young lady,' he said loudly. 'Hands at your sides. I expect better posture than that.'

Everyone turned to look in our direction. Even the children suspended their argument. I straightened myself, but heat blossomed in my cheeks and I pointedly avoided making eye contact with the watchers. I had never known the platform to be so crowded before. I could almost imagine Peter had arranged for that too.

I put my arms down and stared at my feet.

Peter lifted my chin. 'Head up,' he continued, like a punctilious deportment teacher. 'Don't slouch.'

My eyes flicked up to the board and noted with dismay that the next train wasn't due for another six minutes. An eternity. Peter saw it too and his eyes gleamed. There was nothing he enjoyed more than discomfiting me. But again, there was something more than pleasure behind his eyes this time.

Gradually, my arms drifted back up until they were hiding the badge once more. As soon as I realised I dropped them to my sides again. But Peter had noticed the lapse.

'Do you want a smacked bottom, my girl?' he asked, again in a much louder voice than necessary.

Mortified, I pleaded with my eyes. Now even more people were staring. Behind me the French boy sniggered and I heard him translating what Peter had said for his girlfriend. My face burnt so hot it was painful.

'Well?'

'No,' I whispered, cringing.

'No *what*?'

'No, sir.'

'Well, I'm not so sure. I think a smacked bottom is just what you need.' He took me by the hand and led me forcefully to the nearest bench. Still holding my hand, he sat down in front of a giant advertisement for the Royal Ballet.

'Right, young lady,' he said sternly, enunciating the words with crisp and awful precision. 'Over my knee.'

My legs threatened to buckle and I stared at him in abject horror. He couldn't mean it. He couldn't be serious. Not here. Surely he wouldn't . . .

He didn't tell me a second time. He hauled me across his lap and delivered a sharp volley of swats to the seat of my Ravenscroft skirt.

I buried my face in my hands, desperately praying the train would come early and take everyone on the platform away with it. I strained to hear it over the staccato smacks.

'For propriety's sake,' he said loftily, 'I won't lift your skirt. But any more misbehaviour will earn you a long hard session on your bare bottom when we get home. Do you understand?'

'Yes, sir.'

'Am I going to have any more trouble from you?'

'No, sir.'

'Very well. Up you get.'

I scrambled to my feet and clung to him, hiding my face in his chest, determined not to emerge from hiding until the train came rattling into the station. I would die if I had to look anyone in the eye.

But Peter wasn't having that. He made me stand and face him. 'Now, apologise for your behaviour,' he said.

I didn't hesitate. 'I'm sorry, sir,' I said, my voice a pale ghost of itself.

I could feel the eyes of the children on me. They had to be shocked that someone my age was subject to such discipline. Their mother clucked her tongue, making an object lesson of me. The French couple was thoroughly enjoying my shame as well. I caught their superior smiles and I had to wonder if they were into *une bonne fessée* themselves.

The noisy arrival of the train had never been so welcome. The witnesses to my disgrace climbed aboard and I rooted my feet to the ground, hoping Peter wouldn't make me board the same train. Silly me.

I suffered the children's vulgar staring as I stood clutching the stanchion and stared through the doors at the rushing blur of the concrete tunnel. I felt the cool air on my bare thighs above my knee socks. Out of the corner of my eye I saw the old man watching me with smug satisfaction. Probably glad to see that there were still some parents who believed in old-fashioned discipline. The French couple was still eyeing me when we reached our stop.

Though I knew the way, Peter kept hold of my hand and led me to the school. His childish treatment regressed me. It was no roleplay; I *was* a Ravenscroft pupil again. And as the familiar asymmetrical roofline hove into view a thousand memories came swarming back. We rounded the corner and I noted with a little sadness that the immense oak tree was no longer there. It had dominated the front courtyard, partially obscuring the building. Without its cover, the Victorian gothic façade was less imposing than I remembered. Bays of arched triptych windows sparkled in the sunlight, surrounded by multicoloured brickwork. Clusters of brick chimney stacks soared above richly carved gables. It was hard to believe the fussy over-decorated school had ever felt like a prison.

I expected to find the doors locked, and was surprised when they swung open at my touch. I remembered my very first day and the terror I had felt on entering the place. The strange new faces and the grownup responsibilities that awaited me within the massive walls were overwhelming. I couldn't even begin to comprehend the trauma I would have experienced if I'd been left on my own as a boarder.

The corridor was dark and I stepped hesitantly inside. My low-heeled shoes clacked conspicuously on the parquet floor and the noise startled me. Self-conscious, I shifted my weight to my toes. A few paces down on the right was the headmaster's office, where twice I had failed to be caned.

'Where was Mr Chancellor's office?' Peter asked.

I nodded towards the heavy door. 'Just there.'

'The scene of the crime,' he mused.

I couldn't resist going up to the door. Again, I was sure it would be locked. But it gave when I twisted the knob and I smiled delightedly at Peter. He didn't return my smile.

The anteroom brought back another flood of memories. I thought of the time I had sat under the watchful eye of Mrs Willis, swinging my legs and nervously waiting to be called in. My chagrin at the outcome of that meeting had cast a pall over the rest of my school career.

Somehow I found myself drifting to the big oak door of the inner sanctum.

'Knock,' Peter said.

My hand seemed to remember the anxiety as well. The unique sense of dread at requesting entrance to the place of punishment. But there was no one there. Peter was just playing with me. Willing to play along, I raised my hand and rapped softly, obediently.

'Come in.'

The voice jolted me. I stared at Peter, wide eyed, convinced I'd heard a ghost.

'Don't keep him waiting,' said Peter.

As if in a dream, I turned the handle and quietly pushed the door open. My heart stopped. Mr Chancellor sat behind his desk, just as in my dreams, regarding me solemnly. I couldn't breathe.

'Well, don't just stand there, girl,' said the headmaster sharply. 'Come in.'

In slow motion, I did as I was told. Peter slipped in behind me and stood by the door.

I gaped at Mr Chancellor. It had only been a few years, but they had wrought their changes. He was more distinguished; his hair was greyer, his face more lined. And he no longer wore the kindly look I had found so frustrating in the past. He looked at me with narrowed eyes and I felt a rush of fear and excitement.

'Harker,' he said, shaking his head in disapproval. 'Again.'

I glanced over at Peter, but his expression was unreadable.

'Look at me, girl,' Mr Chancellor said tersely.

Like a soldier on the parade ground, I snapped to attention, trying to control my breathing. This couldn't be real.

Mr Chancellor frowned at an open file on his desk. 'I have received a disturbing report about you, Harker.' He removed the top page from the file and began to read. ' "I understand that Dr Morrison has become increasingly concerned about the progress of your research." '

My stomach clenched on hearing the familiar words. Blood pounded in my ears and I burnt with shame as I stood before him, my deceit laid bare.

'"Despite repeated requests you have failed to provide satisfactory evidence of the data that you have gathered for at least three months." '

I wanted to beg him to stop, but I didn't dare interrupt. Though I knew every word of the letter by heart, hearing it from my headmaster was excruciating. I was thankful Peter was behind me. There was no way I could have faced him. I listened aghast as Mr Chancellor went through the entire letter, wincing in anticipation of the phrase about disciplinary action. He emphasised those two words with tangible significance and my insides churned with unease.

He finished reading and laid the letter aside. With a sigh he removed his glasses and regarded me with a look of such disappointment that I thought I would burst into tears. Several seconds passed in unbearable silence while he shook his head sadly.

'I always had such high hopes for you, Harker.'

I opened my mouth with no idea of what to say. What *could* I say? Any attempt to explain myself would be hopelessly inadequate. It would only reinforce the awful reality that I needed stricter discipline.

'You've been punished before for neglecting your schoolwork. But now it seems you've resorted to deception in a misguided attempt to avoid further punishment.'

Deception. The word was crushing. All the more crushing because he was right. My lower lip quivered like a child's and tears welled behind my eyes. Defeated, I shut my mouth and stared in despair at the floor.

'And yet,' he continued. 'There is no question you deserve further punishment. Such flagrant dishonesty demands it.'

Again I searched for words, but nothing would come. Huge sorrowful tears rolled down my cheeks and I scrubbed them away, too ashamed to make eye contact.

He glanced once more at the letter. 'I'm afraid this has its roots in your time at Ravenscroft. Your misbehaviour didn't receive the punishment it warranted, and you came to think you were immune. You got into bad habits.'

I sniffled piteously, my fingers twisting and twining in anguish. I couldn't believe this was the same man who had let me off truancy and outrageous insolence with a scolding and a suspension.

'Look at me, Harker.'

Reluctantly, I raised my head, wiping my eyes with the back of my sleeve like some wretched Dickensian orphan. I had never felt so forlorn.

'Things are different this time. This time I have the authority I need to teach you a lesson.' Mr Chancellor looked over at Peter and they exchanged a meaningful glance. My headmaster's grey eyes, once so sympathetic, were now flinty. 'In a few minutes I am going to cane you.'

I'd been waiting all my life to hear him say that to me. And now it felt like the fulfilment of a prophecy. Light-headed, I clasped my hands in an attitude of penitence. I opened my mouth to protest, but I didn't have the courage to speak.

He continued. 'But first I want you to spend some time thinking about it. Turn around and face the wall. Now kneel. Hands on your head. Nose touching the wall.'

Through it all I hadn't said a word. When I finally spoke it was in a dead voice. 'Yes, sir.'

My sense of shame deepened as I adopted the ignominious position. The parquet floor was hard and unyielding against my knees and I hissed with pain. I laced my fingers on top of my head and leant forwards to put my nose against the dusty wall, terrified of what I knew was coming.

'It is often the case,' said Mr Chancellor, 'that a girl learns to manipulate authority figures. She talks her way out of deserved punishments and takes advantage of lenience, exploiting any weakness she finds. It's impossible to maintain discipline under such circumstances.'

My skin grew cold as I listened. This was not the

Ravenscroft that I had known as a schoolgirl. My headmaster had become a strict disciplinarian.

He didn't acknowledge me further. My tears continued to flow freely and I felt them trickling all the way down my throat, into my collar. I didn't dare break position to wipe them away.

Uncomfortable as his reprimand was, the floor was worse. And I felt it ever more intensely as the minutes dragged on. My thighs trembled from the effort of balancing on my knees and my shoulders ached from the position of my arms. I wanted more than anything to beg him to let me up, but his talk of manipulation made me hold my tongue.

I heard a scrape as Mr Chancellor pushed back his chair and stood up. His soft footsteps crossed the room and a cabinet door creaked open. Some muffled sounds followed and my heart begin to race.

I gritted my teeth and tried to think of anything but the degrading position and the distress it was causing me. But I knew that once he let me up it would be time for the caning. And, just when I thought I couldn't take it any longer, Mr Chancellor ordered me to my feet.

I stood awkwardly on legs of rubber, bracing my hands on the wall to keep from falling. The headmaster flexed the cane in his hands. Then he beckoned me forwards. Part of me expected him to don a black cap and sentence me to death. Part of me wanted him to. I could have climbed the steps to the scaffold more easily than I could cross the few feet between us.

'Please . . .'

'It's no use pleading with me, girl. You are the agent of your own disgrace.'

The undeniable truth heightened my shame and underlined the inevitability of what was about to happen. My tears had stopped. Despite his austere displeasure I could see his fondness for me, his genuine desire for me to succeed. I was overcome by the fierce desire to show him that he could be proud of me again.

His focused intensity compressed the room, creating a

bubble around us, tuning out everything but my unworthy behaviour and the means to correct it.

I had come full circle; this was my second chance.

Standing before Mr Chancellor in my Ravenscroft uniform, in the same office where years before I'd tried to provoke him, I submitted at last to my fate.

He indicated the edge of the desk and I placed myself behind it obediently.

'Remove your blazer,' he said.

The buttons proved a challenge for my unsteady fingers, but I untangled them enough to perform the simple function and slipped out of the blazer. At his instruction I folded it and placed it on the desk. I was acutely aware that each carefully choreographed step brought me one step closer to the caning I had always deserved but never received.

'Raise your skirt.'

My hands fluttered to the hem of my smartly pressed bottle-green skirt. Trembling, I lifted the hem at the back, revealing my regulation school knickers. My knees bumped against each other nervously and I locked my legs in place to still them.

Mr Chancellor moved one step away from the desk. 'Now take down your knickers.'

A rush of heat swept through my entire body. It was the penultimate step. I faltered.

He frowned.

A medley of words and phrases jostled for place in my brain. *Deception. Flagrant dishonesty. Disciplinary action.*

With a moan of surrender I slid them down to my knees, unveiling the vulnerable unmarked bottom he had never seen.

The headmaster offered no further direction. He simply stood silent, waiting, the cane flexed in his hands.

I blushed deeply and took hold of the desk, gripping it tightly to still the shaking in my hands. I looked up at him, a soundless entreaty.

'You know what comes next, girl.'

At last, leaning forwards, I stretched myself out across the expanse of smooth polished wood.

The meticulous ritual was familiar and reassuring. A dance I knew by heart, but that still challenged me. While my bottom was no stranger to exposure or to punishment, the process was always powerful and it always affected me. The preparation was the hardest part, concentrating my mind on both the punishment and the reason for it. With Mr Chancellor it was even more powerful. The dread I felt was profound. The hesitance, fear and embarrassment. And I knew my submission was all the more alluring for my reluctance.

I had gone back in time to reclaim an experience that should have been mine years before. Lying across the desk, my bare bottom was helpless before Mr Chancellor at last. An offering.

He raised the cane and tapped it gently against the smooth pale skin. I tensed involuntarily and he waited for me to relax again.

'How many, girl?' he asked suddenly.

I released the breath I'd been holding in anticipation of the first stroke. 'Sir?'

'How many, girl?'

I blanched and stared up at him. What was the correct answer to that? Too many and he might give me all of them. Too few and he was likely to add more. I floundered, trying to decide what was fair.

How many would Peter give me?

I'd almost forgotten he was there. My eyes stole across the room, where he stood by the door, watching my face intently. But he offered me no assistance. He was merely a silent witness to my punishment. He wouldn't interfere.

My eyes watered again as I contemplated the seriousness of the offence. Deception. It was a test. Peter had deliberately regressed me to the Ravenscroft girl who'd toyed with her headmaster out of morbid curiosity. A schoolgirl who made promises and didn't keep them. A girl who deserved severe punishment. And knew it.

With a shudder of guilt I suddenly knew the answer. I took a deep breath.

'All I've ever deserved,' I whispered. 'Sir.'

Mr Chancellor nodded gravely, understanding. He took up his position and laid the cane against my bottom. He tapped once, twice, and then drew back.

The cane whipped down faster than I'd have thought possible and I sucked in a breath as it struck. Hard. Harder than any stroke I'd ever felt before. The searing parallel lines began to form, blazing, across both cheeks as I fought to steady myself, breathing deeply. I didn't count. I didn't want to know.

He measured out another stroke and it lashed into me with the fearsome velocity of a snake striking, so fast I didn't have time to flinch. I cried out, writhing as the pain washed over me, engulfing me.

Mr Chancellor used his whole arm, stopping the downwards swoop at the last moment and ending with a ruthless little flick of his wrist. Each stroke landed with laudable and terrible precision.

With consummate skill, he aimed and struck again. I managed to swallow my cry as it lashed into me, but the next tore a strangled sob from my throat. The one that followed was harder still, staggeringly severe. I kicked wildly, throwing my right leg up and arching it high over my back, sheltering my agonised bottom.

Mr Chancellor didn't speak. He simply waited for me to compose myself. Embarrassed at my display, I dropped my leg and rooted both feet in place, determined not to move again. I lifted my head, finding Peter's gaze across the room and holding it. I would make him proud.

In complete silence the caning continued and I accepted each stroke as my due. I hissed through my teeth and couldn't suppress a yelp at an exceptionally hard stroke, but I did not break position. It was a matter of honour. I had my second chance, and I was determined to take it. But it wasn't Peter or even Mr Chancellor who would judge whether I had.

A strange calm settled over me as I surrendered to the battering waves of pain, riding the peak and trough of each one, separate and unique. I locked my eyes on to Peter's, and was convinced I could see my pain reflected there.

The cane rose and fell and my mind unfolded its wings. I felt myself climbing, flying, soaring high above the pain. And, when at last it became so intense that it morphed into pleasure, I threw myself off the edge and flew. It carried me up and away, out of my guilt, delivering me.

The birch – what's left of it – slashes into my bottom, scorching me.

'Twenty-three,' I count, my voice ragged and hoarse from crying. 'Th-thank you, s-sir.'

My words are barely intelligible through my unrestrained sobbing. The floor in front of me is wet with my tears. I writhe and gasp over the block, sniffling pitifully. One more to go. Just one more.

It falls at last.

I have to take several huge gulping breaths of air before I can count. 'Twenty-four. Thank you, sir.'

I flinch as Peter's finger traces the punished flesh, inspecting the marks. I don't need to see to know it's a thorough job. It feels as though I've been flayed alive and I know I'll be marked for days. I can picture the scores of red welts criss-crossing my backside, speckled with angry purple beestings where the buds have cut me.

'All right, Angie,' he says. 'You may get up.'

I stumble to my feet, unable to stand without help. Disoriented, I blink helplessly at him for a moment before falling into his arms. Tears stream down my face, soaking his shirt as I pour out my suffering and contrition.

He holds me tightly, resolutely, my tether to reality. The catharsis is nearly as intense as the birching. It leaves me feeling completely drained. But purged. The punishment was severe, but I can't argue that it wasn't deserved. And now that it's over I can begin again with a clean slate.

As my tears subside, he guides me to the bathroom, where he'll clean me up and care for me. The worst of the pain is diminishing and soon there will be a pleasant warmth beneath the burn. I've learnt my lesson.

But discipline is a process. No single punishment elicits a permanent change. I'll slide again. And be brought back in line. And in between we'll play and I'll hate it and love hating it. And, when another severe punishment session is needed, I'll cut the switches and present him with the rod. I'll assume the position and take my stripes, shedding my guilt as I yelp and cry under the strokes. And afterwards I'll thank him. The pain in my bottom tells me he cares.

In spite of everything, it's all I've ever wanted.

Afterword

Apparently I'm the first Nexus author to pose for the cover of her own book. I blithely tossed the idea to the editor one day, expecting that he'd say no. But to my delight he thought it was a great idea – 'unprecedented and radical' – and encouraged me to do it.

I thought it would be simple: just find a friendly lap and someone else willing to push the button on the camera. A cute outfit. A little smacking to pinken my cheeks. Piece of cake, right? Ha.

Positioning the hand went something like this: 'OK, raise your arm a bit. Now turn it out. No, angle it down. Further. A little more. Can you flatten it a bit more? No, that's too much. I know it doesn't feel right; it just has to *look* right.'

We finally got the pose right, but the camera flash kept washing out our efforts. In order for the colour pink to show up at all my bottom had to be glowing red. It was proving a very painful endeavour. Especially once we realised the camera had been set on the wrong speed and we had to start from scratch.

For the second photoshoot we recruited an additional photographer to help with the positioning. And about two hours and fifty pictures later, the four of us thought we had a perfect cover shot. Unfortunately, it wouldn't fit into the Enthusiast series design. Back to the drawing board.

The day before the deadline for the cover art, we tried several different poses. And finally, we got it right. Of the hundred or so pictures we took, the designers were sure they could use one of them. We were happy, the editor was happy, and the people in the cover-design department were apparently 'a bit freaked by the full impact of a spanking in progress'.

Full impact indeed; my bottom was very sore – which is just as it should be.

All in a day's work, really.

Notes & Acknowledgements

Peter's archive is based on the Professor's (though he only has one volume of *My Secret Life*). All the films, books and periodicals described are real.

Angie's thesis was inspired by notes in Ian Gibson's excellent book, *The English Vice: Beating, Sex and Shame in Victorian England and After*. Much of the historical detail came from www.corpun.com and *A History of the Rod*, by the Reverend William M Cooper, BA.

There are too many people to thank, but two of them deserve special mention for their unique contributions. A big thank you to Bailey for her tireless camera work on three separate occasions. We finally got the cover shot in the end. And another thank you to Lucy McLean for providing the Glaswegian slang.

The leading publisher of fetish and adult fiction

TELL US WHAT YOU THINK!

Readers' ideas and opinions matter to us. Take a few minutes to fill in the questionnaire below and you'll be entered into a prize draw to win a year's worth of Nexus books (36 titles)

Terms and conditions apply – see end of questionnaire.

1. **Sex:** Are you male ☐ female ☐ a couple ☐?

2. **Age:** Under 21 ☐ 21–30 ☐ 31–40 ☐ 41–50 ☐ 51–60 ☐ over 60 ☐

3. **Where do you buy your Nexus books from?**

☐ A chain book shop. If so, which one(s)?

____

☐ An independent book shop. If so, which one(s)?

____

☐ A used book shop/charity shop

☐ Online book store. If so, which one(s)?

____

4. **How did you find out about Nexus books?**

☐ Browsing in a book shop

☐ A review in a magazine

☐ Online

☐ Recommendation

☐ Other __________________________________

5. **In terms of settings, which do you prefer? (Tick as many as you like)**

☐ Down to earth and as realistic as possible

☐ Historical settings. If so, which period do you prefer?

____

☐ Fantasy settings – barbarian worlds
☐ Completely escapist/surreal fantasy
☐ Institutional or secret academy
☐ Futuristic/sci fi
☐ Escapist but still believable
☐ Any settings you dislike?

____

☐ Where would you like to see an adult novel set?

____

6. In terms of storylines, would you prefer:

☐ Simple stories that concentrate on adult interests?
☐ More plot and character-driven stories with less explicit adult activity?
☐ We value your ideas, so give us your opinion of this book:

____

____

____

7. In terms of your adult interests, what do you like to read about? (Tick as many as you like)

☐ Traditional corporal punishment (CP)
☐ Modern corporal punishment
☐ Spanking
☐ Restraint/bondage
☐ Rope bondage
☐ Latex/rubber
☐ Leather
☐ Female domination and male submission
☐ Female domination and female submission
☐ Male domination and female submission
☐ Willing captivity
☐ Uniforms
☐ Lingerie/underwear/hosiery/footwear (boots and high heels)
☐ Sex rituals
☐ Vanilla sex
☐ Swinging

☐ Cross-dressing/TV
☐ Enforced feminisation
☐ Others – tell us what you don't see enough of in adult fiction:

____

____

____

8. Would you prefer books with a more specialised approach to your interests, i.e. a novel specifically about uniforms? If so, which subject(s) would you like to read a Nexus novel about?

____

____

____

9. Would you like to read true stories in Nexus books? For instance, the true story of a submissive woman, or a male slave? Tell us which true revelations you would most like to read about:

____

____

____

10. What do you like best about Nexus books?

____

____

11. What do you like least about Nexus books?

____

____

12. Which are your favourite titles?

____

____

13. Who are your favourite authors?

____

____

14. **Which covers do you prefer? Those featuring: (tick as many as you like)**

- ☐ Fetish outfits
- ☐ More nudity
- ☐ Two models
- ☐ Unusual models or settings
- ☐ Classic erotic photography
- ☐ More contemporary images and poses
- ☐ A blank/non-erotic cover
- ☐ What would your ideal cover look like?

____

15. **Describe your ideal Nexus novel in the space provided:**

____

____

____

____

16. **Which celebrity would feature in one of your Nexus-style fantasies? We'll post the best suggestions on our website – anonymously!**

____

THANKS FOR YOUR TIME

Now simply write the title of this book in the space below and cut out the questionnaire pages. Post to: Nexus, Marketing Dept., Thames Wharf Studios, Rainville Rd, London W6 9HA

Book title: ____________________________________

TERMS AND CONDITIONS

1. The competition is open to UK residents only, excluding employees of Nexus and Virgin, their families, agents and anyone connected with the promotion of the competition. 2. Entrants must be aged 18 years or over. 3. Closing date for receipt of entries is 31 December 2006. 4. The first entry drawn on 7 January 2007 will be declared the winner and notified by Nexus. 5. The decision of the judges is final. No correspondence will be entered into. 6. No purchase necessary. Entries restricted to one per household. 7. The prize is non-transferable and non-refundable and no alternatives can be substituted. 8. Nexus reserves the right to amend or terminate any part of the promotion without prior notice. 9. No responsibility is accepted for fraudulent, damaged, illegible or incomplete entries. Proof of sending is not proof of receipt. 10. The winner's name will be available from the above address from 9 January 2007.

Promoter: Nexus, Thames Wharf Studios, Rainville Road, London, W6 9HA

NEXUS NEW BOOKS

To be published in December 2006

SILKEN EMBRACE
Christina Shelly

The Bigger Picture is a radical and powerful organisation of dominant women intent on turning young men into ultra glamorous she-males to become housemaids that serve wealthy women and demanding men. Shelly manages to escape the strict training program and shelters with Mrs Ambrose, a beautiful and glamorous widow who runs a rival academy. But it's not long before the beautiful and severe agents of The Bigger Picture track her down and return her to captivity, where her erotic torments and re-education continue, with an even greater creativity and extremity than ever before.

£6.99 ISBN 0 352 34081 9

WHALEBONE STRICT
Lady Alice McCloud

Petticoats, corsets, frilly knickers, lace, and canes – all part of the Imperial world inhabited by Thrift; a young and naïve foreign office agent sent on special missions on behalf of the empire. In *Whalebone Strict*, Thrift Moncrieff's assignment for the British Imperial Diplomatic Service takes her to the North American colonies, where she is supposed to compromise the position of a politician. In this she is rather more successful than she had planned, leading her ever deeper into difficulties that more often than not lead to the opening of her ankle length corset and elaborate underwear, either for the entertainment of a string of lecherous men, or to have a hand applied to her delectable buttocks.

£6.99 ISBN 0 352 34082 7

IN FOR A PENNY

Penny Birch

Penny Birch is back, as naughty as ever. *In for a Penny* continues the story of her outrageous sex life and also the equally rude behaviour of her friends. From stories of old-fashioned spankings, through strip-wrestling in baked beans, to a girl with unusual breasts, it's all there. Each scene is described in loving detail, with no holding back and a level of realism that comes from a great deal of practical experience.

£6.99 ISBN 0 352 34083 5

This information is correct at time of printing. For up-to-date information, please visit our website at www.nexus-books.co.uk

All books are priced at £6.99 unless another price is given.

ABANDONED ALICE	Adriana Arden 0 352 33969 1	☐
ALICE IN CHAINS	Adriana Arden 0 352 33908 X	☐
AMAZON SLAVE	Lisette Ashton 0 352 33916 0	☐
ANGEL	Lindsay Gordon 0 352 34009 6	☐
AQUA DOMINATION	William Doughty 0 352 34020 7	☐
THE ART OF CORRECTION	Tara Black 0 352 33895 4	☐
THE ART OF SURRENDER	Madeline Bastinado 0 352 34013 4	☐
AT THE END OF HER TETHER	G.C. Scott 0 352 33857 1	☐
BELINDA BARES UP	Yolanda Celbridge 0 352 33926 8	☐
BENCH MARKS	Tara Black 0 352 33797 4	☐
BIDDING TO SIN	Rosita Varón 0 352 34063 0	☐
BINDING PROMISES	G.C. Scott 0 352 34014 2	☐
THE BLACK GARTER	Lisette Ashton 0 352 33919 5	☐
THE BLACK MASQUE	Lisette Ashton 0 352 33977 2	☐
THE BLACK ROOM	Lisette Ashton 0 352 33914 4	☐
THE BLACK WIDOW	Lisette Ashton 0 352 33973 X	☐
THE BOND	Lindsay Gordon 0 352 33996 9	☐

THE BOOK OF PUNISHMENT	Cat Scarlett 0 352 33975 6	☐
BRUSH STROKES	Penny Birch 0 352 34072 X	☐
BUSTY	Tom King 0 352 34032 0	☐
CAGED [£5.99]	Yolanda Celbridge 0 352 33650 1	☐
CALLED TO THE WILD	Angel Blake 0 352 34067 3	☐
CAPTIVES OF CHEYNER CLOSE	Adriana Arden 0 352 34028 2	☐
CARNAL POSSESSION	Yvonne Strickland 0 352 34062 2	☐
CHERRI CHASTISED	Yolanda Celbridge 0 352 33707 9	☐
COLLEGE GIRLS	Cat Scarlett 0 352 33942 X	☐
COMPANY OF SLAVES	Christina Shelly 0 352 33887 3	☐
CONCEIT AND CONSEQUENCE	Aishling Morgan 0 352 33965 9	☐
CONFESSIONS OF AN ENGLISH SLAVE	Yolanda Celbridge 0 352 33861 X	☐
CORRUPTION	Virginia Crowley 0 352 34073 8	☐
DARK MISCHIEF	Lady Alice McCloud 0 352 33998 5	☐
DEPTHS OF DEPRAVATION	Ray Gordon 0 352 33995 0	☐
DERRIÈRE	Julius Culdrose 0 352 34024 X	☐
DICE WITH DOMINATION	P.S. Brett 0 352 34023 1	☐
DISCIPLINE OF THE PRIVATE HOUSE	Esme Ombreux 0 352 33709 5	☐
DOMINANT	Felix Baron 0 352 34044 4	☐
THE DOMINO ENIGMA	Cyrian Amberlake 0 352 34064 9	☐
THE DOMINO QUEEN	Cyrian Amberlake 0 352 34074 6	☐

LICKED CLEAN	Yolanda Celbridge 0 352 33999 3	☐
NON FICTION: LESBIAN SEX SECRETS FOR MEN	Jamie Goddard and Kurt Brungard 0 352 33724 9	☐
LESSONS IN OBEDIENCE	Lucy Golden 0 352 33892 X	☐
LOVE JUICE	Donna Exeter 0 352 33913 6	☐
MANSLAVE	J.D. Jensen 0 352 34040 1	☐
THE MASTER OF CASTLELEIGH [£5.99]	Jacqueline Bellevois 0 352 33644 7	☐
MISS RATAN'S LESSON	Yolanda Celbridge 0 352 33791 5	☐
NAUGHTY NAUGHTY	Penny Birch 0 352 33974 4	☐
NEW EROTICA 5	Various 0 352 33956 X	☐
NEW EROTICA 6	Various 0 352 33751 6	☐
THE NEXUS LETTERS	Various 0 352 33955 1	☐
NIGHTS IN WHITE COTTON	Penny Birch 0 352 34008 8	☐
NO PAIN, NO GAIN	James Baron 0 352 33966 7	☐
NURSE'S ORDERS	Penny Birch 0 352 33739 7	☐
THE OLD PERVERSITY SHOP	Aishling Morgan 0 352 34007 X	☐
ONE WEEK IN THE PRIVATE HOUSE	Esme Ombreux 0 352 33706 0	☐
ORIGINAL SINS	Lisette Ashton 0 352 33804 0	☐
THE PALACE OF PLEASURES	Christobel Coleridge 0 352 33801 6	☐
PALE PLEASURES	Wendy Swanscombe 0 352 33702 8	☐
PENNY PIECES [£5.99]	Penny Birch 0 352 33631 5	☐

PETTING GIRLS	Penny Birch 0 352 33957 8	☐
PET TRAINING IN THE PRIVATE HOUSE [£5.99]	Esme Ombreux 0 352 33655 2	☐
THE PLAYER	Cat Scarlett 0 352 33894 6	☐
PLAYTHING	Penny Birch 0 352 33967 5	☐
PLEASING THEM	William Doughty 0 352 34015 0	☐
PRIZE OF PAIN	Wendy Swanscombe 0 352 33890 3	☐
THE PRIESTESS	Jacqueline Bellevois 0 352 33905 5	☐
PUNISHED IN PINK	Yolanda Celbridge 0 352 34003 7	☐
THE PUNISHMENT CAMP	Jacqueline Masterson 0 352 33940 3	☐
THE PUNISHMENT CLUB	Jacqueline Masterson 0 352 33862 8	☐
RITES OF OBEDIENCE	Lindsay Gordon 0 352 34005 3	☐
SCARLET VICE	Aishling Morgan 0 352 33988 8	☐
SCHOOLED FOR SERVICE	Lady Alice McCloud 0 352 33918 7	☐
SCHOOL FOR STINGERS	Yolanda Celbridge 0 352 33994 2	☐
THE SECRET SELF	Christina Shelly 0 352 34069 X	☐
SERVING TIME	Sarah Veitch 0 352 33509 2	☐
SEXUAL HEELING	Wendy Swanscombe 0 352 33921 7	☐
SILKEN SERVITUDE	Christina Shelly 0 352 34004 5	☐
SINS APPRENTICE	Aishling Morgan 0 352 33909 8	☐
SLAVE ACTS	Jennifer Jane Pope 0 352 33665 X	☐
SLAVE GENESIS [£5.99]	Jennifer Jane Pope 0 352 33503 3	☐

SLAVE OF THE SPARTANS	Yolanda Celbridge 0 352 34078 9	☐
THE SMARTING OF SELINA	Yolanda Celbridge 0 352 33872 5	☐
STRIP GIRL	Aishling Morgan 0 352 34077 0	☐
STRIPING KAYLA	Yvonne Marshall 0 352 33881 4	☐
STRIPPED BARE	Angel Blake 0 352 33971 3	☐
THE SUBMISSION GALLERY [£5.99]	Lindsay Gordon 0 352 33370 7	☐
THE SUBMISSION OF STELLA	Yolanda Celbridge 0 352 33854 7	☐
THE TAMING OF TRUDI	Yolanda Celbridge 0 352 33673 0	☐
TASTING CANDY	Ray Gordon 0 352 33925 X	☐
TEMPTING THE GODDESS	Aishling Morgan 0 352 33972 1	☐
THAI HONEY	Kit McCann 0 352 34068 1	☐
TICKLE TORTURE	Penny Birch 0 352 33904 7	☐
TIE AND TEASE	Penny Birch 0 352 33987 X	☐
TIGHT WHITE COTTON	Penny Birch 0 352 33970 5	☐
TOKYO BOUND	Sachi 0 352 34019 3	☐
TORMENT INCORPORATED	Murilee Martin 0 352 33943 8	☐
THE TRAINING GROUNDS	Sarah Veitch 0 352 33526 2	☐
UNDER MY MASTER'S WINGS	Lauren Wissot 0 352 34042 8	☐
UNEARTHLY DESIRES	Ray Gordon 0 352 34036 3	☐
UNIFORM DOLL	Penny Birch 0 352 33698 6	☐
VELVET SKIN [£5.99]	Aishling Morgan 0 352 33660 9	☐

WENCHES WITCHES AND STRUMPETS	Aishling Morgan 0 352 33733 8	☐
WHAT HAPPENS TO BAD GIRLS	Penny Birch 0 352 34031 2	☐
WHAT SUKI WANTS	Cat Scarlett 0 352 34027 6	☐
WHEN SHE WAS BAD	Penny Birch 0 352 33859 8	☐
WHIP HAND	G.C. Scott 0 352 33694 3	☐
WHIPPING GIRL	Aishling Morgan 0 352 33789 3	☐

- - - - - - ✂ -

Please send me the books I have ticked above.

Name ....

Address ....

....

....

.... Post code ....

Send to: **Virgin Books Cash Sales, Thames Wharf Studios, Rainville Road, London W6 9HA**

US customers: for prices and details of how to order books for delivery by mail, call 888-330-8477.

Please enclose a cheque or postal order, made payable to **Nexus Books Ltd**, to the value of the books you have ordered plus postage and packing costs as follows:

UK and BFPO – £1.00 for the first book, 50p for each subsequent book.

Overseas (including Republic of Ireland) – £2.00 for the first book, £1.00 for each subsequent book.

If you would prefer to pay by VISA, ACCESS/MASTERCARD, AMEX, DINERS CLUB or SWITCH, please write your card number and expiry date here:

....

Please allow up to 28 days for delivery.

Signature ....

Our privacy policy

We will not disclose information you supply us to any other parties. We will not disclose any information which identifies you personally to any person without your express consent.

From time to time we may send out information about Nexus books and special offers. Please tick here if you do *not* wish to receive Nexus information. ☐

- - - - - - ✂ -